25th
Happy Birthday
Susan,

with love,

Square and Oz

Anouchka Grose Forrester was born in Sydney in
1970. She moved to London at the age of two
and has lived there ever since

Also by Anouchka Grose Forrester

RINGING FOR YOU

Darling Daisy

Anouchka Grose Forrester

Flamingo
An Imprint of HarperCollins*Publishers*

Flamingo
An Imprint of HarperCollins*Publishers*
77–85 Fulham Palace Road,
Hammersmith, London w6 8jb

Flamingo is a registered trade mark of
HarperCollins*Publishers* Limited

www.**fire**and**water**.com

Published by Flamingo 2001
9 8 7 6 5 4 3 2 1

First published in Great Britain by
Flamingo 2000

ISBN 0 00 655157 2

Printed and bound in Great Britain
by Clays Ltd, St Ives plc

For Roslyn and Peter

Thanks:

to Javier Marchán for his fantastically idio(ma)tic translations, Darian Leader for being a good friend and generous reader, Jonny Geller for being on my side, Rachel Hore for being uncorporate and bookish in the very best way, Jennifer Parr for being a far more talented (not to mention nicer) editor than H.P., and Patricio Grose Forrester for being prepared to wake up and chat at any hour of the night, for being patient and, most of all, for being so much fun to live with.

Editor's Introduction

It took me a while to decide whether or not to do what I am on the verge of doing right now. After wrestling with my conscience for the greater part of four months I feel I have no choice but to go ahead with what may turn out to be one of the most unscrupulous and dishonourable actions I have ever performed. Before I tell you what it is, let me attempt to justify my decision. Firstly, I am a writer and, though I say it myself, a rather mediocre one. You've probably read other things of mine – maybe without knowing. I usually write under a pseudonym as at least I have the good sense to feel ashamed (one of the many things that enables me to feel superior to my contemporaries). I live by writing and have done so for a number of years – journalism mostly, for magazines, tabloids, broadsheets, journals, monthly newsletters and any other form of publication that pays. I have written books on Italian architecture (for children), shellfish, and the paranormal, not to mention a couple of forays into ghost writing. I am also the proud progenitor of two novels. These I had counted on to pull me back from the brink of utter nonentitude. But perhaps because I had higher hopes for them, the novels are the efforts that really make me squirm.

The time has certainly come for me to embark on a new project. I've been very undecided about whether or not to give up all hope of redemption and just write some more hogwash. Or to consider the possibility of *attempting* to write something I can live with. (An urge exacerbated by the passing of my fortieth birthday.) My pride is still recovering from a recent literary fiasco, the upshot of which was that I found myself unable to keep up my mortgage repayments (not to mention the large sums I am obliged to pay to my dear ex-wife) and ended up moving from a smart flat in Bayswater into a spacious but exceptionally grotty house in New Cross – owned by a very good friend of mine.

The reason I'm telling you all this trivia about my life is that I found something when I moved in. Something truly sad and awful in a lot of ways, but I suppose you could say it appealed to the sadist in me at the same time as it spoke to something kinder and more concerned about people. Someone had left three hand-written books behind in a box full of papers. The box was mixed up with a load of other boxes and black binbags full of rubbish – apparently abandoned by mistake. I was a little concerned at first – I rather felt for the person who lost it. Her name was Daisy, she came from America (Las Vegas of all places) and I had free access to her secrets.

It's always strangely thrilling to read things one isn't meant to, but what makes this case unusual is that Daisy was peeping at all her housemates' letters, notes and even film scripts, then photocopying them in the fax machine and keeping them on file. After I found the box I spent a couple of days piecing the whole lot together according to dates on letters and mentions in the notebooks of what was going on alongside passages in the photocopied texts. Most surprisingly, the whole thing came together into something resembling a story. So much so, in fact, that I momentarily suspected a hoax. The beginning may seem a little directionless, but if you persevere it gradually begins to deliver the goods; our heroine suffers a conflict of love interests, slides into a slough of despondency, develops anti-social habits which land her in suspenseful situations and radically changes the course of her life. There are even a handful of sub-plots concerning peripheral characters, some of whom could feasibly be said to 'develop'. However, I ought to warn you that Daisy is a difficult girl to like. If you read books largely for the sake of forming imaginary friendships with people more glamorous, intelligent or morally upstanding than either yourself or the flawed, fleshly creatures of your acquaintance, I suggest you put this down at once.

My work on this project has involved an odd combination of impartial studiousness and indefensible intrusiveness. Do archae-ologists deciphering secret scrolls feel any qualms or are they fully assuaged by the idea that the reticent authors are long since dead? There's something rather worrying about resuscitating the chicken scratchings of characters who are probably quite capable of coming back to wallop you in the face.

I tried to imagine what the girl must have felt about leaving her books behind. I'd be frantic if I lost a whole manuscript. I suppose *she's* not in it for the money. I'd love to ask her what she *was* in it for. There's something about her notebooks which prompts me to speculate that she desperately wanted someone else to read them: she explains all the background details. You surely wouldn't do that if you were only writing for yourself. She also revises and corrects occasionally. I don't believe she thought what she was creating was great literature. She probably didn't realize it was at all interesting simply because it was in her own handwriting. This is one of the greatest problems with the contemporary literary scene. The people who want to be writers try to dignify their trite ruminations, typing them out in an authoritative Times typeface, double-spaced with justified margins and fool themselves into thinking they have written something great for the sole reason that, on a purely material level, it looks like the other great writing they know. If they had written it in green biro in a tatty spiral-bound pad they might not feel so confident. At the other end of the scale there are people who like writing but don't think of themselves as writers. They scribble away in funny books with shiny floral covers or on stacks of handmade Indian paper, using a pen they liked the design of in a gift shop. I have to confess to belonging to the first group. Daisy falls firmly into the second.

My agent specializes in heartfelt confessional writing and thought it was a potential hit (although I haven't yet told her that I'm not making it up – I just said it was a story about a flatshare in London to which she replied that there was another extremely popular book like that and that it ought to do very well). I apologize to the strangers I'm about to betray but I'd just like to point out before you come after me with a pickaxe, a letter-bomb or a lawyer that I am not claiming to have written your things myself, that I've made little changes so that no one will know it was you, and that if you want a share of the money you can get in touch via the publisher.

The reason I have decided to go ahead with this plan isn't simply that it saves a lot of time and avoids me having to come up with an idea of my own. I excuse myself by saying that it's better to put a book into the world that was written with some intention other than persuading people that it was penned by a great author (or a nice person). So many books exist for the sole purpose of winning admiration for their creators. All the delicate characterizations, narrative pyrotechnia, political astuteness and linguistic innovation function as little more than advertisements for the writers' superior being. You must have heard the saying that anyone who wants to be the Prime Minister is therefore unfit for the task – well I think the same can be said for writing. Anyone who wants to be a famous author should be prevented by law from touching keyboards, pens and paper except for making lists, writing basic business letters, and sending cards (but only on very special occasions).

I'm also saying this in the defence of the texts I have found and edited into this book. Although they may not be the most erudite pieces of writing in the world they do at least have the merit of not having been written for the sake of impressing anybody (excluding, perhaps, the film scripts).

Where I felt it necessary I have corrected spellings, inserted punctuation marks, italicized and restructured sentences, but mostly I have left it as I found it. I have also added chapter headings and the occasional note of my own, but only where strictly necessary. Daisy's signatures are, I feel, of particular interest, so these have been reproduced in their original form.

H.P.
London
July 1999

First Notebook

(plastic cover with embossed daisy, ruled)

Landmarks

The wallpaper in our room is pearly pink with nubbly white diagonal slashes. The carpet is a swamp of clumpy brown hellfibers. Our drapes are gray with lilac roses and are made from a textile that could probably build up enough static to start a storm. We have a mattress that feels as though it's been stuffed with unripe oranges and a closet whose doors have to be held shut by a slab of wood jammed between the handles. Apart from that it's great.

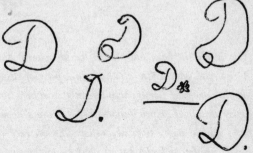

I just went to see Big Ben and the Houses of Parliament. When I got there I didn't know what I was meant to do next. Like most great buildings Big Ben is stuck on the side of a road. It was smaller than I imagined it would be, although the Houses of Parliament were pretty huge. I thought there might be guided tours but I couldn't even find a door, so I never worked it out. I stood at the bottom of Big Ben for a while, desperate to notice something interesting. In the end I found myself feeling quite impressed by all the frizzly stonework and thinking of each little gnarl being handmade by a real person. I find it incredible that these giant famous things were ever not there and that they had to be made. I don't really mind seeing construction work being done – I mean it looks tough but the guys are usually chatting and listening to the radio. But when you see something all finished and like it always existed it's terrible to picture it being pieced together a bit at a time.

I wouldn't exactly say I enjoyed my outing, but it was nice to have a break from being Leni's secretary. She gets so many phonecalls – all from people called things like Polzer and Tank.

[Ed: Inside the box, underneath the abandoned diaries, was a thick A5 notepad with a biro attached via a piece of string. It contains six months' worth of (largely uninteresting) telephone messages. I assume Daisy must have swiped it shortly before her final departure. See overleaf for a sample page. (I firmly believe the presence of the phone pad further justifies this publication: why be so thorough unless hoping to be discovered?)]

for	from	when	what
LEVi	OLi	TUE-AM	CALL
"	TANK	TUE-AM	PARTY FRI. — TOOTS?
"	TANK	TUE-AM	TELL OLi
"	POLZER	TUE-?PM	Oi!
LEVi	DADDY	WED-AM	CAN'T MAKE IT TOMORROW
LEVi	TOBES	THUR-PM	PERFORMANCE/VIDEO NIGHT MAXTON☐
Sophia	Mother	THUR P.	TOMORROW £13. ??? (think she'll call back!)
LEVi	GREETS	FRi-AM	WHERE WERE YOU? WAITED FOR AN HOUR. CALL ON THE FRIENDSHIPS OVER.
"	tank	Fri a.	red lob or sensy? (What are your friends on about? Jo!)
LEVi	Rom	SAT-7M	→ WANTS POLTZER'S № NO MESSAGE.
Jo	IAN	Mon-AM	
Daisy	Rob	Mon	To come late of the library.

Jo and Sofia should be home soon. I'm already learning the rhythms of the people in the house. Those two are easy because they both have regular jobs. Leni's more erratic. Her whole life seems to happen elsewhere. When she's at home she makes you feel like being at home is something to be ashamed of. I don't know how she does it because she goes on as though being here is a real big treat for her. She makes out it's OK as long as it's not for too long or too often and that you spend the time either in the bathtub or on the telephone. She wants to do some kind of postgraduate film course in New York. I wonder what her movie scripts are like. I asked her what she was working on right now and she said something dopey-sounding about identity. It seemed to be about a small girl growing up in a small town. Why are all short films about growing up? Is it because they're anxious about being short themselves and want to grow up into big films? I asked her if it was autobiographical and she said that she grew up in West London and the small town was a metaphor, although she didn't say for what. Anyhow, it sounded like a total crock.

Rob ought to be back around seven. (I just heard the door, but I can't tell whether it's Jo or Sofia. If it's Sofia I'll go have a coffee with her, but if it's Jo I think I'll stay very quietly in here.) He goes to the library after lectures because he can't read or write at home. It's true that when he's here I tend to want to chat, but he says that even when he was single he couldn't do it. He'd keep getting up to make himself coffees or re-order his CDs. (It's Jo – I just heard the TV go on. Sofia doesn't do that. Actually, I think I'll go see how she's getting along.)

. . . What a mistake! She just clapped on about all the people in her office, calling them by their first names as if I knew who they were. She told me that Sarah really annoyed her because she asked Tony if she could swap lunch breaks with her without even consulting her and she missed her hairdressers' appointment because Sarah had already gone and Tony wouldn't let her go at the same time. Then one of the people she telephoned in the afternoon insulted her when her questionnaire went on for too long and the coffee from the machine tasted of mushroom soup. I know that a lot of annoying stuff happens to people over the course of a day but they shouldn't just tell it to anybody. She has a boyfriend. Why can't she just call him and get it off her chest and then tell me some other things instead? The problem with Jo is that you can't imagine what the other things would be. In her own way she's pretty enigmatic. When I hear her talking about crap in a crap way using endless crap expressions and interpreting the world in all its intricacy using the most limited set of crap ideas I know there must be more to her than I'm seeing and I start wondering what it is. I try to imagine her with an American accent to see if it helps me understand her more. I sort of see her as one of these dumb people from Maryland who are always on TV talking about their views on marriage or something.

The accent thing is weird. I really and truly believed all my life that I had an English accent. But now I'm realizing that even Dad wouldn't sound English to people if he came here.

I'm really missing Rob today. I'm still only just getting to know him and he's hardly ever around. It's probably a good thing because we moved in together quite quickly. At least this way there's no danger of us getting on top of each other (in the wrong way!). I think it's tough for him that we met just when he was awarded his scholarship. He told me that when he was at University back home he led a pretty monastic existence. He works really hard. He's not exactly geeky – he's mostly really well adjusted (much better than me) – but he gets very excited about astronautical things and it doesn't seem to him like a sacrifice to devote most of his time to them.

When I start missing him his face comes up super-clearly in my mind. He has one of those faces that still has a lot of kid in it. He only needs to shave every couple of days and his hair is all light and sandy. He has the whitest, straightest, most braced-out teeth ever to have come out of America. Dad would never let me go to an orthodontist because he thought it was too vulgar and Yankee. Sometimes I feel proud of my screwy tombstone teeth because I think they're pretty cool and individualistic. But when I think of Rob's, which are like two rows of cinema seats, I get a massive rush of envy. He should be here in about half an hour. I love thinking of him getting on the tube and the tube going through all the tunnels and under the houses and then knowing roughly what time he's most likely to be walking up the road to the front door. He's a very on-time kind of person so I often know roughly what he's up to without him having to tell me. Sometimes I think of him walking up the road, coming up the steps and reaching into his pocket for his keys at exactly the moment it's actually happening. It's a skill I've been developing over the past couple of weeks, since I gave him the keys to my apartment back home. Usually I have to do it a few times during the ten minutes in which he's most likely to get back. But even when I get it nearly right (I imagine him halfway up the street when in fact his keys are already in the door) after heaps of miscalculations it still feels like there's something fantastic in the near-simultaneity of my thoughts and his actions.

I'm not in that kind of mood today. I think I'll have a bath before Leni comes home and hogs it.

I've had a weird last few days. The first weird thing was that I went to the Tower of London. What a hellhole! The second weird thing is Sofia. The third weird thing is that Jo has organized a house outing to the pub either tonight or tomorrow (depending on when Leni can make it, naturally). People like Jo always do stuff like that. I know it's important that we all get along if we live together but I really don't feel like pushing it. I don't want to have to talk to my housemates without the option of disappearing into my room or pretending I have to go to the Post Office. She announced this gorgeous occasion a couple of days ago with a really creepy note on the toaster. *[Ed: The note itself turned up in the box. It reads: 'Hiya all, Howzabout a swifty Thursday or Friday? Let me know which is best. Here's a pen – USE IT! Last to sign buys the first round. JOxxx.' Underneath there are two columns marked Thurs. and Fri. In Daisy's writing it says, 'Either is fine, Daisy +Rob', across the two columns. Sofia writes, 'Thank you Jo – I come both days – Sofia'. And Leni has written, 'Might be able to do Thur. but would pref. Fri. although might have to rush off. If you think I'm buying the drinks think again bunnies. L.']*

Jo's writing is all big and babyish – exactly what you'd expect from someone like her. I'd love to analyze it (graphology is one of my big things at the moment) but I'd need a little more to do the job properly. Still, you don't need to be the world's greatest graphologist to see in Jo's clunking, copy-the-teacher letterforms that she's a hopeless conformist and desperate to be liked.

Rob was quite keen to accept the invite just because he's had almost no conversations with any of them so far and thinks he probably ought to. He was concerned about sorting out the gas account and checking the deal with the telephone. He seemed to approach the occasion as a purely practical thing. He's cute like that. I get all ratty because our housemates aren't exactly my idea of fun, but he sees it more like a business arrangement that has to be fixed up amicably in order to function efficiently. We only ended up living here because an older cousin of Rob's who works in a law firm downtown sorted it out for us. We do sort of need to check out the technicalities of the whole thing. I'd have preferred to have an apartment to ourselves but it would have cost more and the guy didn't have time to go sniffing around for a good offer. Leni is the sister-in-law of one of his colleagues so it was the easiest option for him to arrange. I wish it was just Jo and Sofia living here. It would be boring but I really, truly and genuinely can't stand Leni. She's so stuck on herself. She comes in and asks how you are and then makes it clear she doesn't have time for your answer and that, anyhow, she wouldn't give a fuck about it if she did. Her accent is so hoity-toity she sounds like a stupid actress in one of those piss-boring BBC series that people back home think are so upmarket.

Anyhow, back to the point. Sofia is the *weirdest*. A couple of days ago she came home and I went out to talk to her. She gets so jumpy. It makes you think she'd prefer it if you left her alone. But if you persevere it seems like she's really touched that you can be bothered. Sofia's seriously uncool about being a foreigner. She acts like not speaking English is a terrible disease and that she's very grateful to you for overcoming your disgust enough to talk to her. Because she's so stressed about not having

16

enough words to flesh out a conversation she starts saying things she has no real hope of finishing in order to show good will. Even the beginning part of the phrase tends to come out a bit mulched up like she's used some very loose approximations which, put together, don't even nearly make sense. When I asked about her day she said something like, 'Good . . . yes . . . and finishing went over getting behet . . . vehet . . . ai! . . . begetables . . . ah . . . ah . . . ah . . . puta madre! . . . ah . . . I not know . . . perdon . . . Té?'. I looked in the bags of vegetables admiringly just to show that I could see roughly what she was on about and she seemed so encouraged she tried again. 'Yes! This shop man he say . . . ah . . . he say going dance el me . . . old, old, agy . . . euchh . . . his hands!' I think she was trying to tell it like it was a funny story but I wasn't quite sure. She looked all wide-eyed and nervy, but then she does all the time. I didn't know whether she was inviting me to be shocked and disgusted or to think he was a sweet old man. I asked her whether she was OK. She said yes really defensively as if I'd changed the subject. I can't imagine how lost she must feel. I think she really panics almost every time she has to speak.

Then she started fussing around making the tea like she was on stage, exaggerating all her movements and pretending to not know where to find the sugar. Luckily the telephone rang before either of us died of embarrassment. It was her Mom, so we didn't have to drink our teas together. I hung around outside the door for a second just for the thrill of hearing her speak fluently in Spanish. She sounded like a whole new creature.

I think I've written enough for one day. I feel like stopping. The Tower can wait 'til tomorrow.

The weird stuff is really piling up. Something super-strange happened last night. I hope things get back to normal soon as I'm building up a backlog. We'd just gotten into bed when we started to hear a baby crying outside. It was screaming in a horrible way like it was really in pain. We looked out of the window but couldn't see anything. The sounds seemed to be coming from a back garden a few doors down. I was ready to call the police but Rob kept trying to persuade me not to. He said we shouldn't do anything until we were sure there was actually something wrong. But by then it might be too late. The kid sounded like it had a problem with it's voice, like maybe it had some kind of disability and the parents put it outside because they couldn't cope. I was about to go to the phone when the noises stopped. Maybe they took it back inside.

On a slightly lighter note, what about the Tower of London? It's a good reminder of what complete sons of bitches people are. It's full of horrible old men aching to tell you gruesome stories about even grosser people in the seventeenth century and scrungy packs of tourists taking pictures of each other in front of chopping blocks. Everywhere you go there's a little plaque or yellow-toothed guy telling you about some really vile misdeed or punishment. It practically made me throw. There was a tour guide showing round a party of American families. He had them all mesmerized by this patch of grass, telling them stories of all the beheadings that happened there – without exactly sparing any details. He said they'd had to take five chops at one lady. They'd convicted her of being a witch on the grounds that she'd managed to live to be seventy (nice way to treat old people!). After the first hack she got up and started running around with all her blood spurting out. The tourists were almost dribbling. Even the kids.

It was funny to come across those kinds of people off the Strip. Back home we're obliged to see them all the time in
18

their fat-ass shorts carrying their change cups from casino to casino. It's not a pretty sight. But even with their legs covered and their money carefully stored in nylon tushie-bags they still fail to come across as anything like reasonable human beings. I thought I'd go look at the jewels before I punched somebody or puked.

It's the weekend – not that it makes much difference. Rob's at the library and the others have all gone out. I wish there was someone around to talk to because I feel pretty funny after last night. We went to the pub. Our local pub is OK. It looks exactly like a British pub in a movie. It has red carpets, picturesque old buffers and a big wooden bar. Leni looked at me like I'd gone totally neuro for liking it so much, but we don't really have pubs back home so they're a novelty for me.

Jo insisted on playing non-competitive pool. You keep changing teams in this complicated way so that you never get an opportunity to hate your opponents properly. She's full of lame ideas like that. I think she just wants everyone to love each other but doesn't quite know how to bring it about. She was wearing a fluffy pink cardigan and slouchy faded jeans. She has tiny gold earrings and a chain with a little gold sperm on it. Her hair is mousy and nondescript. Superficially speaking, she's probably the most inoffensive person in the world.

After the pool non-tournament we went and sat down. Jo guided us to a small, round table (to stop us taking sides). The pressure to have a great time was intense. I can be pretty slack in situations like that, but Rob is quite good. He was very relaxed and made a toast to meeting the others at last. They asked him about astronautics and were really impressed by the idea of him designing spacecraft (like everyone always is, even Mom). Sofia started to look more relaxed after a drink and asked, although he'd just explained it, 'Eso, you making rocket espacial?' She nodded politely at his second answer and giggled hysterically at something he said. It dawned on her that she must have misunderstood when no-one else laughed. She looked very embarrassed and refused to tell us what she thought she'd heard. Rob gave the rest of his answer in Spanish.

Leni was nauseating, as usual. She was wearing a denim suit with too-long sleeves and some kind of spacey t-shirt. I get the feeling she's confused about being a girl. With girls she's brisk and calls us stupid names, like 'hun' and 'sweets', but with Rob she acted interested and respectful. She seemed to want to let him know that she was a serious and intelligent person. I wouldn't call it flirting. It was more like the opposite of flirting. I felt as though she was trying to identify herself with him, as opposed to us, and make him and her more like boys together. She was speaking in her lowest possible, most monotone voice and sounding as serious as possible while she was just asking him pretty basic stuff about what he was planning on doing in the future. She knew a couple of things about new plans for US space stations and the significance of finding water on the moon, but nothing the average dumb CNN-watcher isn't aware of. Isn't the problem with self-confident people that they're confident that what they say and do is interesting? Sometimes it's not. Jo made me laugh by winding Leni up, interrupting her attempts at serious conversation with klutzy jokes about rockets being 'knob extensions'. She asked me whether 'big car, small dick' was a rule that went for spaceships. Leni rolled her eyes at Rob but he ignored it. He turned and asked Jo what she wanted to do with her life (he can be very cool in that way). Jo got all cooing and excitable about the prospect of the future in general and started saying how she'd like to have a big house with a big garden and a dog and a cat and a job in TV and a family (with her current boyfriend) – 'you know, all the things everyone wants, I suppose.' She said she was going to be twenty six on her next birthday so she needed to get started in a proper job as soon as possible to make sure she had it all fixed up by the time she turned thirty. It was one of the most excruciating life-plans I've ever heard. It was like hearing a pig saying it wanted to be made into bacon.

The idea of her cozy destiny got Jo so excited that she decided to share her bliss by offering us all the opportunity to wallow in the joy that is the future. She did it in this really gawky way like, 'I know, let's go round the table and say what our ambitions are.' I realize it's just her way of handling group situations and I'm sure she meant no harm, but the idea hit me like I'd been whacked in the stomach with a baseball bat. I didn't want to talk about my ambitions in that place with those people. She started with Rob, even though we'd been talking about his ambitions practically all evening. He looked a bit stumped at first, surprisingly. Then he gave this terrible answer – well, terrible in terms of he and I having a long relationship. He said he'd like to work on experiments involving time. He hoped that within his lifetime it would be possible to travel so fast you could leave earth for a year (according to your own body clock) and come back ten years later (according to everyone else's). I was so offended. I'd hate to hold him back – assuming we stay together – but I can't believe he'd go into space and leave his partner, friends and maybe even kids behind to get old while he zipped around the universe like Peter Pan. I even felt offended on any future partner's behalf. The others all found it a fascinating idea and oohed and aahed about it for a full five minutes without even thinking to ask what *I* felt.

Next we turned to Sofia, who looked about as spooked as me at the prospect of defining her future. Or maybe it was more to do with public speaking, as her ideas about what she'd like to do were clear enough once you'd decoded the words. After a spell of eye-rolling and hand-wringing she managed to say that she wanted to travel, learn more languages and maybe work for an international law firm. We were all very encouraging.

I started to sweat and even began shaking. I offered to buy drinks in the hope that they'd have changed the subject before I got back. At the bar I was racking my brain to see whether I could come up with anything. I tried to remember what I'd wanted to be as a child. When I was ten I used to tell people that I wanted to be a psychiatrist. It wasn't a genuine ambition at all. It just made adults go 'wow'. When I was a teenager I wanted to be a hairdresser and then a fashion designer. After that I kind of lost the plot and got a job in a reprographics company. I stayed for a couple of years before going into web design. Now I have a few very good ideas about what I don't want to do, but nothing more constructive than that. I know I don't want to waste my life on junk, but my actual ambitions are as yet undefined. I want to use my life really well but, because I treat it as such a serious undertaking, I'm having a little difficulty working out how best to go about it.

When I got back to the table they were rounding off a discussion about house accounts. As soon as I sat down Jo got on the case again with the ambition thing. It was Leni's turn. Leni handled it as if we were a panel of big money lenders and she was trying to persuade us what a good investment she was. She talked real slow and everything was well worked out. She said she'd first make a short film and then a longer one while she was at college. The short one was nearly finished and she was about to put it in for a few competitions. The longer one was 'more complex' and she was currently in the process of 'approaching funding bodies'. After that she'd be off to New

York to do her postgrad thing. She claimed she would certainly have made at least one feature film by the age of thirty. (Why is everyone so hung up with all that 'by the time I'm thirty' crap?). It was a pathetic plan but she seemed pretty smug about it. I wonder why people think making movies is so fucking clever. Everyone politely said they hoped it would all go well. Leni winked and told us, 'I don't think there's anything to worry about there.' She really and truly sucks.

The whole time she'd been talking, water was practically pouring out of the palms of my hands. I could hardly pick up my drink. I couldn't tell if it was because I was so repulsed by Leni or whether I was anxious about what to say afterwards. I'd spun myself into a frenzy of pure hatred and repulsion by the time Jo turned to me. I remember saying something about going to get potato chips and then quickly standing up. Everyone looked at me like I'd done something terrible. I felt dizzy. I started to see, hovering in front of me, patches of the brown and white geometric patterned wallpaper we had in our dining room back home in Vegas. The patches grew. When finally all I could see was wallpaper and no pub, I passed out.

Pictures

It's crazy to think I can just get on a bus and go see some of Van Gogh's sunflowers or Monet's waterlilies. When I was growing up, things like that felt so far away I hardly believed they existed. In my hometown we had a perfect marble replica of Michael Angelo's *David*, tons of airbrushed paintings of women with long hair, a few kitschy sandblasted glass sculptures and not much else. Now we have Bellagio's Gallery of Fine Art, but I haven't been because I know it'll be full of cornfed turkeys going like, 'Hey honey, ain't it purdy? Boy, that there *Mownaaay* sure noo howdapaint!' Apparently Mr Bellagio is the richest private collector in the whole of America. I guess it isn't surprising with all those sweet old ladies willingly dropping huge gifts into the cute kinetic donation boxes they keep just next door to the gallery.

I'm still trying to work out why I flipped out so badly in the pub the other day. It's true that I don't really know what I'm doing with my life, but I've never felt disturbed enough about it to collapse. Back home my friends are pretty used to me being the way I am, so I suppose I don't feel too pressured around them. I'm not exactly part of an ambitious crowd.

I think I feel even more uncomfortable with my housemates now than I did before. I've been trying to tell myself it isn't just me – that they're kind of edgy amongst themselves.

Apparently they only moved in together a few weeks ahead of us so they don't know each other at all well. Leni had initially gotten the house with two other friends but both of them pulled out at the last minute. Perhaps that's why she seems so dissatisfied with all of us. She had to put an ad in the paper to get two more people as fast as possible or risk not having sorted herself out in time for the beginning of the semester. She'd planned to use our room as a study, but decided to put us in there and keep the money instead. I don't think her parents know. It doesn't exactly make for a situation of love and mutual understanding.

I've been trying to get Rob to tell me what he thinks of the others. He's not very good at stuff like that. This morning he said, most enlighteningly, that they seemed like an OK bunch of girls. He was quite concerned about me fainting, but because I felt so uptight and stupid I couldn't tell him why. I pretended I'd forgotten to eat, so he took me home, made me a giant sandwich and hasn't mentioned it since.

P.S. I haven't heard the crying since the other day. Maybe it was nothing. But if it happens again I'm going to call the police right away.

I'm actually in the National Gallery right now. I've been wandering around for two hours and I need a break. They have so much stuff it's incredible. The first things I saw were the Van

Eycks. They're weird. That picture of the Arnolfini marriage shows every single speck of dust and all the scratches and loose threads in the whole room. Even the tiny glass beads on the back wall have all the shine and reflection painted in. How could anyone make themself notice so much minuscule stuff? It gives you vertigo just to look at it. I saw the Monet lilies just after. That guy was definitely on the opposite tack. Mom has a poster of them in the house, but they're very different when you actually see them. In a bad way. It's like at the ballet when you have to hear the sound of the dancers' feet thudding on the floorboards: when you're used to watching it on TV it doesn't sound very nice. The paint in Monet's paintings looks pretty dull and lumpy compared to the reproduction. The other things I don't get are the Van Goghs. They all have little criss-crossed canvas indentations where the paint was thickly applied. I think he must have stacked his pictures up before they were properly dry. Some even had finger prints where he prodded them while they were wet. I'm really much more interested in details like that than in the paintings themselves, which are nice but I don't know what to make of them.

I feel pretty lonely. I don't think the National Gallery is the ideal place to find soul mates. Perhaps I should make it my policy to be sociable at every possible opportunity. I remember a book my friend's Mom had on how to meet men. It said that you should treat every occasion as a chance to line up dates. I already have a boyfriend, so it would have to be a purely Platonic seduction. I wonder what the line is for galleries. Have you seen other works by the same artist? Why do they all have such small jugs? I'd die.

The only person I have real conversations with at the moment is Rob. I now know all about his school – an Evangelical place where they were taught all kinds of wacko stuff about marriage and the end of the world. I know all about his school friends, his grandparents, his first home, his goldfish, his parents and his ex-girlfriends (none of whom seem to have been very serious). I'm building up a major mental fact-file on Rob but I still feel that I don't really *get* him. He has too few problems. Or too few on the surface. The fact that he's so ambitious and hardworking suggests to me that something is up. I can't help believing this 'good student' thing isn't just an act to cover over some secret heavy shit. But the trick seems to be working for him so why should I try to mess it up? If Rob's troubled unconscious is causing him to work hard on improving the nature of space-travel it's no bad thing. I just wish it didn't make him so incomprehensible to me. I have to know what people's difficulties are in order to develop deep feelings for them. I guess I could try to translate his scientific problems back into normal human terms. Maybe his desire to comprehend the impact of certain forces on certain substances is his way of expressing his need to understand the impact of certain forces on himself. But as I have no idea what these forces are my appreciation of him isn't greatly improved. I'm definitely no shrink.

I've bought some plants for the bedroom and enough posters to hide big chunks of the wallpaper. I got a couple of Monets to help myself recover from the shock of the real thing, a Leonardo da Vinci and a very pretty *Madonna and Child* that Rob can't stand. I've also obscured the carpet with some cheap rugs from a market by Charing Cross station. The last thing I have to deal with is the tiled ceiling, after which it may just about feel like home.

I just had an interesting insight into my housemates' private lives. I couldn't find a pen. I had a really nice one but I must have left it in the gallery. I searched our bedroom, the kitchen and the living room and couldn't find a replacement anywhere. As a last resort I went to look in Jo's room – I thought she wouldn't mind. She didn't have one. After that I tried Sofia's. It was quite a nice room. And a real pen emporium too. She had a whole pot of them on her desk. I borrowed a plastic fountain pen – filled with turquoise ink (as you can see (*Ed: Well,* I *can.*)). I thought it was a little unfair of me only to look in two of their bedrooms so, for good measure, I took a peek into Leni's as well.

Jo's room must be one of the most depressing environments you can find outside a prison. One thing, which isn't really her fault, is that she has probably the worst carpet on the planet. It's dark red with a grid of small brown dots. At larger intervals, the dots are interrupted by fist-sized cream circles with brown lacy patterns round the edges. If you saw it on acid you'd probably kill yourself. Even when you're not it seems to be sending out evil messages. The thing that *is* her fault is that she hasn't hidden it. She hasn't hidden her salmon pink, lumpy flapjack wallpaper either. Maybe she painted it that color herself. I've never come across this particular type of ugly interior first-hand. Before I came here I'd only seen it on MTV and in these artsy movies about miserable English families which I used to sneak into University Film Society meetings to watch. She had a few small, framed pictures on the walls – scenes from *Winnie the Pooh* and a photocopy of *Desiderata* (eeuchhh!!). There was a collection of fluffy animals on her bed. Some looked like she'd had them for years, but others seemed pretty new. I hate cute things and the people who are into them. Who are they trying to kid? Let's face it, the more soft, fuzzy things a person surrounds herself with, the more crimes against humanity she's capable of committing. There was a white formica dressing table with a matching three-way mirror. She also has loads of make-up which she keeps in a box with a twizzling ballerina. It played *Für Elise* when I opened it. There was a row of hairbrushes that looked like she'd lined them up with a ruler at the bottom. I looked in her closet too. The clothes that weren't hanging on the rail were neatly folded on the shelves and coded according to color. All the shoes were in pairs at the bottom. What a sicko.

I checked the underwear, which I now feel pretty terrible about. I just wanted to see whether it was white and cottony like I suspected. The really gruesome part was that her panties turned out to be all black and sexy. It's horrible to think of that slutty nylon crap tucked away underneath her fluffy bunny outfits.

The other funny thing about her room – which I only realize now – was that it had absolutely no books in it. It didn't even have magazines.

On the way out I noticed her pale blue toweling dressing gown on the back of the door. She wears it around the house at night-time and on Sundays. I see her in her dressing gown more often than I see her in her clothes. Because I associate it so strongly with her I had this spooky feeling that she'd been watching me the whole time. I hope it was distracted while I took that flash at her panties.

Sofia's room was an altogether better experience. I felt as if I was finally meeting her with all the difficulties taken out. It was really airy and serene. She had creamy rugs on the floor and a white linen bedspread. I wonder whether she owns her bed. It had an old fashioned steel frame, painted white, and was much too pretty for our landlord to have chosen it. The wallpaper was embossed with a reasonably understated shell pattern and there were a couple of big Art Nouveau theatre posters in clip frames. She had stacks of books. They were mostly by Spanish writers, but she also had translations of Virginia Woolf, Henry James and F. Scott Fitzgerald – one of my favorite writers.

I laughed when I saw Sofia's clothes without her inside. They look seriously Catholic. Nothing's too tight or too short and the fabrics are all cotton or pure new wool. I didn't look at the labels but I guess she gets it all at Benetton or something. I'll never understand how people like Sofia choose their clothes. How can a plain beige sweater distinguish itself enough to jump out and cause you to buy it? It suits her though. She's a really neat-looking, healthy person – no ravishing beauty but you can tell she doesn't have any cellulite or pimples on her back. I bet she washes her hair every day.

Sofia has quite a collection of beauty products. Not tacky ones like mine, but Clinique, Lancome and Clarins. I get really jealous of stupid things like that. I almost get a physical sensation when I see someone else's swanky toiletries.

I didn't look at Sofia's panties. I decided I'd rather not know. But there was a letter on her desk which I'd certainly have read if I could. It was to her family. I flicked through it, just in case there were any bits I understood. I saw the words 'Las Vegas' so she must have been talking about us – but Christ knows what she was saying. I ought to write to Mom and Dad too. I've hardly thought about them since I got here.

I can't decide whether Leni's room was revealing or exactly what I expected. I was kind of shocked when I walked in, but then straight away it started to make perfect sense. It was a mix between a movie production office and a teenage fan pad. The walls were completely covered with movie-house posters and pictures cut out of magazines. She had old stuff, like a horrible picture of Doris Day flicking a whip on the *Calamity Jane* poster, and the *Casablanca* promo with the three main characters' heads. There was a *Big Lebowski* poster and lots of Chinese and Japanese stuff for movies called things like *Tetsuo* and *Hana-bi*. The one that annoyed me most was the *Leaving Las Vegas* poster. I hate movies that glamorize that place. When you've lived a normal, boring life there it pisses you off to see people thinking all these stupid things about it. I remember on our third night here Leni asking us about what it was like 'down there' (like, sure, this is the top of the planet). She didn't listen to what we said, she just kept going on about some book she'd read called *Learning From Las Vegas*. It was really annoying. It seemed to be about architecture, making Vegas out to be the best place in the world. But it's not just the architecture that makes a place what it is. Las Vegas might have some of the most state-of-the-art signposts and buildings on the planet, but it doesn't mean it's not full of racist, sexist, redneck, queer-bashing, fucked-up assholes. In terms of human relations it's probably one of the most backward places in America. And half the people who live there never even go to the Strip anyhow, they just live in regular apartments or bungalows.

Leni's magazine cuttings mostly showed women on their own looking either sulky or mean. Some were actresses or writers, some were models and some were people with pierced cheeks or tattoos on their foreheads. But all of them had in common this way of looking bad-tempered and self-absorbed. It was a helpful insight into where she's coming from, but I wonder whether all those women actually carry on looking like that once they get home. I think Leni's going a bit far doing that face in a domestic set-up. She should save it for when she's in front of a camera and meanwhile try out being a bit more human and vulnerable.

Leni had a load of technology hoarded up in her room. There was a great big Power Mac with a printer, scanner and modem. She also has her own phone-line and fax machine. It's as if she's planning a world take-over. I wonder what she uses it all for. She's never at home anyway. Spoilt witch. She's pretty messy too. Her bed was unmade and the floor was covered with scrunched up bundles of clothing. I didn't need to poke around in her drawers to find out that she wears *cK* underwear. Her dress sense is badly unimaginative, but I'm sure she thinks that's what's so cool about it. I've rarely seen her in anything other than combats and a sporty top. I hadn't noticed before – they all look the same to me – but she has four slightly different pairs of newish Nike trainers. I hate that way of dressing. It's a world-wide problem. Combats and Nikes are just a youthful version of the pinstripe suit.

Leni's bookshelf was pathetic. She only had about ten books, all of which had the words 'gender', 'gaze' or 'sexuality' in the title. I looked out for the Las Vegas one, but it didn't seem to be there.

All my housemates have double beds but, right now, Jo is the only one who has someone to share hers with.

I really wonder what Sofia said about us in her letter. She seemed to have very interesting handwriting.

33

The Tate's great. It's the best place I've visited so far. Much better than the National. I think I have pretty contemporary taste. I love Andy Warhol and Roy Lichtenstein. They have an amazing collection of Lichtensteins here. There's a big painting of a bed that really gets me. On the one hand it's all banal and horrific and on the other it's really vivid and beautiful. You can't work out what to make of it. I like things like that. They also have that really famous painting with the cartoon fighter plane that says 'Blam! Blam!'. Unlike with the Monets they weren't at all disappointing in real life.

It's like

Christ knows what I was about to say. I think I may have made a friend yesterday. I'm not sure how I feel about it.

I was sitting in the Tate café, scribbling in my pad, when this guy came up and asked what I was writing. I told him it was just notes. He was tallish with floppy pale brown hair. He wore a lilac shirt and brown wool jacket (a better outfit than it sounds on paper). He must have been in his early forties. I guess he was good-looking if you're into mature types. His accent was seriously upper-class – like Roger Moore or even Hugh Grant. He persisted with his questions about my notes, asking whether I was a reviewer or a playwright or something. It was all very flattering. I didn't want to disappoint him by telling him I was a bored, out-of-work person, so I pretended it was poetry – which sounded even worse. If there's one thing I really hate it's poetry. I can't believe I pretended to be writing some. He asked whether I'd mind if he sat down. I said I wouldn't. I did actually mind a little, but mostly because of the moronic lie I'd just told. He introduced himself as James Wissen. When I told him my name he said it was very pretty. People always tell you that when you say your name's Daisy. It must be because they think it's polite to say something more than just 'oh'. He asked which part of America I came from. When I said I was from Las Vegas he said he'd always wanted to go. He's about the last person I could ever imagine seeing there so I asked why. He said he'd wanted to visit since reading this fascinating book called *Learning from Las Vegas*. Perhaps I ought to check it out.

As soon as the names and nationalities were done he got back on the poetry case and started asking which poets I liked. The fact is, I hate them all. I find the whole notion of poetry 100% disgusting. But I didn't want to get too picky too soon with the only person who's shown any interest in me since I got here (apart from Jo). For an embarrassingly long moment, I couldn't remember any poets – even shitty ones. I was about to resort to Shakespeare when I remembered the name John Wieners. I don't know where it came from, but I was glad it did. James said he'd heard the name but hadn't read his poems. My mouth became very articulate on the subject. I guess it was glad to have someone to chat to. All this stuff came out about America in the 1950s, Wieners's schizophrenia and guilt about his homosexuality, and his love poems written in the persona of a woman. It almost made me want to read him.

James told me he was an architect, but that he was sick of it. He said he fantasized about going to live in the French countryside. He claimed he'd rather be a bit poorer and do more of the things he really enjoyed, like painting. I asked what type of stuff he did and he said he was very interested in Cézanne, but that he hadn't done enough painting himself to have developed his own style. I admired him for wanting to take a drop in salary in the name of enjoying his life, but it depressed me to think that he'd also be doing it in the name of some lame-sounding paintings. He said it was great that I

35

was devoting myself to my poetry while I was young, because the older you got, the harder it got to get back to the things you cared about. Apparently, the worst decision he had ever made was to study architecture rather than art. He asked whether I published my work. I wished I hadn't told him such a dumb lie. I said not yet. He told me about a friend of his called Souazik who edits a quarterly poetry journal. I can't imagine anyone I'd have less in common with. He said she was particularly keen on discovering new poets from around the world and that he was sure she'd be interested in my writing.

The whole time we were talking, I couldn't tell whether he was hitting on me or not. I'm very naïve about things like that. My best friends, Heidi and Luce, have, at different times, tried to drum the idea into my brain that any man who talks to a girl out of the blue only does it because he wants to jump on her. I don't think this is true. How can he know whether or not he wants to jump on you until he's checked you out? He might start up the conversation because he thinks you have nice legs, a nice face or are alone and therefore an easy target. But it's not until he's talked to you that he can begin to decide whether or not he actually wants to take it further. Luce tells me that I only think like this because I don't have the first clue about men – although I'm not sure where she gets her authority from as she's only ever dated women.

After about twenty minutes' batting the breeze James suddenly looked at his watch and said he had to go home to pick up some documents for a meeting. He told me it'd been really nice to meet me and that he'd love to read some of my poetry sometime.

I stood up with him and he asked whether I was in a rush to go anywhere. When I said I wasn't he looked really pleased. He said it'd have to be a 'fleeting visit' as he was in a 'tearing hurry', but that if I'd like to come with him to his flat he had 'a marvelous little present' for me. I must have pulled a terrible face. He laughed and said I could wait for him on the sidewalk if I felt nervous. The offer made me feel safe, so I accepted.

His flat was just along from the gallery. It was in a beautiful white building overlooking the Thames. The lobby was really smart, with turquoise carpets, cream walls and an old elevator with sliding brass doors. I would have felt like a dork waiting outside, so I went up with him.

The place was fantastic. He left me in the living room while he arranged his papers next door. He had some great stuff – a mix of minimal modern furniture with Persian rugs, carved African figures, paintings (which looked interesting at the time but which I now can't remember) and hundreds of books. Most of them seemed to be art books, but I noticed he had a massive philosophy section going all the way from Plutarch and Epicurus right up to Derrida, Baudrillard and some others I hadn't heard of. I wonder whether he's read it all or whether he's just showing off.

He reappeared in the living room with his briefcase in one hand and a playing-card-sized chunk of green glass in the other. He held the glass out to me. I took it out of his hand and looked at it admiringly. It was about a centimeter thick and one side was glazed with a metallic speckle. The edges looked quite sharp. It was pretty appealing, but I wondered what in hell had inspired him to give it to me. Maybe he'd been lying about the gift and the glass chip was the only thing that came to hand when I actually agreed to come home with him. He said he had to rush and that he'd tell me all about it next time. What a tricky bastard.

There was a big silver car parked right outside the front door. He was driving up to Covent Garden and asked whether I needed a ride anywhere. I didn't feel like getting into his car so I said I was going the other way. He reached into his pocket for a business card which he pressed into my palm and then kept hanging onto my hand, looking me straight in the eye, as he said, 'Call me'. It was pure cheese but my legs went wobbly anyway.

I went back to the Tate to have a look around the gift shop. I bought a really great book called *Shoes*. It has hundreds of pictures of different amazing shoes. I love shoes. I really believe that it doesn't matter how shitty your clothes are, if you have good shoes, people will believe you're stylish. Horrible clothes with the right shoes suddenly look witty and ironic. I wear mostly thrift-store stuff or things I make myself, but I spare no expense with footwear. The ones I have on at the moment are a pair of two-tone golf shoes.

I can't keep secrets so I thought I'd better tell Rob about James Wissen. Rob's often told me that he's not the jealous type, and I hadn't done anything wrong anyway. He got a real rant-on about danger. He couldn't believe I'd gone up to a stranger's flat on my own.

I'd probably describe myself as quite a paranoid person. But not when it comes to personal safety. I'm always worrying that the people I know don't really like me or that they say shitty things about me when I'm not there. But I'm not particularly concerned about strangers trying to murder me. I remember Lara used to load her purse up with mace sprays, rape alarms and small, hard objects but I've never been too concerned with all that. I hate to draw conclusions from anything as arbitrary and unfair as Lara's accident, but I think it's right to say that, as you can't predict the thing that's finally going to get you, you might as well not panic too much meanwhile. (This comparison has made me feel really guilty. In fact I think it ought to go.) It never *seriously* occurred to me that James was dangerous.

38

Rob made me swear not to do it again. I felt he was treating me like a child. I don't see why my house-call should upset him so much. Maybe he *is* jealous after all. I hope so. I decided not to tell him about the piece of glass.

I didn't expect to miss my friends nearly as much as I do. They're so unlike the people here. My main friend Heidi is a personal fitness trainer. She really likes it and wants to stick with it. She doesn't have any other things she'd rather be doing. Luce, my other good friend, is a silver service waitress at the Flamingo Hilton. She says she'd like to have her own bar or café, but that it's hard work and a big risk. Right now she prefers to get a weekly pay check (plus tips) and not to have to worry about running a business. They're both really clever. The absence of a big plan is in no way a sign of a brain deficiency. I guess when they get older they'll probably train as therapists or something but, for now, they're happy as they are. My other friend, Lara, died. She was definitely the most ambitious of all of us. She wasn't like Leni, though. I guess she was the best friend I ever had. I was lucky to have her too. Basically, she saved me from five years of bullying at High School. In my first year I got picked on all the time for my accent, my way of dressing, the type of stuff I said, and for generally being the wrong person. Lara arrived a year later, straight in at sixth grade, without knowing anyone. She looked a little lost so I showed her around and we just got along. She was so pretty and perfect she could've dumped me after that first week and got straight in with the cashmere set but she didn't. People must have decided that there had to be *something* right with me for Lara and I to be such good friends, so they cut out pushing me around or were even occasionally nice. That's when I made friends with Heidi and Luce, who were in the eighth grade and the type of misfits who manage to fit in anyhow. Luce is pretty uncompromising and not worth picking on because she never cries and always has something to say back. She used to come to school dressed like a young Elvis Presley – something nobody else could have gotten away with. Heidi was weird and goofy-looking but extra sporty, which meant people had to be careful with her. Our teachers were pretty protective of the sporty ones. When *I* got called names or kicked in the kidneys nobody minded too much. But if it ever happened to one of the school's precious sports stars the guilty ones would be put on library duty for an entire semester.

Lara was going to be an actress. She looked a bit like Audrey Hepburn, only with freckles. Her Mom and Dad were against it, but the drama teacher at school went round to their house to tell them she had a gift and that it was their duty as parents to allow her to use it. After school she spent a few years doing TV commercials and pretending to be a Roman slave or Medieval wench down on the Strip. But then a quite big director gave her a tiny part in his movie. She was run over by a police motorbike two weeks before shooting was due to start. I bet she would have been a famous actress by now. It happened a couple of years ago and I think it may have been one of the things that prevented me from just getting on with pissing away my life and not worrying too much. You can't believe it when one of your friends dies. It's crazy to imagine all the things they might have done if bad luck hadn't got in between. When I think about Lara I still can't quite get over the fact that the great future we all pictured for her won't actually be happening. When I look at Nicole Kidman or Kate Winslet I get mad. All

I can see is that the only reason they're rich and famous is that they haven't been knocked over by a bike yet.

It's dumb, but I've really been wondering what Sofia said about us in her letter. I peeped in her room today and it was still on the table. I think she'd added more since the other day. I'd love to know what she thinks of us. I noticed the word 'simpatico' near the Las Vegas bit, so I guess she thinks we're OK. She probably has a Spanish/English dictionary on her bookshelf – maybe I could work it out. The problem is that I can't really remove the letter from her room, and it makes me nervous to stay in there too long. One idea I had was to photocopy it in Leni's fax machine. It would only take a minute. It sounds a bit pervacious [*Ed:!*] but I don't see any harm in it really. If she's saying friendly things about us, then it makes no difference. And if she isn't, I think we should know. It's probably as good a way as any to get to know her while conversation is so difficult. I know for a near-fact that neither Jo, Sofia nor Rob will be back for another couple of hours. You can never be sure about Leni, but an element of risk will only make it that bit more diverting. Leni's room is upstairs at the front. It wouldn't be hard to sneak out and into the bathroom next door. I think I'm going to do it. It'll be fun – as long as I don't get caught. Here goes . . .

I made it! I've got the letter! It was excellent! There was something really satisfying about pulling it off. I grabbed it, took it into Leni's room, and copied it without a hitch. I felt glad to be putting a piece of her gadgetry to good use. The only annoying part was that I didn't manage to find a dictionary. I've seen Sofia with one before but maybe she carries it around in her bag. I don't really mind. I enjoyed *getting* the letter so much that I'm not so bothered now about actually reading it. Maybe I could do a bit of graphology on it. I must be going cracko. Oh well. I've had a healthy shot of adrenaline for the day so I can get on with the boring stuff. I've been neglecting my washing for too long. It might be time I changed the sheets and hoovered too. I've been such a full-on tourist I've ignored some of the more basic aspects of existence. I think I've also been a bit slack because I'm confused about what these things mean when you're in a relationship. When I lived on my own I was quite good at cleaning up after myself. But since moving in with Rob I've felt conflicted about the housework. I never know, when I'm washing my own clothes, whether I should stick his dirty underpants in the machine too. Or if I should tidy his bits and pieces when I'm clearing up the room. I feel petty if I don't, and resentful if I do. So far he's never done anything like that for me. He's too busy at college. Maybe if he lived on his own he'd just let everything rot and not worry about it. I don't see why he should be forced to live up to my exacting standards of hygiene, but I don't want to live in a pit. If I just tidy my stuff and not his, the room's still a mess and I might as well not have bothered. I can't understand why the fact that I have feelings for someone should mean I have twice as many boring household things to deal with. I think it may be very unnatural to have a boyfriend in this day and age.

[Ed: Here is a transcript of Sofia's letter. I have followed it with a translation for non-Spanish-speaking readers.

3 de Octubre

Querida Familia:

Especialmente cuando voy al trabajo y vuelvo en un autobús de esos de dos pisos, es cuando más pienso en vosotros sentados en la galería on en le jardín en El Ortondo.Que difícil de comprender las diferencias que hay entre los mundos que vivimos. Todas esas escapadas de rebajas a Madrid poco me prepararon para mi vida en Londres. Las dos primeras semanas como ya sabeis fueron horribles. Espero no haberos preocupado demasiado con todas esas lágrimas tontas por teléfono. Ayer conté un mes desde que estoy aquí y mi piel ya se va pareciendo más a una corteza de tocino de Hebra.

Las cosas en el trabajo están yendo bien. Dadle las gracias a Josefina por su consejo -el Sr. Gurruchaga no me ha tocado la roddilla desde entonces.

La gente con quien vivo sigue siendo extraños. La chica morena que me entrevistó por la habitación casi nunca la veo. A la otra la veo cuando toca, pero a ésa no hay quien la entienda. Me habla como si yo fuese una jili, y no se si lo hace porque es educada o porque es lengua mala. Una pareja de Las Vegas se ha mudado a la casa recientemente. El es simpático, incluso habla un poco de Español, pero la novia es un caso más complejo. El tipo de mujer por quien el tío Alfredo perdería la cabeza y luego se quejaría llamándola histérica sin remedio. Ahora que hay menos gasto con el alquiler llamaré más por teléfono. Ya vereís.

43

Manuela – ¿Cómo van tus cosas? Espero que note estén haciendo estudiar demasiado duro. ¿Me has robado toda o sólo una parte de mi ropa? Si la lavas con suavizante prometo no matarte cuando vuelva estas Navidades. ¿Como lo llevas ahora que no tienes a una con laquien pelearte? No importa cuanto mejora mi Inglés, jamás encontraré aalguien que me arranque los pelos como tu lo haces -¡de pura raíz! No te preocupes por el curso. No te piden que lo entiendas, sólo que te aprendas los nombres para que no hagas el ridículo cuando sales ha cenar.

Diego -!La universidad no puede ser tan mala como todo eso que cuentas! Las premeras semanas son siempre horribles -y eso va para todo, créeme. Por lo menos en la universidad nunca te obligan a lavarte el pelo. Eso es ideal para los Heavy Metals y para un mamarracho como tú. El resto del mundo es menos amigable para los mal olientes genios matemáticos. Y que conste que una no quiere marimandonearte como una hermana mayor, pero creo que deberías continuar. Escríbeme.

Parece que estoy madurando un poco, pero no lo suficiente para ya no echaros en falta.

Dear Family,

Particularly on the way to work and home again, on one of those buses with two floors, I think of you all sitting in the gallery or in the garden at El Ortondo. How hard it is to understand the differences between the worlds we are living in. All those trips to the sales in Madrid little prepared me for my life in London. The first two weeks, as you know, were horrible. I hope you were not too preoccupied with all my stupid tears on the telephone. Yesterday I counted that I'd been here two months and my skin is becoming more like a rhinoceros's. {Ed: The literal translation would be something more like 'the tough rind on a piece of cured meat from Hebra', but I decided I'd rather take liberties.]

Things at work are going well. Please give thanks to Josefina for her advice — Mr. Gurruchaga has not touched my knee since.

The people with whom I live continue to be strangers. The black-haired girl who interviewed me for the room, I hardly ever see. As for the other, I see her when it's time, but no one can understand her. She talks to me as if I were a silly billy and I don't know whether she does it because she is polite or bad-mouthed. A couple from Las Vegas have moved to the house recently. He is sympathetic as well as speaking a little Spanish, but the girlfriend seems to be a more complex case. The type of woman uncle Alfredo would call a hysteric without remedy. Now that there is less to spend on the rent I'll call more often. You'll see.

Manuela — How are things? I hope they are not making you study too hard. Have you stolen all or only some of my clothes? If you wash them with fabric conditioner I promise not to kill you when I return to the house for Christmas. How is it going without having me to fight with? It is not important how much my English improves I will never meet anyone who will grab me by the hairs as you do — straight from the roots! Do not worry about your course. You are not supposed to understand, only to learn the names so as not to be ridiculous when you go out to dinner.

Diego — University cannot be as bad as you say it is! The first few weeks are always horrible — and that applies to everything, believe me. At least at University no one obliges you to wash your hair. It is ideal for Heavy Metallers and for a big scribble like you. The rest of the world is less amicable towards stinky maths geniuses. Although this confirms that I am one, I do not want to boss you around like a big sister, but I believe you should carry on. Write to me.

I think I may be maturing a little but not enough that I miss you any less . . .]

★

I called Mom and Dad last night. It was OK to talk to Dad, but Mom was her usual self. She's pretty annoyed about me coming here for all kinds of reasons, although she was trying hard not to show it. It made me mad. Why should she care if I want to visit my own birthplace? Mom is so fucking controlling. First she made my Dad and me move to Boston, which was bad enough already, and then to Las Vegas, which is about as terrible as it gets. Just because she has a swanky job title (she's a big-time endocrinologist) and the government can't stop throwing money at her she thinks she's licensed to push us around. Well it might work on Dad, but I'm not letting her do it to me any more. She's practically ruined his whole life that way. They met at Cambridge – he was doing an English degree and she was studying medicine. He's from London and she's originally from Connecticut. (Do normal people put shit like this in their journals? It's either my fantasies of being discovered or it's because I don't have any brothers and sisters to discuss family stuff with.) My Dad is a writer, although he doesn't publish his work. I think he takes it too seriously ever to send it to mere agents or editors. He won't even show it to me. He's been working on the same book for thirty years now. I have no doubt that it's a work of genius, I just wish he'd publish it to give Mom something to suck on. Because she gets so much funding she's allowed to make all the decisions about where they live, what they eat, where they go on vacation, what he wears. It's so unfair. He got the highest mark ever given by his University to a Literature student (according to Mom, who likes to brag about him even though she's done everything possible to prevent him from doing anything with his life). She supposedly supports him so that he can get on with his work. In reality it's just meant she's had the last word on everything and that she makes him go on stupid pepper-buying missions every day like he's the butler or something. I hope sometime soon he manages to show the world what a smart guy he is.

Our first move to Boston happened when I was four years old. I don't remember it that well, but I don't recall thinking it was too terrible or anything. Mom got some sort of research post at the University and it seemed like a great opportunity (for her). We stayed there for seven or so years and it was OK. When I was eleven, and just about to start at a new school – with a cool gray and red uniform – Mom was head-hunted for a new research post opening up in Vegas. Dad could hardly believe it. He quite likes Hunter S. Thompson and all those kinds of swingy Sixties writer types, but I don't imagine he ever saw himself living a tame domestic existence with a wife and a kid out in the suburbs of Sin City. I don't think he really wanted to go – and I made no secret of the fact that *I* didn't. I had no idea what Las Vegas was at that age, apart from things I'd half-noticed in the news. I just knew I didn't want to live there. I had friends in Boston, I knew my way around, and the last thing I wanted was to go to this place where all the stupid people went and where only dumb or bad things happened. Over the years my opinion of it didn't change much. The ceiling at *Caesar's Palace* is nice the first three times or so, you can go swimming for free (if you don't mind the sight of the tourists) and the thrift stores are some of the best in America (because nobody else shops in them so you can always get cool stuff). Apart from that it sucks.

It's funny that I've started writing now I'm here. Dad gave me this notebook as a going away present. I never write – I think the last time I did was in a school exam eleven years ago. I thought it might have put me off forever, but it's actually not so bad. I was pretty surprised by his choice of farewell gift – which I think he noticed – but he just said I should jot down whatever came into my head and at some stage in the future I'd be glad I did.

Shops

I bought some great shoes. I think they must be Japanese. They're made from red leather, come halfway up the leg and are split between the first two toes.

The first place I went was Covent Garden. It was OK. The market part was horrible but there were some really good places on the other side of the station. There was a little street with about eight shoe shops. I must have tried on a zillion pairs before I bought the ones I did. I hope I made the right choice. I decided the split toes would help me more to fit in. You'd never see anything like them in Vegas.

After the successful shoe-buy I went to Oxford Street. It was seriously depressing. I may love to shop, but I hate to see too many other people doing it too. Human beings look terrible when they're shopping. The shoppers in Oxford Street seemed to fall into three main types. The majority were ditzy people milling about in the hope of stumbling into some consumable that might help keep the lid on whatever hideous void was threatening to eat up their lives. Then there were the ferocious shoppers who probably needed something urgently for a wedding, job interview or critically important date. And finally the smallest, and most annoying, category were the euphoric day-trippers. The first kind are the saddest and the ones I feel most sympathy with. The second come across as straight-

49

forwardly evil. But the third are genuinely disturbing. Why are they so pleased to be shopping? And why do they have to show it by screaming, giggling and running around? What is it about going in and out of department stores that makes them so crazy? Are they excited about the ways in which their new things might change their lives for the better – making other people like them, admire them or feel envious? Do they get some kind of freaky thrill out of financial transactions? I always feel terrible when I spend money. How do they manage to buy things *and* laugh so much? They must be nihilists.

To make it all worse, now that I'm not earning every expenditure feels like a major loss. I just spent £50 on those shoes. That's more than my week's rent. Because I bought them I'll have to start dealing with my career crisis even sooner than I might have, and I'm sure there's not an employer anywhere who would accept me if I wore them to an interview. Economically, I now see they were a very bad move. But if they make me feel more settled I guess I could think of them as an investment.

Here I am again! I just can't stop writing. What a bunch of assholes. I'm too embarrassed to go back, but it's intolerable to sit on my own in this shitty bedroom.

Rob hates my shoes. He said they were the most disgusting things he had ever seen on anybody's feet ever, even taking into account his entire family's verruccas, bunions and corns.

He said it in front of the others too. He asked how much they cost and then looked at me like I'd committed a truly odious crime (I even knocked £10 off the real price because I felt guilty). It's none of his business how I waste my savings, but he had the audacity to seem annoyed. Fuck him. I think he's been waiting to get mad at me since the James Wissen incident. He's too hung-up on pretending to be perfect to admit to feeling jealous. Jo said she thought my shoes were funky. Great. Leni said 'Oh dear', and Sofia giggled and said something to Rob in Spanish which he found completely hilarious and refused to translate. I loved my shoes when I bought them and imagined the whole world would love them too. What's everybody's problem?

Now I feel like they're all having a housemates' bonding experience at my expense. I can just imagine them laughing about my shoes and the way I stormed out of the room. I can almost handle that sort of shit from the others but it makes me really depressed to think that my boyfriend is a feelingless asshole with conservative taste. I don't mind *him* wearing his stupid fratty-bagger button-downs but he can't expect me to join him. People are so screwed up about clothes.

Sofia was the worst. How dare she talk behind my back in front of my face to my own boyfriend? This is the most home-sick I have felt so far. I wish I could call Luce or Heidi. But I feel like I'd need to talk for hours and it would cost about a billion dollars. Plus the telephone is in the kitchen and I couldn't face going in to get it. (I just heard the doorbell. I wonder who it is. But then again, who cares? I know for a fact that it can't possibly be anyone for me.)

Luce, Heidi and Lara are the only people I feel like talking to in the whole world and two of them are thousands of miles away and one of them's dead. How come life got to be so terrible? Lara was buried, not cremated. I'd never let anyone do that to me. I have two very clear and conflicting pictures of her right now. I remember her drinking a coffee milkshake. And then I see her body putrefying in a moldy, satin-lined coffin. The horrible thing is that, when I think of her, one of the biggest feelings I get is self-pity. I think it's so unfair that I can't see her any more.

Rob and I managed to sort out our row last night, which is lucky as I was almost thinking of killing myself. He brought me a plate of the pasta they'd all cooked together. I was gushing tears. He sat down on the bed next to me, stroked my hair and started going 'Poor, poor Daze.' It made me so mad. I told him the fact that he called me Daze was clear proof that he didn't even know me or understand the first thing about me. I also told him he was a clothing-fascist-jock. He sat there very calmly. I told him the food looked like a plate of dog vomit.

I was crying like a nut and banging my fists on the bed when we started to hear strange noises from upstairs. Jo's boyfriend had come round to the house for the evening and they were clearly making the most of it. I hate to hear other people humping. Even in the cinema I find love scenes irritating. But Jo banging away in her porno undies a couple of meters above my head was too much. Rob hardly knew what to do with himself.

Some of Jo's noises seemed a little fake. But the ones that didn't were the worst. The bits I found unconvincing were the cute girlie moans. I'm sure they were only for the sake of politeness. The most realistic stuff was the panicky yelping and gurgling. She made such ugly sounds you had to assume she meant them. The boyfriend was more down-to-earth and straightfor-wardly sporty. He stuck mostly to grunting and panting. When he spurted he let out a growl like an engine winding down. They kept it up for hours. Rob and I have never gone for it quite so much in one sitting. When we first heard them we were really embarrassed, but after a while we started laughing. I couldn't sit there feeling suicidal with cutesy Jo making such stupid sounds upstairs. It really stopped our row though. By about bang number four Rob even said he was starting to like my 'cloven hooves' (giving me an insight into why he hated the shoes so much – him being a well-indoctrinated Evangelist and everything). I felt a real idiot for making such a fuss. I'm glad I'm still here.

I can't decide what to do today. Maybe I could ring James Wissen. Then again maybe not. The idea makes me nervous and I don't think Rob would be too thrilled.

I went to Deptford Market because Jo recommended it. It was a good tip. I'd never seen anything like it. Deptford Market has a kind of colorful, carnival atmosphere mixed with under-tones of really deep misery. I've seen enough of *that* where I come from, but not like they do it in Deptford. You can get every single possible color of nail varnish for 50p a bottle. There's also a guy selling a carpet cleaner that can apparently remove horrible marks and stains without scrubbing. I would have got some if I believed it might remove the horrible marks that make up the designs of our carpets. The best part of the market was the old clothes section. They had some interesting ideas about pricing. There was one cart guarded by a tiny boy with white hair. When I asked how much something was he told me it was 'One for 50p, two for a pound, three for a pound, four for a pound, five for a pound, six for a pound or seven for one pound twenty'.

I bought a strange purse made out of a rolled up copy of *Playboy*. I doubt I'll actually use it but I wanted to own it because it was such an amazing thing. Why would a woman want to walk around with a pretend copy of *Playboy*? I can't imagine. It's my bag now though, so I can spend the rest of my life working out why a girl (like me) would be drawn to such a dumb gimmick.

I also got a black crêpe 1950s dress for £1. I couldn't understand why it was so cheap. I asked the stallholder – a woman in her sixties who looked like she could do with a break – if she was sure about the price. She looked at me like I'd totally flipped and said, 'I can only eat one dinner, luv.' What are these people on?

Leni stuck a really bitchy note on one of the cupboards this morning. She left a pair of trainers in the kitchen the other day and they smelt so bad someone – either Sofia or Jo – must have put them outside. Leni went mad looking for them only to find they'd been shredded and scattered all over the garden. It's a bit spooky to think about who did it, but I'm sure it wasn't any of us. And what was she doing leaving her reeky fungus breeders in a communal space anyhow?

It seems like there are some pretty unwholesome things going on in this street. The back gardens are really dark at night and there's a train track at the bottom so I guess all sorts of scary people might be able to sneak in. But why would they rip up a pair of shoes? Maybe they tried to break in, failed, felt angry and decided to do a little damage. I can't really force myself to care too much about Leni's trainers but at least now we know we ought to be really careful about locking up.

[Ed: Leni, this note almost makes me love you.

My Darling Housemates,

My angels! my pets! How privileged I am to be sharing my life with you. But my property is still my property and not yours to toy around with as your whims dictate. If I leave a pair of costly, beautiful and relatively new trainers in the kitchen I expect to be able to revisit them there, exactly as I left them. But no! One of you has taken it upon yourself to deny me this right and to subject my precious shoes to the cruelest of fates! What had they ever done to you?

As we all know, the kitchen is not the most inviting room. If your intention was to make it lovelier, why not wash the dishes, mop the floor or empty the dustbin? Did offering my shoes to the Beast of Brockley do anything to alter the fact that all our cutlery is coated in a fine veneer of filth? Or to shift the slippery vegetable pulp from the plughole of the sink? I rest my case.

Truly, sincerely and above all angrily,
Leni.]

★

Last night when we were all asleep, Mom and Dad rang and left the most pathetic message ever. Well, Dad's part was sweet, but Mom's was really annoying. I don't think she noticed that the ansaphone wasn't me. Maybe she even chose to ring so late because there's no chance of the machine disagreeing with her or telling her to shut up. She still seems pretty annoyed with me for having left. Not because she enjoyed me living nearby, but because she can't understand why I would abandon a perfectly good career in web design to chase a boy halfway across the world. She saw it as some kind of miracle that someone as ill-educated as me had managed to get a respectable job, and thinks this marvel is unlikely to repeat itself during my lifetime. She didn't mention any of this in her recording, thank God. She just left her message in such a terse voice that I could tell she was still seething. Although I'm twenty-nine I have a very adolescent attitude towards my mother. Basically, I wish she didn't exist.

Dad asked how the journal was coming along. I wonder why it matters to him. I think it's going quite well. It's not exactly *Robinson Crusoe* but I really enjoy writing it – although I'm not too convinced that in the future I'll be glad I did. If Mom ever read it she'd spontaneously combust on the spot.

Because I've failed so far to get hold of a Spanish/English dictionary I've decided to go ahead with a graphological study of Sofia's letter. I feel quite passionately that graphology is a legitimate means of finding out about a person. It makes sense. If one person has tiny, squished-up writing and another makes giant, swirly marks then that difference must surely mean something. If Sofia and I can't talk too much to each other, I might as well get to know her in other ways. It's important to see how each writer lines up their margins and lays out their lines, and whether they form their letters the same every time or whether each *g, t* and *y* is different. The book I use is called *Understanding Graphology* by Hubert Desenclos. I love it so much I brought it to London with me (along with my copies of *The Great Gatsby, Tender is the Night, The Beautiful and Damned* and all the short stories including Zelda's). Desenclos is a very serious man, trained by the Paris Société de Graphologie. My own graphological portrait was perfect, only it didn't tell me anything new. It basically said I was confused and uncertain with an inquiring mind and need to love. Rob's seemed accurate too. It said he was methodical, rational and capable of enjoying life, although he had to watch out for his sado-anal tendencies in relationships. This last bit was something I was glad to be made aware of.

[Ed: I have included a sample from Sofia's letter. Perhaps, given the evidence, other budding graphologists will disagree with Daisy's conclusions.

Although I feel I ought to keep my opinions to myself I can't refrain from confessing that I find all of this a heap of bogus bunkum.]

con quien vivo sigue
siendo extraños. La
chica morena que me
entrevistó por la habitación
casi nunca la veo. A la
otra la veo cuando
toca, pero no esa no
hay, quien la entienda.
Me habla como si yo fuese
una jili, y no se si lo
hace porque es educada
o es lengua mala. Una
pareja de Las Vegas se
ha mudado a la casa
recientemente. El es
simpático, incluso habla
un poco de Español, pero
la novia es un caso
mas complejo. El tipo
de mujer el dió

Sofia's character comes as a great surprise to me. I'd never have guessed she was like this from the little I know of her. But that's what's amazing about graphology – you get right under the surface without having to ask permission. Employers use it all the time these days. The main thing I didn't realize, probably due to her language difficulties, is that Sofia is usually extremely talkative (seen in her messily aligned words with animated writing style). Her social side dominates both her intellect and her inner feelings meaning that the persona she projects into the world is probably more important to her than how she actually feels. One of her best features is that she is emotionally responsive and has a great capacity to empathize (close-packed lines with overlapping stems). She also gives the appearance of being exceptionally cheerful – although this may be a bit put on. Her enthusiasm and adaptability ought to make her a good housemate, although another part of her chart suggests that she can be argumentative and difficult to live with (crooked *g* stems with pressure on paper and marked *t* bars). With luck this will be compensated by her loving nature (full o with wide, irregular word-spacing).

On a less positive note, she is liable to be headstrong, inconsiderate and exceptionally aggressive (lively script with stress on ending strokes). She can also be pretty slack and indecisive, disguising her negligence under the appearance of an easy going nature (unemphasized capital letters with soft, rounded forms). Her stubbornness and ungovernability are liable to aggravate those friends not already alienated by her desperate need to compete (*h* and *d* tops leaning to the right with pronounced *t* bars).

She is also clearly an aesthete (streamlined simplifications with plenty of connective movement).

Who'd believe you could get so much from looking at someone's writing? I can see it all now. The other day when Sofia talked in Spanish to Rob about my shoes she was just being characteristically aggressive and competitive. And all her friendliness is just her desperately trying to hide how fucked up she feels. Poor her though, being so talkative and not being able to speak. I guess there are Spanish speakers at her office but with all that anxiety and inner turmoil she must go nuts when she can't just relax and chat at home. I think before I did her reading that I was starting to hate her but now I feel a little more tolerant. I know it said she was going to be a difficult person to live with but at least if you have an insight into why it can make things easier.

I'd like to call James Wissen but guilt is holding me back. I'm not exactly hot for him and affairs are very much against my principles, but I feel like having a conversation with somebody outside our house. I also wouldn't mind finding out about that bit of glass. I'm getting quite attached to it. When Rob asked what it was I told him I found it in the street. I suppose it comes from a bowl that got broken by the cleaner or something. James is a creep for not telling me. It's working though. Curiosity is finally overcoming my conscience enough to allow me to ring. No one will be back for at least another half hour so I'd better get on with it. I'll try him at his office . . .

. . . I've got a lunch date for tomorrow! He called me darling. We're going to the proper restaurant at the Tate – not the café. Maybe he chose it because it's so near his house. I don't think I should go up there again though. He sounded all schmoozy on the phone. Maybe he was whispering because he was at work. I bet architects have open plan offices. What have I got myself into? I really hate lying but I don't feel I can tell Rob – not because I'm doing anything wrong, more because I'm not. If I say I'm having lunch with that guy whose house I went into after meeting him in a café he'll go nuts. (Or worse, he'll go secretly nuts and bitch at me for some unrelated reason a couple of days later.) But the fact is that nothing's going to happen. I might as well save Rob a dose of angst by not telling him. I know I'm not interested in sugar-daddies, but Rob may have trouble believing me. So the best thing I can do is just keep quiet about it. It's the ethical solution.

I also lied to James *again* about my writing – I told him it was going fine. He asked if I'd show him some of my work. I said maybe. He mentioned someone called Souazik, saying he'd try to introduce us. He referred to her as if I'd know who he meant. I couldn't remember what he was on about so I just said, 'That's nice', although frankly it was pretty annoying. I remembered afterwards that she was the poetry woman. I'll just have to make excuses.

There's the door. I wonder who it is. I haven't spoken to Sofia since she was such a witch about my shoes the other day. I'd better go sort it out. Maybe it's Jo. I'd love to know what she thought of Leni's note. Oh well. I'll have to do some PR for myself after flipping my wig in front of everyone. Whoever it is I'd better just go and be nice to them if I want to have some hope of a happy domestic future.

Lunch with James was really something. I'm still in shock. I read a Jilly Cooper novel once. (I must have been about twelve and was very interested in sex, although I couldn't quite believe anybody actually did it). James is exactly like one of those guys. I thought it all sounded pretty moon-assed on paper, but I guess I hadn't met any sophisticated middle-aged English men at that point in my life – apart from Dad, who's my Dad and doesn't count.

It was good to have a reason to dress up. I tried not to go too over-enthusiastic, but it was a chance to christen my crêpe dress. We met in the foyer and he guided me down to the restaurant by the waist. I always thought this was a pretty vile gesture, but I think it may depend on who does it. If Rob tried any waist-guiding stuff with me I'd probably either laugh or throw, but from James it seemed quite acceptable – perhaps because it was balanced against all the advantages that come with being over forty, like lack of gaucheness and a cool out-look. While Rob's ambitions tend to make him see his future as enemy territory that has to be conquered and brought strictly under his rule, James seems to have a more relaxed relation to his own lifespan. If Rob is going all-out to triumph over the rest of his existence, James is more interested in finding out ways of enjoying himself.

The Tate restaurant is quite cool. It has some schlocky murals of castles and forests on the walls, but the food was delicious. I had smoked salmon blinis followed by venison. I haven't been to many restaurants in my life – particularly not swanky ones – so I find it pretty thrilling. It isn't so much that I haven't been able to afford it, more that it's never been a priority. My parents hardly went to restaurants either and when they did it always felt like they were doing it against their better judgement. We'd never have a first course and after the main dish they'd suggest that we had coffee and ice cream back home. I suppose the truth is that I've always seen eating out as a waste of money, although when it happens I love it.

We talked about a load of things. I told James I'd come to London quite suddenly, but that I'd been trying to escape from Vegas for ages. I also told him about Rob. I felt reluctant to mention my boyfriend situation as I was afraid it might ruin the cozy atmosphere, but James didn't visibly react to the information at all. I was half glad but wondered why. Although I'm not going to have an affair with him, I still wish he'd shown some kind of disappointment. I told him I wasn't sure exactly what I was doing with my life. That really set him off. He's absolutely fixated on the idea of me being a poet. I don't quite understand why, but it seems very important to him. He went on and on about how meaningless a career was in relation to a vocation. Naturally, I had to live. But I shouldn't worry too much about a *career*. He insisted that, as I was sure I needed to write, if I forced myself into a career against my will I'd only look back with remorse in fifteen years' time. He also said that it was worse to find yourself on a four-poster deathbed in a mansion feeling like your life had been wasted than on a poky little deathbed feeling like your life had been eventful and worthwhile. I told him I didn't want to start thinking of myself on any deathbeds for ages. (And as the whole poetry thing is a great big fish story anyway I can hardly expect it to save me from a tormented old age – although I didn't tell him this part.) Maybe he only likes me because he thinks I'm a poet. Maybe I could get into poetry. But I hate the idea of justifying my existence with some pathetic fantasy of a vocation, meanwhile dressing in rags and thinking that anyone who can afford to pay their own gas account is a sell-out.

James told me a little bit about his marriage, which ended seven years ago. He was pretty evasive. One thing he did say was that he occasionally found himself wishing he had kids, although he was very glad he'd never had any with his ex-wife. I found his confession pretty embarrassing so I didn't ask why. I think I would have liked to know but I can be quite shy about asking intimate questions. I love to hear all about people's lives and their feelings but I don't want them to think I'm just nosy. What of any value would I have to say to James about the breakdown of his fourteen year relationship anyhow? I don't even know what it's like to date the same person for more than eighteen months.

I asked him about the glass chip. He looked at me mischievously and said he'd tell me over coffee. I'd had a few glasses of wine by then so I told him it'd better be good or I'd be forced to try out my coffee trick on him. I don't know what made me say it. My coffee trick is extremely unpleasant and not at all funny. Nobody I have ever played the coffee trick on has ever been impressed.

The coffees came and I said 'So?' He told me his company had been working with the set designers at the National Ballet a couple of years ago on a production of *A Midsummer Night's Dream*. Oberon's costume had apparently involved a heavy glass lower torso. The day before the opening one of the wardrobe assistants had knocked it off its stand and smashed it to pieces. My piece of green glass was a remnant of the king of the fairies' codpiece. It was a good enough explanation and didn't deserve the coffee trick at all but he seemed to want to know what it was.

The coffees were hot. I dropped a couple of lumps of sugar into mine and left the spoon in the cup while they dissolved. I asked James some kind of boring question about whether he'd enjoyed working for the ballet. This was all part of the trick. He started to answer and when he looked reasonably off-guard I lifted my spoon out of the cup and calmly placed the hot metal on the back of his wrist. His reaction was terrible. I really regretted the joke. He gave out a loud yelp and his whole body convulsed, spilling the rest of his drink all over the white tablecloth and knocking one of the wineglasses onto the floor. Either the wail or the smashing glass brought the waiter rushing over. James got really flustered and told the guy rather irritably that it was all fine and that we'd like the check. I was mortified. He started dabbing at the splashes on his jacket and not looking up at me. I went mad apologizing, without much hope of redeeming myself. I could see a nasty red smutch forming where I had hot-spooned him. It was one of the most painful and embarrassing moments of my life.

When the waiter came back I was still firing off apologies and James hadn't spoken. I insisted on paying, even though it was about £75 and I definitely shouldn't spend that sort of amount on lunch. It cost even more than my shoes making it certain that I won't be able to talk to Rob about it.

We put on our coats and left the restaurant in silence. He guided me by the waist again but this time it just felt embarrassing and uncomfortable. When we got out onto the steps I felt I wanted to get away from him as quickly as possible. I apologized again and he turned his head aside. I looked down at his hand. The blotch was even redder in the daylight than it had looked under the dim restaurant lighting. I stared at it for an impossibly long few seconds as if to check out how much damage I'd done before saying a final goodbye. The thing that snapped me out of my trance was noticing the hand come suddenly to life and click its fingers. My eyes shot upwards to catch him looking directly back at me. He seemed very serious. I couldn't imagine what he was about to say. He said, 'Would you like to try having another coffee at my house?' I said, 'Oh!', stupidly. The one thing I promised myself I wouldn't do today was to go up to James's house. After the hot-spoon thing I would have gone a long way to make it up to him, so going round to his apartment was a probably a very bad idea. I said something like, 'Err . . . aah . . . um . . . I . . . I . . . I think I'd . . . I'd better get back . . . You know? . . . mmm. But thanks. Er . . . goodbye.' I felt that he would be able to see perfectly clearly what my stuttering meant (something along the lines of, 'Basically yes please but I really like you and I have a boyfriend so there's no way I could trust myself to be alone with you in your apartment.') But perhaps he understood it as something more like, 'No thanks, you petulant bastard' or, 'Get away from me you depressing, middle-aged creep'. Whatever he understood wasn't given away by his reaction, which was virtually non-existent. He just said, 'OK darling, give me a bell and we'll see if we can organize something with Souazik.' We politely kissed each other goodbye and I ran off down the steps without looking back. The whole experience left me with a feeling of really deep shame and inadequacy worse than anything I have suffered since puberty.

I'm going to have to start hiding my notepad from Rob, although I still refuse to allow myself to have an affair. I don't know why I object to affairs so strongly. I've never had one, none of my boyfriends has ever hurt me by having one and no one in my family, as far as I know, has ever done it either. I have no real right to hold anything against affairs as they have never harmed me or anyone close to me. I just don't believe in them. I believe that if you find yourself liking someone while you're with someone else you should make a decision in favor of one or the other person and stick with it. I think it's greedy and pathetic to imagine you can have both as long as you are a good enough liar. I guess there are relationships where you can sleep with other people without lying to your partner, but I'm not in one. I'm quite sure that if I went to bed with someone else Rob would leave me. Thinking about it now I wonder whether it's *me* Rob likes or the fact that another human being is exclusively his to sleep with. Maybe the conditions of the relationship are more important to him than *I* am. Perhaps having an affair would be the way to work out whether he really loves me. I could never do it. It's just too shitty. It's

Oh my God! I didn't hear Rob come in last night. He saw me scribbling away and asked what it was. I told him it was just all my impressions of the trip so far. He said he'd like to read it. I told him I'd find it too embarrassing as it wasn't meant for anyone else to see – or at least not during my lifetime. I said he'd probably find it boring. I'm sure he would too, except the last part, which he'd find unforgivable. He must have been in an extra frisky mood after a hard day at the library and started trying to wrestle the book from me. I put up a pretty good fight, luckily, and managed to pin him to the floor with my knee on his chest and to fling the book into a corner.

(Ed: This notebook is the most buckled and battered of the three. I presume much of the damage took place during this particular incident.) It was really fun to be able to be stupid with Rob and roll around on the floor and tickle each other. I'm sure I could never have so much fun with serious old James. I don't even want to have an affair any more.

This is the last time I'll be writing in this book as I don't feel safe leaving it lying around. I'm going to pretend I left it on a bus and get a new one. I guess I'd better use this last opportunity to talk about something I care about. One of the things that's really on my mind at the moment is the future – particularly mine. I wish I had a better idea of what to expect. It must be great to know what you'll be doing – although I suppose you never actually *know*, but at least if you believe you do you don't have to drive yourself crazy worrying about it. Rob and I are totally different in that way. I guess you could say we're good for each other. I have no idea what I ought to do, nor have I ever had one. When I was at my first school the teachers got it into their heads that I was some kind of prodigy – only they never worked out precisely which kind. My big thing as a teenager was Classical Studies (which must be why I keep a special place in my heart for *Caesar's Palace*). I don't know why I liked it so much. I guess I enjoyed the way it was quite eclectic and you looked at architecture, religion, clothes, drama, politics and ordinary people's lives. Like, one class would be about telling a Doric column from an Ionic one, and then next week you'd talk about schoolboys being advised to smooth out the imprints of their butts in the sand to avoid arousing the older guys. Maybe I could have become an ancient Greek historian or something, but I hated school. I liked learning, I just couldn't stand having to go to such a dumb place to do it. My high school didn't exactly love me either. I never did anything really bad, I just used to come and go and not show much interest in anything. They kicked me out after eleventh grade – which really delighted Mom. I read quite a bit now. I know a little about a lot of things, but my knowledge is seriously unformulated. Dad always had a load of books at home. He wasn't too big on fiction – it was mostly sociology, anthropology and history, with a bit of critical stuff like studies of Eighteenth century literature and analyses of various forms of the novel. I tried to pick up as much as possible, but I'm not sure how much I actually 'got'. Rob really impresses me because the thing he studies is so specific. I like the idea of outer-space too. I think if you're going to limit yourself to one thing you'd better make it a good one.

Rob says he likes to be around me because I have a relaxed attitude to life. I don't know where he got *that* idea from, but it's sweet of him to believe it. He also says he's surprised that someone who's done so many different things could like a guy who's obeyed all the rules and always done everything he was meant to. All I've really done is a handful of dipshit jobs, but because his whole life has been entirely directed towards a single goal he thinks my flakey existence sounds exciting. It's true that he and I look like an unlikely couple. We dress pretty differently – I guess he's kind of *Brady Bunch* while I'm more *Adams Family*. *And* he's three years younger than me (although I'm sure it doesn't show). But I think differences are important in a relationship. If he met someone as single-minded as he is they'd only meet up about once a month. And if I tried dating someone as abjectly directionless as me we'd probably fall into a swamp or depress each other to death.

I'm hoping something of Rob's way of being will rub off on me. I'm really sick of all the lame stuff I have to do just to get by. The computer design job I had before I came here was fairly well-paid. But it was a drag (literally). It mostly involved designing websites for two-bit companies in Nevada. I managed to save up enough to leave so I suppose it wasn't a complete waste of time. I knew I was going to come to England, I just didn't know when or how. The morning after our first night together Rob got the letter confirming his scholarship. I asked if I could come with him and, without hesitating, he said yes. I was amazed. He was too. It'd been an enjoyable enough night and everything, but it seemed a bit over the top to disappear into the sunset together because of it. It wasn't exactly an intense evening – we just got on really easily. I hadn't dated anyone for ages (my boyfriend before Rob was a full-on manic-depressive nutcase who I don't even want to think about ever again). So when I met someone I felt so relaxed with, and who seemed so together, I felt like hanging on to him.

What I believe is, if you meet someone you like you ought to do everything possible to be together until you don't like each other any more. Just hanging around while it's convenient is terrible. I'm actually pretty crusading on the subject. But it's tricky when you meet someone who's on the verge of doing something drastic. For Rob, part of going for the scholarship was about getting away from Vegas and I'm sure he wasn't banking on a bit of it coming with him (not that I like to see myself as a free-floating piece of Vegasness – a girlsize gambling chip or living coin-cup). He's lucky to have me to chat to after all those zitty engineers though. I even get a bit of a wife-on every so often and wash something of his, or cook. It's funny round here when I cook for him. Leni can't believe it. She thinks it's an outrage that not only do I not have a definite career but that I might occasionally cook for my boyfriend. I just don't see the world as clear-cut as she does I guess.

Second Notebook

(hardback, William Morris print cover, ruled lines)

Home

Why do some people say they find blank pages intimidating? I guess they're worried about writing crap. It doesn't bother me. Now I've started with the writing thing the only problem I have is making myself stop in order to get other stuff done. Not that it's an issue right now. I've spent so much money in the last few days I think I'd better stay in to compensate. I don't really have anything else to do. I can't watch the TV. I find English TV completely uninteresting. I know it's famous for being great and everything, but it's not. And it looks pretty cheap. The soap operas are miserable and I'd rather chew my own toenails than watch those dumb dramas about good old British bobbies.

I wore my new shoes to the corner shop this morning and got nothing but abuse. There was a load of schoolboys sitting on a wall, smoking. They went completely nuts when I walked past. They were calling me a Mutant Ninja Turtle and laughing. I think a couple of them actually spit at me – although, if they did, they missed. I had to walk past them again on the way back. They must only have been about ten years old, but they were some of the meanest kids I ever met in my life. To make it worse, I felt so flaked out I dropped my pint of milk and they started calling me a silly bitch and a fucking useless twat and stuff. What kind of lives must they lead? I tried to get less upset by making myself feel sorry for them, but I was still shaking when I got back to the house. They made me feel like an all-out loser for spending money on designer bullshit that doesn't even look good. I wish I could remember what it was I liked about my shoes before everybody started telling me how gross they were.

I don't feel like going out again after that. Perhaps I could do some more room-research. It's free, it's entertaining and it doesn't *really* do anybody any harm . . .

The two things I can gather from today's investigations are that Jo is an even more puzzling person than I'd imagined and Leni is a talentless shmuck (good). I left Sofia pretty much out of it because she's been the main subject of my inquiries so far and deserves a break. (I did actually take a quick look just in case but didn't spot anything worth bothering with.)

When I went into Jo's room this time I was horrified to find it *exactly* the same as the last time. I know Rob's and my room hasn't been refurbished by an interior designer or anything, but at least some of Rob's books have moved from the top of the closet to the bedside table, I've changed the duvet cover from a blue one with gothic writing to a cream one with birds flying around on it, and we take our shoes off in a different place every time. Jo's room looks like one of those spooky bedrooms where the person has died and their parent or spouse has kept everything precisely as they left it. I wonder what makes her line up her hairbrushes in that way.

I wish Jo wrote a diary, but there was no sign of one any-where. I looked in all her drawers and everything. I'd sincerely like to know what goes on inside her head. I'm aware that I could try asking rather than snoop around her room when she's out. But I don't think she'd answer me truthfully. I think she'd just spout the usual bullshit. I should probably just accept that this bullshit constitutes the entirety of Jo's psyche, but I don't believe it's possible. Maybe if I spent a long time listening to her and building up trust she might begin to become more interesting. But I practically feel like smashing my head into a wall after two minutes in her company.

I'm full of schemes like this. I always imagine I'd like people if I had a bit more patience. But why can't I just allow myself to dislike them and not worry about it? I think it may be because I notice how unfair dislike is when someone does it to me. If someone likes me then I think that's OK. But if someone dislikes me I feel like they're ignoring all the good things about me and that they can only sustain their antipathy because they don't know or understand me well enough. It's very flawed logic and could work equally well in the opposite direction (the people who like me only do it because they don't know or understand the more unsavory aspects of my character). But I set a great deal of store by it anyway. So when I find myself feeling repulsed by somebody, I try to imagine a side of them I might be able to empathize with. This could all be very sweet and philanthropic, only it doesn't work out that way. Just because I have the fantasy that I may be able to love the people I hate, it doesn't mean I'm actually able to make it happen. What normally happens instead is that I hate myself for not being able to adore some sad airhead, *and* I carry on hating them too.

Leni's room was more fruitful. In her favor the mess had moved, at least giving some indication that she is alive. Her remaining Nikes were in a stinking bundle on her bed and the closet doors were wide open showing a big empty space where the wrinkled heaps of clothes might one day hope to hang. (I think I may be becoming more poetic. Perhaps I *will* eventually have something to show to Souazik.)

Under Leni's desk there was a folder. In it I found what must be the script of that short film she said she'd made. It was the lamest thing – worse than anything I'd imagined. She must have used every single cliché she could possibly dredge up. It's the story of a little girl who's too special to cope with being the offspring of a really grim Mom and Dad. Like sure, Leni, how could you be the daughter of mere mortals? Not autobiographical my ass. It's just the sad fantasy of someone who thinks they're too spectacular for their own life. The other annoying part is that half the film takes place in Morocco. Did her family pay for her to go there or did she hash the scenes together in Deptford souk? (I guess it must be the second as I'm sure that if it had been the first she would have found an opportunity to boast about having gone to Africa to make her blockbuster.) Either way it's a travesty. I took a copy of it and read it in here just so I didn't have to inhale too much of her gruyere and rubber-glue bedroom aroma. It makes me ill to think that particles from Leni's spoilt, sweaty feet have actually invaded my lungs. She can be as condescending as she likes about my taste in shoes. At least my socks couldn't be used to evacuate buildings.

★

Last night was so bad! Rob and I were alone in the house and the crying came back. It sounded slightly nearer than I remembered, but it was still hard to tell which house it came from. I called the police and they said they'd be straight over, but it took about twenty minutes. The screaming kept on all the time we were waiting but as soon as the cops arrived it disappeared. I think the baby's parents must have seen the flashing light. I hope they didn't do anything too desperate to make it stop.

Rob and I showed the police out to the garden anyhow, hoping we might hear *something*. The sounds could have been coming from one of three houses. I was practically hysterical, begging the policemen to go round and knock on some front doors. But they were too lazy and half-witted. They said they couldn't go search people's houses without a good reason, and hearing a baby crying wasn't enough. I tried to explain that the parents were locking the baby out. But, as I hadn't actually seen it, there supposedly wasn't enough evidence to justify getting people out of bed at eleven o'clock at night.

The police were exactly like the ones on the Britcop shows. One was tall and porky with colorless hair and the other was small, dark and ferrety. They both seemed quietly amused by the whole thing. I thought they were supposed to prevent crime, not sit around the station eating Battenberg Cake until a worthwhile crime had been committed. They told me to call if the noises came back but that, for now, there was nothing they could do. I've been watching out the front window all day, trying to work out who lives where, but I haven't seen much. There was one lady with a small child, but the kid looked happy and they crossed over to a house on the other side of the road.

I haven't heard the noises for a couple of days now and it doesn't seem as though any of the neighbors has a baby. Of the three likely houses, one is inhabited by an elderly couple, another by a group of three men and the third by students. Rob says I should stop obsessing and that it probably isn't anything serious or the police would have heard about it from other people too. I wish I could believe him, but I can't stop worrying. Why would a child make such a desperate noise if everything was fine? Still, it seems to be true that there isn't much I can do until the next time it happens. Looking out the window all the time is just plain unhealthy. When you have all these horrible ideas in your head *everyone* starts to look like a potential child batterer.

One of the things I like to do to relax is to make cakes and cookies. They are, in my view, the best kind of food to experiment with. I guess some people (like Leni) think it's to do with some pathetic need to *provide* or something. But I prefer to see it more as a scientific exercise backed up by a need for a material relation with history (only joking). I just love to see how different combinations of substances respond to heat. I get really fascinated observing how changing the ratio of fat to flour or flour to sugar affects how the cookies spread, crumble or crack. I also like to try out other people's elaborate recipes, like short-bread with a Florentine topping, chocolate, almond and pis-tachio wheels and cream-filled ginger snaps which you shape around the handle of a wooden spoon.

Our kitchen isn't the most welcoming environment for a fledgling pastry chef. It's a kind of no-man's land between the hallway and the spare shower. There's a table but no one ever eats off it. It's never very clean in there, even when someone makes a real effort, and there's a desperate shortage of gadgets. You can tell it was put together by someone who had no intention of ever living here. The sink has no draining board, the stove lacks a grill and the floor is carpeted. Why would anyone put a carpet in a kitchen? It's as if the landlord would like to make our lives as inconvenient as possible. It's strange that we all live in a house that belongs to someone none of us have met (even Leni has only ever seen the agent from the letting office) nor probably ever will, and yet we all suffer the consequences of his stupid and careless choices every day of our lives. He probably sees himself as just an average guy, but for us he has the status of a god or a politician. *[Ed: I must remember to tell him you said that.]* We have to keep him happy and stick to all his rules (pay the rent, don't damage the walls or pull up the carpets) at the same time as we have to suffer the idiocy of his decisions.

No one here is at all interested in cooking. It's as if cooking is a shameful thing that people aren't meant to do any more. Leni only eats toast, Jo only eats things from packets and Sofia only eats stews, soups and things that don't require more than one pan. I think she must have orchestrated that pile of slop the day I bought my shoes. Rob is really into takeaways and

79

would always choose them over home-made things. I quite like cooking for utilitarian reasons, although not as much as I love baking for entertainment. I try to combine the two and make spinach soufflés or stuffed things but, in this house, my heart's not really there. The kitchen is a grim room to hang out in and I have to shoulder the general disgrace of being seen as an at-home-in-the-kitchen type of girl. It's just mindless discrimination. If I was a guy I bet they'd all be really impressed.

Still, yesterday I had a major baking success. Baking doesn't seem to come with so much stigma attached as general meal-cooking. I think there's a reason — if the others want to get a cookie they have to earn it by being nice. It's produced some interesting results. I had an almost civil conversation with Leni. She arrived home just when the cake had come out of the oven. The smell was really filling up the house. She came in to see what was up and started work straight away trying to get a piece. For the first time she asked how things were going with me and actually gave me time to answer. I told her I was finding London pretty interesting. She asked what I found interesting about it. At this point I decided she deserved some cake. I cut her a slice and told her I'd enjoyed seeing the stuff at the Tate and I liked the way London felt like a place where interesting things happened, unlike Vegas which is exactly the opposite. She said it was nice to hear someone say that because most Londoners only ever thought about getting away. I also told her about the noises, but she seemed completely unmoved, like it was the least interesting thing anyone had ever said in her presence. I realized it must be because she didn't know how to talk about matters outside herself, so I asked how the course was going. She burbled on about how hard it was and that they made her write theoretical essays, which were OK but basically irrelevant when it came to the business of making movies. She said her film had been short-listed for some kind of prize. I tried not to act too shocked. How could all those other competition entrants have written worse scripts than hers? Maybe her Mom was on the panel of judges.

Leni said she couldn't wait to finish college and get on with her life. This bit almost made me explode – I only managed to bite my lip because I'm still campaigning to redeem my reputation at home. But how boneheaded can you get? Only someone from Leni's background could come up with a dumb idea like that. As everybody knows, real life is disgusting. Maybe her parents will protect her from it enough for her not to notice. They'll take care of her rent and keep her in trainers until the movie-making starts to pay – which won't be too long if enough strings get pulled. My parents would probably bail me out of prison (provided it wasn't too expensive) or help with the rent if it was a question of me being made homeless. But either of these would come with a huge lecture on how I needed to take responsibility for myself and make sure it never happened again. Mom and Dad are really into the whole independence thing, which I think is basically good (although I sometimes can't help seeing it as an ongoing punishment for my academic failure).

I don't know whether Leni's position is enviable or sad. I like to understand life in a heroic way. When I start feeling bad about not knowing what to do I think of the first cells and amoebas fighting for existence. They must have had such a hard time. It's incredible that so much ingenuity came from things without brains. Then I move on to the first apes roaming around the prehistoric jungles, scrabbling for food and applying all their intelligence to not being eaten themselves. I think about how each individual monkey must have battled with starvation, winter, illness, predators and other monkeys, in order to survive and bring up babies. Apparently there were a few moments when it looked as if the whole population was about to die out. But thanks to a few tenacious primates, here we are today. When I find myself stuck on the question of what I'm supposed to do about being alive I try to see myself as part of a long chain of resourceful creatures doing their best for no real reason other than a compulsion to continue their existence. If Mom was prepared to pay my accounts up until the moment some larger institution took over then I'd never be able to relate to my primeval benefactors. Poor Leni. I don't think she was even telling the truth about the 'real life' thing – straight after saying it she went off on one about how she was looking forward to living in New York for a year. She took the opportunity to mention this dumb thing about how much more sophisticated New Yorkers are than other Americans. Who gave her the right to say *that*?

Sofia got a letter today. *And* she left her dictionary behind in the kitchen. I've got nothing to do, nowhere to go and I need a bit of entertainment. I've peeped into her room already, so I know it's on the table just waiting for me to come in and pay it some attention. Think of all the pounds I'll save on bus fares, gallery admission and expensive shoe-shopping trips!

[Ed: The following letters were printed on a single stretch of fax paper although I presume they were written on separate sheets. As before, a translation is supplied for non-Spanish speaking readers (or those not

equipped with the relevant dictionary). However, I have put my own attempt after Daisy's translation so as not to ruin the poor girl's effort before you've had a chance to enjoy it.

1 de Noviembre de 1998

Querida Sofía,

!Que contentos nos pone saber que estás bien! ¿Pero dónde están todas esas llamadas que nos prometiste? No te preocupes. Te perdonamos si nos dices que es porque te lo estás pasado bomba. Papá te manda un beso muy grande y dice que te echa de menos. La casa no es la misma sin ti. Te puedes imaginar, Manuela perdida sin su rival preferido y Diego sufriendo tu ausencia como sufre por todo lo demás.

Tenemos nuevas telas para este invierno y todo el mundo pregunta por ti. ¿Te gusta tu trabajo? Ye has echado ya un novio inglés? (¡No se lo diré a Joaquín!!!) ¡Vaya un lío tuvimos con la que te reemplazó . . . ! La muy urraca no se acordará de escribir en el libro pero si de robar cosas pequeñas. Menudo drama se armó. Y si te parece poco, el fin de semana pasado no se le ocurre otra cosa que escaparse con el marido de la mejor amiga de su madre. A alguna gente no se le ocurre otra cosa que hacer cosas dañinas y malas.

Por lo demás la vida aquí es como siempre. La abuela no está bien, pero a perro viejo todo le son pulgas. Menuda guerra nos está dando. Ya conoces su juego, no vivas y no dejes vivir. Prefiere continuar enferma y así ver si puede enterrarnos a todos conella. Pregunta por ti y en sus momentos más lúcidos cree que ella ha sido la única afortunada a la que tú has visitado. Pobre. Yo me callo por Papá y por no desilusionarla.

Todos esperamos verte estas Navidades.

Besos

Mami.

Querida Sofía:

¡Que morro tienes! ¡Odio tu ropa! La mía está mucho mejor y si te comportas tal vez te la preste. Aunque agradezco no tener ya esas alopécias que tus tirones me ocasionan, la verdad es que estoy mucho peor sin tu caracter malévolo. No queda nadie con quien hablar sobre las estúpidas cosas que Mamá y Papá me dicen que estudie. Incluso a Papá se le escapó decir que con una personalidad como la mía voy a necesitar encontrar un trabajo bien remunerado ya que nadie se querrá casar conmigo. ¡Ja! Ese todavía piensa que vivimos en los cinquienta.

¿Sale a cuenta el sacrificio con los hombres Londinenses? Si me dices que sí me cojo el primer avión porque Martín me está volviendo loca con sus celos y sus ideas bizantinas sobre los anti-conceptivos. Yo usaría la píldora, pero con él ya sabes que es como hablar con la pared. ¿Qué más le dará a él?

Joaquín ha estado hundido desde que te fuiste.Sofía, aunque sea por caridad pero escríbele.

¿Quién es el chico en tu casa? ¿Está bueno? ¿Qué le pasa a su novia? Por favor escríbeme y cuéntame con pelos y señales. Ya te llamo cuando no esté Mamá.

Un beso muy grande.

Manuela.

Querida Hermana Grande:

!Es injusto!!!!! Sólo porque tenga una facilidad inmediata con los números no quiere decir que tenga que casarme con ellos. !Jo!!!, no estoy bromeando. La universidad no es mi lugar. No tengo nada en común con el resto. Cuanto más me obligan a hacer lo que más odio, más desgraciado me siento. Tarde o temprano tendré que hacer lo que a mí me de la gana. Dile a Mamá que ya tengo pelo púbico bajo el sobaco. Estoy descubriendo muchas cosas nuevas aunque aún no se bien-bien lo que son.Se despiertan posibilidades nuevas en mí. El globo está hecho por más cosas de las que un genio apestoso pueda nunca llegar a contar.

Diego.]

This all seems to be tougher than I'd expected. Half the words aren't even in the dictionary and I can't figure out why. Maybe Sofia's family have very unusual vocabularies. There's no way I'm going to get on the whole graphology trip again. But after the date and the 'Dear Sofia' I get completely lost. I can see that the letters must be from her mother, sister and brother. The only bit I could work out from the beginning of the mother's letter was the 'contentos' – but as for who or what it applies to I have no idea. After that there's a bit about Papa and very big kiss. Then it says something about Manuela and a favorite rival (meaning Sofia?) and Diego and absence. I can't find 'sufre'. I wonder whether it has anything to do with suffering. Surely that would be listed. No wonder Sofia is having problems with such a shitty dictionary.

In the next paragraph there's a word that might mean either web, skin or material followed by a mention of winter. Then it says something about work, something about English, something about a book and something about small things. Then there's some stuff about a weekend, more work, a husband (Sofia's dad?), a friend, a mother and damages. What is this woman on about? After that there is tranquillity, a grandmother, a dog, fleas, a piece of news, disillusion and a reference to Christmas. I hope it isn't anything too serious. I guess it must be mostly OK as if the grandma was seriously ill it would probably be at the top of the letter. Maybe she's caught the dog's fleas. From what I gather Sofia must have quite an interesting relationship with her mother. Mom would never mention anything heavy like disillusionment. She's far too caught up with the facts and superficial problems of day to day existence.

The Manuela letter starts off with something about a snout and talks about hatred and clothing. Is Manuela saying she hates Sophia's clothes? That's unbelievable! It mentions a bad character, silliness, Mama and Papa, studying and work. Then it goes on to men in London and someone called Martin who seems to have stupid, anti-conceptual ideas. I guess it could either be her boyfriend or someone she studies with. Then there's a mention of someone called Joaquín (who also got a mention from 'Mami'). After that there's a question with the words 'small' and 'house' which is followed by two other questions. I like the way they have the upside down question mark at the beginning. I wonder why. I suppose it tells you early on that the sentence you are reading is interrogative – which must be helpful for live newscasters and radio performers.

Manuela sounds like a nightmare. I sometimes feel jealous of people with brothers and sisters, but when I think of having someone who thinks they can insult you and mess you around just because they have the same parents I see it might not be all it's cracked up to be.

The last letter looks really sweet and funny. Diego must be Sofia's little brother. It started with 'injustice', 'immediate' and 'numbers' and went on to talk about University. Maybe he is finding his course difficult. He seems to be taking it well though judging by all those exclamation marks (I'm assuming they signify a joke). At the end he says something about an alarm clock and new possibilities so maybe he'll pull himself out of it. If I could choose a sibling I think I'd like a little brother.

It's interesting to build up a mental picture of Sofia's family and how it functions. I wonder what they look like. Maybe the reason she moved here had something to do with her difficult relationship with her sister. I've heard that in Spain it's normal for people to carry on living at home until quite late. It must be horrible if you don't get along with your family.

[Dear Sofia,

    How happy we are to hear that you are well! But where are all those phone calls you promised us? Don't worry. We will forgive you if you tell us it is because you are having a bomb of a time. Papa sends you a very big kiss and says he misses you. The house is not the same without you. You can imagine. Manuela, lost without her favourite rival, and Diego suffering your absence as he suffers the rest.

    We have some new fabrics in for the winter and everyone is asking after you. Do you like your work? Have you got yourself an English boyfriend? (I won't tell Joaquín!!) What a fuss we had with your replacement. The little magpie did not remember to write in the book but did remember to steal small things. It built up into quite a drama – and, yes, I'll describe it a little. Last weekend nothing other happened than that she ran away with the husband of her mother's best friend. To some people it only occurs to do damage and bad things.

Apart from that, life here has been tranquil. Grandma is unwell, but an old dog is all fleas. You know her game – don't live and don't let live. She prefers to stay ill and to see if she can bury us all with her. She asks after you and, in her more lucid moments, believes she is uniquely fortunate enough to have received a visit from you. Poor thing. I shut up for Papa's sake and in order not to disillusion her.

We are all looking forward to seeing you at Christmas.

Kisses,

Mami.

Dear Sofia,

What a cheek! I hate your clothes! Mine are much better and if you behave well I might lend them to you. It is true that I am worse off without your malevolent character. And there is no one to talk to about all the stupid things Mama and Papa tell me to make me study. Including Papa's comment that with a personality like mine I will need to find good work as no one will ever marry me. Well! That man thinks we are still living in the 1950s.

Are the men in London worth the sacrifice? If you say yes I will catch the first aeroplane as Martín is driving me mad with his jealousy and Byzantine ideas about contraception. I would use the pill but it's like talking to a brick wall. What difference should it make to him?

Joaquín has been sunk since you left. Sofia, even out of charity, write to him.

Who is the boy in your house? Is he nice? What is happening with his girlfriend? Please write to me and tell me with hairs and signals! I will telephone you when Mama is not around.

A very big kiss,
Manuela.

Dear Big Sister,

What injustice!!!!! Just because I have an immediate facility with numbers it doesn't mean to say that I have to marry them! I am not joking. University is not my place. I have nothing in common with the rest. The more I am obliged to do what I most hate the more unfortunate I feel. Sooner or later I will have to do what I want. Tell this to Mama. I am discovering many things, although I don't yet know very well what they are. There are awakening new possibilities in me. The world is made of more things than even a stinky genius can count.

Diego.]

★

It seems hard to write in the bath but I'm going to try it anyhow. I wonder what I've been up to these last few days. I checked out all the parks nearby. There's one called Hilly Fields which has a cool view over suburbia and one called Telegraph Hill which faces the other way and has a great view of the whole of London. I also went to a cemetery in a place called Nunhead. It had loads of really old graves in one part and really new ones

89

in another. People have definitely gotten more boring about gravestones in the last hundred years. In the nineteenth century almost everybody had a big stone angel, imposing crucifix or ornate raised tomb (except the poor who were probably just dropped in a pit). Nowadays it's meter-high shiny granite rectangles all round. I suppose it would be quite embarrassing to go for anything too outstanding, like you were desperate to brag about how special you are, even when you're no longer around to benefit from the claim.

The bathroom is one of the better rooms in the house – although it suffers from being shared by people who aren't exactly best buddies. If people who cared about their home lived here it could be a great place to sit and relax. Even now it's alright, but it could do with a few plants or seashells or something. Everything's white. The knobbly wallpaper is white. The floorboards are painted white. Even the underdrape is hanging on to its whiteness, although it could do with a wash. There are no pictures or ornaments anywhere, just loads and loads of different bath products. Everybody has their own corner of the bath for their soaps and shampoos. Rob and I have one between us. I haven't been told who owns the others (the corner thing is an unspoken house rule) but it isn't hard to work it out. People's choice of cosmetics seems to have little to do with empirical differences between skin and hair types and a lot to do with who they think they are. Rob uses two-in-one shampoo for normal hair. Sofia's are all Spanish products – which is good, as with her grasp on English she'd probably buy fabric conditioner instead of shampoo. Leni and Jo's stuff is slightly less obvious, but in the end you have to assume that Jo's are all the ones with words like 'sensitive', 'gentle' and 'delicate' on the labels while Leni's must be the products that claim to provide 'shine', 'movement' and 'strength'.

This is a pretty uncomfortable place to write. It feels unnatural to have the top half of your body all dry and doing something civilized like writing while the bottom half is submerged in warm foamy liquid. (I use shampoo for damaged hair and bubble bath scented with herbs to 'encourage relaxation'. What does that say about me?) Life's not exactly boring at the moment I just don't have much news.

I've found out what the noises are! Rob and I were in the bedroom getting ready for bed at about eleven thirty last night and there was a screech right outside the bedroom window. It was a *horrible* sound, like someone being killed. I froze for a second in a pure panic and then raced to the telephone. I started yelling at the operator, telling her to get someone over as fast as possible as a child had been murdered in our garden.

Rob wouldn't let me go outside in case the guy was still around, and I wouldn't let him go outside and leave me alone in the house. I don't know where all the others were. I think Leni and Jo were out and Sofia was fast asleep – although I can't understand how she slept through such a vile noise.

The police turned up a little quicker than last time. It was the same two guys. They said there was an ambulance on the way and asked what we knew. We told them about the wail and said we hadn't been outside to check as we were too scared (which made Rob pull a really peevy face at me). Just then there was another squeal a little further away. I must have gone white. The porky policeman looked at me with his best smug-copface and asked if that was what I'd heard before. I couldn't tell why he was looking so unmoved. I started ranting at him like, yes, of course it was, so why was he just standing there like a tree-stump instead of racing over to find out what was up? The ferrety one asked where I was from. I didn't get why he was throwing me such an irrelevant question. I went, 'Las Vegas, OK? Now will you go start acting like a policeman instead of some kind of creepy door-to-door salesman?' 'So they don't have too many foxes out that way, then?' he asked. I went, 'No. Why?' before realizing that they were both chuckling away like they were in some corny Ealing comedy.

It turns out that the wailing is the noise foxes make when they're on heat. It was a pretty embarrassing way to find out (especially when the ambulance men arrived) but I'm glad it wasn't anything more gruesome. I didn't realize foxes lived in cities. The policemen said there were loads of them and that I might even get see one if I looked out of the window late at night or early in the morning. How absolutely cool.

Books

I just read the most incredible book, all in one go without stopping. It must belong to either Leni or Jo because I found it in the living room. As it turns out, the living room is a great place to pick up info. I'm always catching up with the world via the out-of-date papers and magazines lying around in there. This book was called, *The Man Who Loved a Polar Bear* by Robert Akeret. It completely blew me away. It's about this sixty-year-old shrink who follows up five of his patients thirty years after their treatment to see whether or not they lived happy lives after therapy. At the start, one of them was in love with a polar bear, one of them thought she was Spanish when she wasn't, one fantasized about cutting women up, one believed she'd killed her father by thinking nasty thoughts about him and one had writers' block. Akeret pretty much managed to cure the whole bunch, but later found himself wondering what had become of them. So he tracked them down and went to pay them each a visit. The Spanish one, the psycho and the dead-Dad lady were all pretty pleased with their lives so far. The polar bear guy was doing S/M shows in the evenings and lecturing about the circus in the daytimes – not exactly happy, but OK. But the writers' block guy had gone totally freako. He'd moved to Paris and become a big literary star, on chat shows all the time and everything. He'd written a novel about his alcoholic wife that was so horrible she dropped dead after reading one chapter, and another about a guy who finds his wife's head on the doorstep and then spends the whole book working out that it was actually him who killed her. He was planning on writing an unpunctuated monologue about the lead-up to his own suicide and then really killing himself at the end. When he'd first gone to see Akeret he'd told him not to try to shrink his soul and Akeret got all worried about the guy's narcissism. But in the end the therapy only fed the guy's vanity by making him more and more interesting to himself. With Akeret's help he got over his block by finding himself so fascinating he was sure never to run out of subject matter.

I enjoyed reading it so much, but at the end it suddenly occurred to me that it might be a spoof. I don't believe the patients were real people. Not because they were too nuts to be genuine – I'm not *that* naïve about human nature. More because of the last story. If it was true then I ought to be able to go into a bookshop and buy the famous French writer's books. But I just don't think it's plausible. The books themselves sound too fako and fictional. The cheesiest part was that he apparently included a character called Akeret in all his novels in the role of the main character's shrink. No way. Akeret sounds too much like 'accurate' not to arouse suspicion. I guess it could be true, but I think I like it better as a put-up. There's this note at the end saying, 'If you think it reads like a novel that's because I got my good friend, the novelist, *Whatever Whatever* (another phony baloney name), to help me write it'. Who's he trying to kid?

It certainly helped to pass the time though. It's dark already. I might go see if I can spot a fox.

I re-read a little chunk of diary and realized I've had very little to say about Rob recently. I think I feel like he and I may have reached some kind of minor crisis in our relationship, although it would be easy to let it pass unnoticed. It's like we're both losing the basic idea of what it means to be together. Now that the thrill of running away to England has kind of worn off it's hard to see what the actual connection is between us. The better we know each other the more we seem like strangers. I feel that if I can be in love with Rob I could be in love with anyone. There's a randomness about the whole thing of choosing a partner. Like everybody could be loveable somehow.

Rob is very caught up with college at the moment. I'm realizing more and more how much his studying means to him. It's not as if he's just learning a skill so he can go earn his living. He's seriously obsessed with rockets. Rob is truly passionate about all the mathematics and physics and sophisticated engineering skills that go towards putting things into outer space. I don't quite know how to feel about it. Theoretically, I think it's good for people to have an overwhelming drive to do something particular. But in practice I feel quite excluded and irritated by it. I might as well face it, his course is far more interesting and important to him than I am. If he had to choose one or the other it's perfectly clear that the spaceships would win. Naturally, I'd never make such a stupid demand on him. I'm just not sure I'm compatible with a person who can devote so much of his life to his work. I wonder who I *would* be compatible with. I'm reconsidering whether someone older wouldn't make a better partner for me. It'd probably be my ideal to be with someone who had a good part-time job and read books, went to the movies and enjoyed eating out. Rob is just too focused. He does what he loves best all day long, so when he gets home he just likes to relax, eat take-aways and chat about unproblematic stuff. Cinemas and restaurants are more like places to go to compensate for the rest of your life. Maybe if you find yourself doing exactly what you want you no longer need them.

I don't quite know how to handle this stage of our relationship. Realistically, I think it's a good idea to concentrate on whatever we've got than to start fantasizing about what we imagine we'd prefer. But isn't that a way to get yourself stuck in a miserable situation? What if I really could be happier with a guy like James?

I think I might try writing some poetry.

I had quite a good evening at home yesterday. I was so bored by the time Jo got back that I went into the living room to watch TV with her. She'd just been for an interview at a corporate identity and branding company in Soho. They had a job going as office manager, i.e. buying toilet paper and coffee and making sure the flowers always look good. She said the person who interviewed her was really sweet and she thought it might have gone OK. It sounds like a total snooze but I hope she gets it. It's really well paid – £22,000 a year. If she gets it she'll do an accounting course in the evenings and, with the experience from the job and another qualification, her adult life will finally begin. Her next question would be whether or not to marry her boyfriend. She's been with him now for three years and really feels sure she'd like to stay with him forever. I asked her how she knew. She looked at me like I was totally off my bean and said, in a kind of moony way, 'He's just the most gorgeous man on the planet.' It's incredible that she could feel that way about a man who looks like a potato and seems to be at a permanent loss for words, but I suppose that's love for you.

Sofia came home and joined us in front of the *Network South East News* (which was all missing cats, school dinners and extremely violent killings a couple of blocks away). She and Jo get along quite well. One thing which probably makes Jo special is that people feel they can relax around her. Because she's unthreatening and non-competitive she's an easy person to hang out in the living room with. She talks real slow to Sofia, but Sofia doesn't seem to mind. In fact I think she may even appreciate it as she answers back much better than she does with either Leni or me. Maybe we're so worried about not patronizing her that we actually make things worse. Sofia said she was bored with her job and looking forward to going back to Spain for Christmas. She told us she was missing her family – especially her brother and sister, which I found a bit surprising. She asked Jo how the interview went, so I guess they chat together quite regularly. It's funny how little I actually notice about what goes on around here.

Some program about pop culture in Europe came on TV. There were a couple of songs that got Sofia all excited. One had a really stupid dance to go with it – which she showed us. It was all ass-wiggling and jumping around. Rob got home and we all went to the shop together to buy a couple of bottles of wine. I persuaded him against a take-away and we cooked a really delicious lasagne. It was probably our best evening in this house so far. It's good to cook, eat and wash-up with people. I think friendships often work best when they're accompanied by functional activities.

Over dinner Sofia told us some funny stories about her little brother, Diego, with translation support from Rob. Apparently he's some sort of math prodigy, but pretty out of control (so I guess that was a bit of wrong translation on my part the other day). He goes on long sleepwalks and wakes up in the neighbors' sheds and is always being arrested for stealing – although he says he doesn't consciously notice himself doing it. He's one of these people who can memorize the order of a pack of cards and count whole stacks of toothpicks in under a second. The family don't know what to do with him. He got into University aged sixteen but hates it. It's clear he's really gifted, but he doesn't find numbers at all interesting. Jo suggested he get into gambling.

After the washing up we all went into the living room with our coffees and Leni came home. She said she'd been to the Y.C.A. with *all* of her friends from college. She looked a bit put out by the fact that we'd obviously been having a good time together without her and, after a few minutes spent trying to impress us with the fantasticness of her evening, she went up to her room. We carried on chatting wherever we'd left off, but I noticed Jo glance at me as if to check my reaction to Leni's pathetic behavior. I've been trying to think better of Leni since the other day but it made me quite happy to realize that Jo doesn't like her either.

I saw my first fox! I woke up real early and went to the back window. I only had to wait about ten minutes. It came up from the bottom of the garden, snooped around a little and then disappeared under the shed. I hung about for a while but it didn't reappear. It was beautiful – all gingery with a big, bushy tail. I used to read a load of Beatrix Potter as a kid. Foxes were given a pretty bad press – they always wanted to eat the main character. But this one looked more of a victim than a villain. I can't imagine New Cross being the ideal neighborhood for a fox.

After that I went back to bed for a couple of hours until Rob got up and went to college. Leni had left another of her charming notes in the kitchen. She must have been pissed at us for enjoying an evening without her and needed to hit back. It was all about the money we owe her. She made it sound as if we'd been avoiding her, but I don't think any of us even knew we owed it.

[Ed: After a note like this I'm sure I would have paid up at once.

Petals,

As if the gas and electricity bills weren't burdensome enough, we have just received a phone bill. And at £230 it's hardly a snip. I know my name appears on the envelopes, but I cannot take the rap for your blow-heaters and Transatlantic calls. However, because I love you all so dearly, I have taken it upon myself to work out roughly what each of you owe:

Sofia – a measly £65

Rob – a mere £70

Daisy – a piffling £70

Jo – a rather weightier £85 (for extra use of phone and electricity – and what about that £69.99 for the trainers?)

If you feel I am demanding too much or too little, let me know and I'll hand over the bills for you to work it out for yourself. But either way, HURRY UP or the phoneline will be cut and we'll freeze.

Thank you in advance for your speedy cash deliveries (the bottom line being, arse about and you die).

Leni.]

★

Today's book-find wasn't quite so fantastic as the last one. This time I'm certain it belonged to Jo. It was called *The Magic Eye* – one of those trashy 3D books that you have to stare at for ages, giving your eyes time to rearrange the patterns into pairs of jumping dolphins, skulls or monkeys on bicycles. This book must have had about thirty pictures and I managed to convert them all. It's really satisfying when the little flat shapes turn into one big 3D shape, but it's creepy to feel your hands holding a thin thing, while your eyes see it as a gigantic cavernous space. I noticed as soon as I put it down that everything looked and sounded different. It made me really uncomfortable. The psycho character in the Akeret book said this thing about inhabiting a universe slightly to the left of everyone else's. I really related to it at the time, but after straining my eyes on the dot book I felt it more than ever. I need to go jam my fingers into some soil to get myself back to normal. You've really got to watch out what you pick up around here.

Alone
I am looking out
At myself
Looking . . . I can't! I really don't have it in me even to pretend to write poems. Crap. I don't know where to start. I'd like to do it just because it's the only way I can really justify calling James. But Christ knows how people go about writing that stuff. I imagined it might just be like any old writing but with shorter lines, either rhyming or a bit more blown-up than average. But I can't do it.

The other evening at home taught me that the best way I can get on with James without suffering the not-knowing that might lead to an affair is to have something concrete to do with him. If I can hang out with him and meet Souazik to talk poetry it should diffuse any tension and we can all just get along. I'll have something to do and some hope of meeting other people. I just have to get it together somehow to get something down on paper.

I'm going to do a cake to help myself think . . .

. . . I've got it. It's a bit low-down and cheap but it'll do for a start. The plan is that I take the little bits of writing from my book on shoes, switch the main words for ones a few places along in the dictionary and BINGO! – surrealist poetry. It couldn't be simpler. I'll be a real poetry factory. I'd just better check that there's an English dictionary in the house somewhere . . .

. . . Here comes a first attempt:

Federal Governments of Fanfare

Fatality was at its
most sumptuous during
La Bellringer Equation, a timekeeper
of rarefied tatting, when
A Parisian armadillo
might be seen
sipping chanceries from a
laid paper. Finely embroidered
silver litany
stocks (facing pain)
complemented lustrous
silken slobs,
drawing attention to the annexe.

It works! It's a fucking masterpiece. Who'd have guessed it was originally about French silk slippers at the end of the nineteenth century? *[Ed: Out of curiosity I tracked down a copy of the book. It's called* Shoes, *by Linda O'Keeffe, and only costs £4.99. It's actually rather lovely – an ideal present for someone you don't know too well. I found the original text, which reads as follows: 'FASHION WAS AT ITS most sumptuous during La Belle Epoch, a time of rarified tastes, when a Parisian aristocrat might be seen sipping champagne from a lady's slipper. Finely embroidered silk lisle stockings (facing page) complemented lustrous silken slippers, drawing attention to the ankle.']* I wonder whether Souazik will spot me as a humbug. I actually think it's OK – better than a heap of crap about love or suffering or something. It's quite satisfying. I might as well do another while I'm on it.

The Shooting Stick Must Go On

A multi-colored pavé
week sander with tubular stratocumulus
was partisan to the cottage
exactitude fashioned for
Claymore Cold Storage's
scribble clerk.

A decanter later
he modified
the despair, making
it practical for
stri-
ati-
on.

My Nobel Prize is in the bag. Maybe those line-breaks at the end are a bit much, but I thought it looked more pointy and poetic. I'm so excited I feel like the real thing.

I'll go call James right away . . .

Great! I'm going to meet Souazik and James in a café in Earl's Court next Thursday evening. He said I should bring along a portfolio of poems for her to read. Over the next six days I could put together a whole book, no problem. Now I've got something to do. James was quite husky and sexy on the phone again at first, but after that he got all businesslike. He really throws my head around. I think he was glad to hear from me again, but then decided not to act too pleased. Or maybe he was pleased at first but it wore off when he realized that I'm not actually all that exciting. When he did his sex-voice I came back with a kind of polite, efficient reply in the hope of avoiding any sticky situations. But perhaps James isn't too interested in sticky situations and would just like to have a flirty chat for the hell of it. I can be so uptight. I have to learn to take things less seriously.

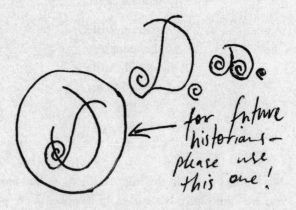

for future historians — please use this one!

P.S. Jo is trying to keep up with the new note-writing craze. She left one on the bin today. It was so witless it put me right off taking the rubbish out – something I don't normally mind doing at all.

[Ed: I know what you mean:

Poor me. I'm just a well-meaning dustbin trying to do my job. But I need help. PLEASE, EMPTY ME, and I will be forever grateful.]

Guests

I had a great weekend with Rob at home. He was studying for some end of term exams and I was writing poetry. Leni went to the country with her Mom and Dad so I asked whether I could borrow her computer to type up my stuff. I felt reluctant to tell her it was poetry but luckily, as there was no cake around, she didn't ask any questions – she just looked a little surprised. I assumed it was because she doesn't think I have a life – or at least not one that involves writing things on computers. But I realized later that it must have been because she wondered how I knew she had a computer in the first place. Oh well. I'm sure she must have had at least a little orb into *our* bedroom at some point. It's freaky to live in a house and not know what's in some of the rooms – like in *Bluebeard*.

Rob was slightly stunned by my sudden urge to write poetry but didn't seem to find it too strange. I think he was pleased I had something to keep me busy. It was nice that we were both working at home. He said it had been unusually easy for him to concentrate. The whole house had a kind of hushed, studious feel to it. Jo was with old potato head in Crilben and Sofia goes to English classes on Saturday mornings and then comes back and does her homework in the afternoons. On Sunday she spent all day writing letters. I went into her room this morning but they weren't on the desk. I guess she must have sent them already. I got loads of poems done and they came out really well. Getting that shoe book was a major piece of luck. *[Ed: This, of course, is a debatable point. I have the poems here. There are thirty-seven altogether. In my professional opinion it would be altogether too tedious to include them. If you want to know what they are like you can go and buy the book and do it yourself at home.]*

Rob was my first literary guinea pig. Because I'd written everything in Leni's room he had no idea how I'd come up with it. I think he couldn't decide whether I was a genius or sadly clueless. He asked where I got my ideas. I decided to carry on with the game as I didn't want to tell him it was all a scam to pave the way for a Platonic relationship with that guy I'd met in the Tate. I said they just came to me. He said he liked the image of a helicopter made from fat but couldn't see how the title related to the poem. *[Ed: Okay, okay. I concede. I'll have to include this particular masterpiece:*

Helicopter of Fat

Closed-circuit television-like ovules
Called paupers were
Strapped onto fine, fragile
Shooting stars to protect them
From muddy European
Stretchers. Matching shooting star-and-
Pauper settees were popular
In the eighteenth cerebrum.]

It wasn't exactly an overwhelming ovation, but I didn't really expect one from Rob. He claims not to understand art and literature, so the fact that he made an effort to express some kind of opinion (however jugheaded) was enough. I'll look forward to hearing what Souazik has to say.

The other thing I noticed while using Leni's computer was a folder titled 'Script 2'. I wish I'd remembered to print it out while I had the chance. Now Leni's back and she's got a really bad cold so she probably won't be going out at all for at least a few days. My indoor studies are being squashed from all sides. The only progress I've made is with Jo – although it's not a happy story. We were woken up this morning by elephantine thudding on the staircase marking the arrival of the mail (a regular occurrence in the days following Jo's last job interview – she even rang from her boyfriend's at eight thirty on Saturday morning to see whether any news had arrived). After that there were sniffing noises from the kitchen followed by a violent slamming of the front door. Poor Jo. The offending letter was resting on top of a pile of apple skin and coffee grounds in the kitchen garbage can. I braved the yuckiness and read it. It was one of the most thoughtless rejection letters ever. How can people allow themselves to be so clumsy when it's human lives they're dealing with? A string of rejections like that and Jo might never marry, have babies or do any of the things her heart is set on. It made me really mad. I almost felt like ringing the person who wrote it, pretending to be calling from the hospital, and telling them that their mother had collapsed and died. *That* ought to give them an idea of what it's like to have some asshole stranger come along and randomly trample all over their feelings. The only thing that stopped me was the thought that the person's mother might be dead already. [*Ed: Minus names, dates and addresses the letter reads like this:*

Thank you for your interest in our company.
Unfortunately the job has gone to another candidate. Best
of luck in future.]

I hope she's OK. I'm sure she's better off not working for a
person capable of putting such a heartless piece of junk in the
mail.

Luce and Heidi rang. We stayed on the phone for about quarter
of an hour. It was so great to talk to them – although my voice
went a bit wavery when the time came to say goodbye. Luce
has fallen in love big-time and Heidi's got a deal training up
actors for an action movie. It all sounded pretty exciting and
made me wonder why I tend to see Vegas as such a dull place.
It was excellent to speak to people who are so familiar – I'd
almost forgotten what it was like to feel *known* by somebody.
I told them about Rob, James and everyone here. Heidi said
James sounded 'bitchin twichin'. I hadn't heard anybody say
those words in the way she says them for ages. It really cheered
me up. The only strange thing about the conversation was that
for the first time since the accident I almost forgot that Lara
wasn't there. I was on the verge of asking how she was when
I remembered. Why did my brain play such an evil trick on
me?

Jo had a dinner party last night. She was in a terrible mood — probably because she's going to have to carry on being a market researcher for a little while longer. She said we could all have drinks in the living room with her friends before the meal, but that she wasn't going to cook for us. Her cooking sucks anyhow so I was pretty relieved. She tried to make this macaroni cheese that she'd seen a woman called Delilah do on TV. Apparently the trick is to buy the most expensive macaroni you can get, otherwise it won't be 'right'. Jo had spent £5 on an average-sized bag of pasta and another £10 on the 'proper' cheeses. I hate stuff like that. I wonder whether her guests noticed it was special or whether she had to tell them.

Jo's friends were bad news. In fact I'm not even sure these ones *were* her friends. I think most of her pals are back home in Altringham and the ones she's made so far in London are just out of desperation. She seemed really keen to impress them, which was good for the rest of us because she took half a day off work to clean the coffee slops off the side of the dustbin (I hope it said thanks) and to scrape the sticky stuff off the kitchen cupboard doors. One was called Tony, who I think is her supervisor. He phoned at the last minute to ask whether he could bring his new girlfriend, Zara. Jo was really annoyed, partly because it was one extra person to provide for and partly because she'd organized the whole thing so that Sarah, who's also from work, could get to know Tony better. I've never heard Jo say anything about Sarah that wasn't horrible so it was pretty hard to see why she was doing her such a big favor. Maybe she was planning on telling them what a pair of dipshits they were before resigning. Ian came too, not that anyone seemed to notice much.

I would have hidden in the bedroom all evening if it weren't for Rob. He likes social occasions in general, however lame. He came home with a couple of bottles of wine especially. I think if I hadn't been there Jo probably would have invited him to eat with them as he was the only person who had any kind of knack for casual conversation. Sofia was mostly silent and Leni left after two minutes, saying she had to go work. Tony and Zara were terrible. They hardly seemed to know each other. Maybe they'd been together a week at most. They spent the whole evening trying to let everyone know how little they liked each other. Maybe Tony had thought Zara was interesting and exotic, but then realized she was just a self-obsessed loony when he saw her in the context of his office buddies. I bet they met somewhere noisy with low lights. She was the best thing that could possibly have happened to Sarah, who's a real mouse. It'd take some weirdy boofhead to make her look appealing by comparison. Tony practically made it his mission to show everyone how much he preferred her to his girlfriend, cutting Zara off mid-sentence and telling her to listen to what Sarah was saying. It would have been really annoying if Zara hadn't been quite so despicable. She was Italian and worked as a reflexologist. She had a huge, shapeless fuzz of black hair with a horrible, floppy bow in it, orange lipstick and a body that was hanging somewhere between voluptuous and saggy. I think she may have been a few years older than Tony, who seemed to be in his early thirties. She said Rob looked really tense and offered to give him a foot massage right there. He told her he didn't think the rest of us would be too pleased if he took his shoes off, so she forced a head and shoulder massage on him instead. She pummeled him around pretty roughly for a few minutes and then told him to relax completely. When she decided he was calm and unsuspecting enough she yanked his head around to the side so hard we all heard a crack. Rob went 'Shit!' and started rubbing his neck. She told him to relax as if she was going to do it again. When he said that maybe once was enough she told him it had to go the other way or it would mess with his alignment. He thanked her and said he'd rather have a pain on one side of his neck than on both. After that the attention turned away from Zara for a few seconds while the others talked about their office. She asked me what I did. I told her I was taking time out to work on a collection of poems for a London-based journal. (I felt I ought to say *something*.) She told me she was a writer but that she couldn't publish her work because it was 'too much for people right now.' I asked her what she meant and she told me she'd written a novel but that she wasn't going to send it to anyone because it was 'too real, too dangerous.' I tried to find out what it was about and she spouted some bull about drug-smuggling and international terrorism. The others had run out of conversation and were listening blankly, but she clapped on as if she had everyone's rapt attention. She started saying she was a natural storyteller and that writing came easily to her. She told us that the few close friends who'd read her book had all cried. I almost felt like crying too. If she was such a good storyteller why didn't she try telling some stories instead of hooeying on about her 'gift'? I didn't like the way she tried to make me feel like my poems must be bogus because someone was actually going to print them (which is far from a sure thing anyhow). Tony was looking at her really disgusted, but then again he was one of those rat-like men who look disgusted most of the time. Sarah said it sounded very interesting but that she couldn't understand Zara's anxiety as there were plenty of pretty hardcore thrillers around and they didn't bother anybody much. Zara gave a self-satisfied sniff and told her to wait ten years and then she'd understand.

When the macaroni was ready and they all got carted off the three of us stayed behind laughing our heads off and doing impersonations for hours.

Play

Rob woke up in a really odd mood yesterday and wouldn't say why. He seemed all absent and melancholic. I tried pumping him with questions but he only got irritated. When he left for college he kissed me goodbye without looking me in the eye. I felt terrible. The phone rang about twenty minutes later and it was Rob at London Bridge Station saying sorry. I told him not to worry and asked whether he had any idea what it was that was making him feel funny. He said no and then said goodbye and hung up a little too quickly. The call left me feeling even worse. I tried to imagine what it could be. He'd seemed fine the night before. If it was a problem with me surely it would've shown up earlier. Perhaps because of my own guilty conscience I started to imagine all sorts of terrible things – like that he'd met a girl at college and had arranged some kind of assignation for today and didn't have the guts to tell me straight out. The more I thought about it the more angry and upset I got. How could he do something like that? I imagined the girl being all libraryish and academic. Rob is all I have here. If we split up I'd have to go home and I don't feel at all ready. I couldn't afford to rent a whole room in London for myself without getting some kind of job, which I really don't want to do yet. It's shitty to be this dependent. The more furious I got with Rob the more angry I became with myself – half for being so pathetic and clingy and half for being prepared to do to Rob what I couldn't stand him to do to me. I felt like ringing James to cancel right away. (Until I remembered that the meeting with him was purely professional.) I really saw how complicated Rob's and my relationship is. It doesn't just depend on whether or not we like each other, but on all these other things too. I guess that's what adult relationships are. It must get even worse when you start having babies and buying houses. How can you ask yourself truthfully whether you're still in love when so much external stuff rides on it? The consequences of either Rob or I not being in love any more are just too terrible. I really understood why it'd make him act so peculiar.

In the middle of the afternoon the phone rang again and it was him. I could hardly speak. I couldn't decide whether to start yelling or to burst into tears. He sounded more cheerful than earlier, so I kept myself under control. He invited me to meet him by one of the lions in Trafalgar Square at seven o'clock that night. I asked whether he was feeling any better and he laughed and said he'd tell me all about it later.

I was so nervous that I arrived half an hour early. Rob was there already. I could see him as I approached, sitting on the lion's back and looking into the distance. He spotted me as I got a little closer and started waving and blowing kisses. As I drew alongside he hoisted me up so we could sit facing each other. The lion was so icy cold I thought my ass might freeze off but Rob looked pleased to see me and I didn't want to start griping. We kissed for a full five minutes before saying a word. I don't know whether it was something Rob did or the freezing lion between my legs, but it was the sexual high-point of our relationship so far. I felt it everywhere, in my teeth and toes, and even spreading out a couple of feet beyond my body.

Afterwards Rob held me away from him and stared me hard in the face without speaking. He looked more intense than I'd have thought he was capable of. I wondered what it all meant but was kind of enjoying the mystery. I raised my right eyebrow to see what would come out. Rob just said, 'Oh Daze, it's my birthday, I'm really sorry.' I can't believe he never told me. In fact I'm sure he once said it was in June.

It turns out that Rob is one of those screwy types who flips out on their birthday. He'd only turned twenty-five but you'd think he'd turned a hundred. Apparently his uncle had told him once that he'd never really believed in death until he hit his quarter century, after which it suddenly seemed like a real threat. Rob said he woke up feeling totally morbid and like he'd never, ever get everything done in the short time he had left. I had to bite my lip to stop myself laughing at his stupid face. It even had a small teenagery zit on it as if his own skin was putting him on for being so nerdy. I told him he was one of the few people who had nothing to worry about. He was doing the right stuff and wasn't in any danger of letting his life slip by. He's so tough on himself. Not everyone can expect to start writing symphonies aged seven. I asked why he was looking at me so funny and he said he was trying to imagine me as a mother. I just let it go with the understanding that it would probably pass at midnight. Luckily he noticed the time on one of the big clocks at the bottom of the square. He'd bought tickets for the theatre. What a clunk. He jumped off the lion, helped me down after him, and then dragged me off to a big place to the left of the National Gallery where they show opera in English. It was the last thing I'd expect him to be into. He said he wasn't necessarily, but that it was his birthday and he'd seen a sign outside the theatre door announcing the fact that they still had tickets for that night's performance of *Falstaff*.

Opera audiences are different to all the other audiences I have ever seen. They have a load more old people in them – *really* old people who can hardly move and stuff. About ninety percent of the audience had gray hair. The people who didn't really stood out. I asked Rob if he still felt old and he punched me on the shoulder. There was also a large quota of solitary people. One woman looked like a cross-dressing writer from the nineteen thirties, with cropped hair, breeches and a massive hook-nose. Luce would have gone crazy if she'd seen her. There was another with black hair and heavy operatic make-up caked onto to her wrinkly skin. I noticed a hippie couple who looked like they hadn't washed since the sixties and who spoke in loud, aristo-type voices. There were only two other people who seemed to be in their twenties, so we all smiled at each other.

The opera was excellent. I'd never seen one before. The songs were beautiful and it was impressive to see the people just standing in front of you and singing so well.

Rob had to get up early this morning for a tutorial and we had breakfast together in the kitchen. Jo was up too so we asked how the second half of the dinner party had gone. She said the food had come out really well, but didn't mention anything about the people – except Zara. Tony had told her the next day that Zara was a psychic. She said that Rob was going to get some kind of contract within the next six months and that he and I had a load of problems ahead. Apparently Zara said I was more complex than Rob and that this wasn't going to be a good thing for our relationship. What does she know? Rob seemed pretty unmoved, but I felt really pissed off. What business is it of hers what happens in Rob's and my relationship?

I felt like sending a message back saying that I definitely wasn't a psychic but that it was perfectly obvious to me that she and Tony weren't going to last a month.

The big day's here. My poetry is about to find its audience. I actually feel really nervous. I don't know why I get myself into stuff like this. It's alright for me to mess around at home pretending to be a poet and thinking it's all very funny and easy, but now I have to show Souazik my stuff I realize how embarrassing it will be if she thinks it's garbage. I also haven't mentioned anything to Rob and I realize it'll look a bit odd if I'm not at home this evening. I have no friends to pretend I've gone out with. I could tell him I went to the movies on my own, but I imagine he'd suspect something. I should probably leave a note so he doesn't panic.

I took the poems down to a copy shop and had them bound together in a white folder. I got some Letraset and put a title – *Shooting Stars* – on the cover. It looks very professional. I hope they like it.

It's odd, but I actually woke up this morning feeling homesick. It wasn't my parents or the weather or my friends that I missed. What did it for me was remembering this funny picture we had in the hallway at home. It's a cartoon strip showing Snoopy with a typewriter on top of his kennel writing what's supposed to sound like a really terrible novel. It wasn't until I was about eighteen that I got the joke. I always thought his novel sounded quite good. It starts with a series of unrelated events – gunshots, screaming maids and a pirate ship appearing on the horizon. Then it goes on to a farm in Kansas where a small boy is growing up. Charlie Brown looks disapproving but Snoopy tells him that in part two he'll somehow tie it all together. In the last square Snoopy goes to the mail-box and drops his novel in. I can't remember what it says, but it's this picture of Snoopy putting his novel in the mail that got me so homesick this morning. I think the suggestion is that Snoopy's about to be cruelly disillusioned. Maybe I am too.

We all met in a tiny café called *The Troubadour* which is on exactly the opposite side of London to here. Apparently Souazik lives a couple of minutes' walk away. The café had all sorts of old musical instruments hanging from the ceiling, like lutes, trumpets and mandolins. They piped out very soft classical music and everyone spoke pretty quietly. Souazik told me that they had regular poetry readings in the basement and when it wasn't busy you could play chess. It was all very bohemian. Everyone smoked – even James, who I'd never seen smoking anywhere else.

Souazik fitted in perfectly, but turned out to be such a nice person that I could only hold her black turtleneck against her for the first ten minutes. She had a mild French accent and came from Quebec. I'd guess she was about five years older than me and was in London doing a PhD on a French writer called something like Abollognere. She seemed incredibly nervous but not in a way that was irritating or pathetic. It was like she was so curious about people and things that she got all tangled up and confused in her desperation to absorb information. She'd ask a question that would include three more questions in concentric brackets and then apologize for not having remembered the first part. When you tried to answer she really listened and then carried on with more questions related to what you'd just told her. She laughed appreciatively at jokes and did almost everything a person could to make you feel OK. If I had a more suspicious mind I'd say she was too good to be true, but I don't think she was doing it for any reason other than genuine interest and magnanimity (I must've picked that word up from her – it sounded great with her accent). James acted a little like she was his best old buddy and a little like he was completely in love with her – I couldn't really tell which. At certain moments, like when he put his arm around her and said, 'Yes but Souazik darling that's because you're extraordinary,' (for actually enjoying reading some of the more miserable, cliché-riddled efforts she receives in the mail from people hoping to appear in her journal) I felt sure they must be sleeping together. But at other moments, like when he put his arm around me and said, 'Daisy, you're a miracle! An anomaly! An absolute freak of nature, isn't she Souazik?' I thought she might be just an old friend of his and that he was more interested in the contents of *my* panties. A couple of times during the evening I actually felt quite distressed by it all. I felt I'd been invited to join in some sort of game without having been told the basic rules beforehand. I didn't know whether James was using Souazik to get at me, me to get at Souazik or whether I was being a paranoid shmuck and nobody was meant to be getting at anyone. The thing that probably made it all work out in the end was that Souazik is clearly no idiot and if she suspected any funny stuff she handled it by being so friendly to me that I didn't feel any need to compete with her. Perhaps I could meet her on her own some-time and ask her a few questions about James. I sort of wish she was his girlfriend so I could stop thinking of him as a possibility.

After meeting Souazik and being forced to acknowledge the fact that she was a real – not to mention likeable – person, I got more and more embarrassed about the prospect of showing her my poems. I'd half forgotten that James would probably want to see them too. When I started doing them it was as a sort of smug gesture to show how pitiful poetry is. But now I'd put them in a binder and was sitting in a café full of smoking turtlenecks it felt like a whole new deal. I didn't want James and Souazik to think I was some kind of sad sack. And I certainly didn't want to fall into the category of bad poets through whom Souazik proves her extraordinariness by liking. The more I thought about it, the less I wanted to show them my stuff. But after an hour of drinking coffee and responding to Souazik's friendly interrogations James suddenly clapped his hands and said, 'So, on with the real business Daisy darling. May we see the fruits of your labor?' I'd been doing the suave thing for a bit too long and it was time for payback. From chatting happily and feeling mostly quite smart and OK I turned instantly into a total honker. I started stammering and mumbling and trying to explain that 'it didn't quite feel . . . like it wasn't . . . you know . . . the right . . .' and all this other cack. I would have said I'd forgotten to bring them if they hadn't been sticking out of the top of my bag all evening. I looked down at the Letraset title and felt profoundly humiliated. How could I have given it such a shitty name? I only called it that because 'shooting star' came a few words down from 'shoe' in the dictionary. It wasn't like I had a thing about shooting stars or thought they were really poetic or anything. I felt like all the efforts I'd made to be nice and interesting were about to be irreversibly undermined by the badness of my poems. I imagined that as soon as Souazik and James started to read them their faces would drop, their manners would become instantly cooler and, at the first opportunity, they'd make their excuses and leave, trying not to laugh too hard until I was safely out of earshot. I considered telling them that the poems were a bad joke and that I hadn't really written them. But then I would have had to come clean with James about the stupid lie I'd told him. The more I twitched around trying to wriggle out of the situation the more adamant they became. They were being soothing but also, I felt, quite stern. I realized that there was really no way out of it without coming across as a self-centered fruitloop. The only way to save face was to hand over the binder and cope with the shame. I passed it to Souazik. James pulled his seat up next to hers. I didn't want to be there when they started reading so I used the opportunity to go to the toilet. I scuttled down to the bathroom and sat there peeing with my head between my knees and my arms wrapped around my thighs. I've never peed like that before but it was quite a comforting position so I stayed in it for a while, delaying the moment when I'd have to go upstairs and face their verdict. After pulling my panty hose up I immediately wanted to go again. I got back into position and realized that it was just nerves. I yanked up my pants a second time and spent a few leisurely minutes washing my hands and drying them very, very thoroughly. I kept asking myself 'What the fuck do I want?'. I couldn't work it out. Why was I down in the bathroom spinning out over a middle-aged guy and a girl I need never see again, reading some poems that I hadn't even done myself and definitely didn't care about?

I used this logic to get me up the stairs, although I see now that I wasn't being entirely honest with myself. I really like Souazik and would appreciate having such a switched-on friend in London. I do have some sort of weirdy crush on James too, although I can hardly stand to admit it. I also think my poems are quite good. And if I didn't write them, who did?

When I got to the top of the stairs I saw Souazik and James laughing between themselves. I felt so humiliated I wanted to leave at once. I would just have slipped out leaving the poems behind if my bag wasn't sitting on their table. I felt pretty furious, but more with myself than with them – it wasn't *their* fault I knew nothing about poetry. I thought of the heaps of typewritten trash I'd inflicted on them and felt my insides implode. They carried on laughing, clearly having no idea that I could see them. I approached the table, expecting them to stop, but instead they looked up at me like I was some sort of heavenly body and said, 'They're brilliant!'. James said I was 'a genuine comic genius' and Souazik told me it was exactly the sort of work she was interested in. She said she always felt nervous when people she liked showed her their writing because she was pretty narrow and particular in her interests, but that we were obviously on exactly the same wavelength. It was so unexpected I didn't know how to react so I just smiled my goopiest smile. Souazik asked whether she could hang onto the folder for a few days to show it to the other woman who runs the journal. She said there might be space in the next issue, but if I could wait until the following quarter they were thinking of devoting the whole thing to American poets. She reeled off a list of names of people as if she thought I'd know them, but I didn't. She also asked whether I'd let her reproduce my poem, *Punch and Cissy*, in her thesis as part of the section on Bollign-iere's legacy. I must find out who he is. I was so relieved not to have made a complete ass of myself I sort of stopped listening and absorbing information. [*Ed: For the sake of thoroughness over editorial discretion, here comes another poem:*

The béchamel
Sauce of the basic
Punch is that a simple
Ortolan can effect a
Dramatic chant with its
Perspiration. Its twine
Buds can be
Clipped on for
Funerals to
Add a toupée of
Placental]

★

We all left the café together. James's car was parked on a street off to the right, Souazik's house was to the left and the tube station was over the road and straight ahead. I said goodbye to Souazik first and thanked her for being kind about my stuff. She laughed and told me not to be silly. She said she'd get my number from James and would call in a couple of days. I didn't mention that James hadn't got my number as I'd decided it was about time I gave it to him. Now I have the poetry excuse it should be OK if he rings. James said goodbye to Souazik, taking her by the shoulders and kissing her on each cheek. It wasn't exactly a sexy kiss, but afterwards I heard him say softly, 'Call me later'. I wondered what it meant.

Just as I was about to say goodbye to James he offered me a

lift to the station. Earl's Court station was about two minutes walk away so it seemed kind of pointless. He asked if it would be any use if he took me to Victoria instead. I was pleased to see him so keen to hang onto me so I accepted.

Inside the car there was an embarrassing silence. It was as if I'd been failing to notice and appreciate him all evening and suddenly there we were on our own together in a confined space and I couldn't ignore him any more. I remembered the last time I'd seen him – the coffee trick and subsequent invite to his apartment – and felt kind of dumb. It's a pretty regular occurrence that I find myself with nothing to say and this was another of those moments. I spent a minute silently appreciating the interior of his car, which was cream leather with mock tortoiseshell panels and bits of chrome. It was quite low to the ground but really comfortable. I didn't notice how fast we were going until we jerked to a standstill at some lights. Even the jerk felt well-sprung and expensively smooth. James turned to me with a half-sweet, half-maniacal smile and said, 'Well done darling'. I thought he was talking about the poems and said thanks. 'No, really, I'm awfully proud of you', he carried on. To which I said something like, 'Er'. 'You were absolutely no trouble. Six cups of coffee between us and no-one got burned. Perhaps soon I'll even dare to invite you for lunch again.' I was so grateful to him for saying it. I smiled, apologized and he burst out laughing. When he laughs he's gorgeous. He's like this really upright, adult guy most of the time, but when he laughs it's as if he could be any age or drive any kind of car, he stops being some generic Englishman and feels really familiar. I relaxed straight away and asked what he was doing for Christmas. He said he'd probably go see his family in Berkshire. It made me glad to hear that even bona fide adults like James still have to spend Christmas with their parents. He asked me what I was planning on doing and I told him I'd be spending it in

New Cross. He asked whether I'd be stuck on my own. I said no and there was another silence.

Because things inside the car had managed to get my attention so successfully, I hadn't noticed that we'd already arrived in Victoria. The journey had been really nice in the end and I was sad it was over. I remembered I had to give James my number and asked whether he had a pen. He pulled out a gold fountain pen from the inside of his jacket, but didn't have his phone book with him. As I wrote my number out on the back of a receipt I noticed my hand shaking slightly and hoped James couldn't see. I handed him back the pen and paper and told him not to lose it. I also said he'd be more likely to get me if he rang during the daytime. He gave me a look that I didn't understand mainly because it didn't have anything dramatic to distinguish it from other looks – no raised eyebrows, winks or grimaces – and leant forward to kiss me goodbye. I aimed for his right cheek but the kiss landed really clumsily. The same thing happened on the other side. His lips landed more on the corner of my mouth. I didn't look him in the eye until I had pulled away. I couldn't tell, but it felt as though he was staring at me particularly intently. I felt a huge rush of jumpy fear. I wrenched open the car door and practically hurled myself out onto the sidewalk. Once the physical gap between us felt wide enough I went back to acting friendly again and waved him goodbye. He drove off without looking back.

On the bus back home I couldn't stop going over and over the goodbye kiss. If my brain was made of videotape the memory would have worn out before we got to Camberwell. What was he trying to do? What was the deal with Souazik? Was he on the phone to her now telling her all about it? Did he invite her along to check me out? Maybe she hates me because of the way I left with James. He must have known nothing was going to happen if he asked her to call later. Maybe he just thinks a farewell kiss on the lips is a normal enough thing between friends and can't understand why I reacted so strangely.

I got so stuck thinking about all this stuff I forgot to think about Rob and how I was going to explain my absence to him. Because I was so riveted by the whole set-up with James and Souazik I didn't really notice how long and steep the hill between the bus stop and our house is. I arrived all out of breath and slightly glazed over. The light was on in the living room so I went straight in. The TV was showing the late news, but with the sound turned right down, and Sofia and Rob were sitting on armchairs on opposite sides of the room. Either they hadn't been talking for a while, or they'd stopped when they heard the door. Rob stood up suddenly as if he was going to rush towards me but then sort of froze. He looked at me really weirdly and went, 'Daze, are you alright?'. I guess I must have looked as though something pretty terrible had happened. I stood there panting for a second, trying to snap out of my James-induced trance and back into my normal way of being. Rob looked so disturbed that my first instinct was to let him know nothing was up. Tactically, this was a bad move. I smiled and said, 'I'm fine,' to which he replied, 'Well, I'm not. Where the hell have you been?' I decided to base whatever bullshit I could come up with on Souazik and the poems. I said I'd met a girl in a bookshop. I mentioned her journal and said that she was going to do an issue on American poets. I told him I'd happened to have the poems in my bag with me and that I'd shown them to her. I said she was doing a PhD on Bollière and liked my work. He said, 'Who?', a little too rudely. I said, 'Bollière, you know, the French poet.' I could see we were getting well away from the point. Sofia, who was looking really embarrassed, got up and said goodnight. Rob broke off scowling for just long enough to smile and say, 'Buenos noches'. When she was gone I felt suddenly more relaxed about being shitty and said something like, 'Look Rob, what's your problem? You go out all day every goddamn day and do the things you want to do, but if I go out for one evening it's like I've murdered your mother or something.' He came back with a retort along the lines of, 'I always come back when I say I will, and if something changes I call you. You're so fucking selfish. I've had to sit here for the last three hours imagining you dead in a ditch and then you come home and tell me you've been out drinking with some poet lady while I've been here thinking of you dead in a ditch.' He's definitely not very used to arguing. Although I clearly occupied the moral low-ground I could see I had the upper hand in terms of rowing skills. I hit back with, 'Nobody asked you to spend three hours fantasizing about my dead body. Maybe you'd like me out of the way so you can have a *buenos noche* with your new best friend.' Then he said, 'That's so like you, Daze. That is just so like you,' and stormed out. What makes him think he knows what I'm like?

There was no way I felt like sleeping with him so I waited in the living room until he went upstairs to brush his teeth. I crept into the bedroom, snatched the duvet and made myself comfortable on the couch. He didn't put his head around the door or do anything to bring about a reconciliation and I wasn't in any mood to be reasonable either. I stayed awake for hours wondering what I wanted to happen next. From an objective point of view I believe that rows are a vital part of any relationship. But when I find myself having one I feel like it's the end. Maybe the healthy rows are the ones about toothpaste squeezing and lid replacement. They allow couples to appreciate their fundamental separateness in order to carry on being together on more realistic terms. But I'm scared this little spat with Rob might have heavier implications. At the base of it, it feels like we're very unsure of whether or not we want to be together. Or at least in the way that we are now. I'm reluctant to patch things up as I feel it wouldn't be honest. But I don't feel like being honest either. I don't even think the whole problem can be put down to James. It's certainly true that if I hadn't been out doing something I felt guilty about I would have called home. But if I was happy at home I wouldn't be out doing something I felt guilty about. It's like things with Rob got too domestic too quick. That wouldn't necessarily be so bad if Rob and I were more compatible in the first place. But the longer I spend with him the less fascinating I find his stories, his ideas and his ways. I hate to admit it to myself but I think I find him really boring. I guess I was so desperate to get away from Vegas I blinded myself to Rob's obvious inappropriateness in order to give myself an escape route.

The more I think about it the worse I feel. I'm all achey from having spent the night on the couch and even a two hour bath couldn't fix it. Rob's due home again in a few hours and I don't know what I'm going to say. But it does feel as though lying back and thinking of England isn't going to work out (especially as I don't really know what to think about England either). I know I may even be in the wrong, but it's not really about right and wrong any more, it's just about whether or not we happen to like each other.

The more I think about it the more I wish he'd get home so we could sort it out. I also wish he'd get home so that I could stop stopping myself thinking about James and get on with something else. I'm trying so hard not to think about him that I can hardly think at all. I just noticed when I looked over at the alarm clock that a whole hour had passed in the time it took me to write the last few sentences. My mind just won't stop thinking about the kiss, but my writing hand refuses to admit it. Last night on the couch my whole body was going crazy. The feelings were so excessive I didn't even need to touch myself to make myself feel like I was coming.

I wonder when Souazik will ring.

Edit

I came across this exchange of notes in the telephone pad. I don't know precisely when it took place as it isn't mentioned anywhere in Daisy's journals. It's rather nonessential to the story but I enjoyed it.

Sweethearts,

Look at this. It's a note. It didn't take long to write. A little more time than it would take to jot down the average telephone message perhaps, but not long. I did it because I could be bothered. Do you think that when my friends and family ring you could bother to write a little note to let me know? I'd do the same for you.

Leni.

Dear Leni,

As you know, when my Mum rang last week you told her to ring straight back and leave a message on the machine.

Jo.

Darling Jo,

Your mother didn't just want me to tell you that she'd called, she wanted to leave a long message about your sister's husband's father's girlfriend's neighbour's dog. I had more pressing things to do. And you got your message didn't you?

Leni.

Leni,

If you flick back through the pad you'll see that most of the messages are for you and that ninety percent of them are in Daisy's writing. I think you should be saying thank you, not complaining.

Jo.

Sweet Daisy,

Little bud. Precious bloom. Bright eye by day and pearl by night. Your generosity overwhelms me.

All my love, and I mean that,

Leni.

OK?

Movies

I've become a leaf, a jellyfish, a puff of wispy stuff. I've put my fate in the hands of whatever. I've realized it's all I can do. It's freezing inside and out. If I exhale I get a little cloud of condensation even though the gas heater's been on for ten minutes. I've taken a week off doing nothing to do even less (i.e. not even fill up my notepad). It's been very relaxing. I baked, re-read all of F. Scott Fitzgerald's short stories and checked out almost every inscription in the whole of Nunhead cemetery. I also thought about James obsessively.

I've decided to stop trying to work things out and just acknowledge my impotence in the face of life's great mysteries (like what in hell is going on, *ever*). Rob was mad at me for a while and then seemed to forget. Souazik rang and said she was definitely going to publish the poems. She was so insistent that they were good I almost started to believe her. She told me she was busy finishing a chapter of her thesis in time to give it to her supervisor before the vacation, but would ring again when she felt less hassled. James telephoned (in the daytime) and said he had to go to New York for a week but that he'd love to see me in the small gap before his Christmas family visit. Everyone in the house is getting ready to go away. Jo's going to see her Mom and Dad in Altringham. Sofia's headed back to Spain. And Leni's going to spend it in her parents' country house.

Rob and I'll be stuck here alone together, which I guess is a good enough reason to keep pushing ahead with the peace process.

I've had a lot of luck fox-spotting lately. I tend to wake up really early at the moment so I just sit and wait by the back window. I see the fox nearly every day. I've decided it's a she. I think she may even live under our shed because once she goes down there she doesn't tend to come back out. I can't decide whether or not I'd like to be her. She's so lovely the way she goes through all the gardens like she owns the place. And she looks so intelligent. But it must be tough trying to get by in such an inhospitable environment. I wonder what she eats.

Research is going quite well. Firstly, I managed to get hold of another letter from Sofia's brother. Sofia actually mentioned to me that she'd received it, so I asked her how he was. She said she wasn't sure but he didn't sound very well. I don't know how much I actually gathered from the letter myself (I didn't have the dictionary around this time) but, from his crossings out, underlinings and smudges, he seemed to be in a bad state.

[Ed: And, dutifully, here it is:

Querida H. G: Eres muy amable pero estás muy equivocada. ¿Cómo podrías llegar a entenderme? Ni siquiera aunque estuvieses aquí. *La Vida Cotidiana* no significa nada para mí. Me mantengo despierto por días sintiendo todas esas cosas que la otra gente tratan de ignorar. Somos criaturas atormentadas pero algunos dichosos tienen la suerte suficiente para encontrar PAX. Mamá y Papá están P . . . E . . . R . . . D . . . I . . . D . . . O . . . S. Un brindis por el colapso del sistema bancario mundial. Diagolo.

Dear B.S, [I am assuming H. G. stands for Hermana Grande] *You are very kind but you are very wrong. How are you supposed to understand me? Even if you were here.* Ordinary Life *means nothing to me. I stay awake for days feeling all the things other people try to ignore. We are tormented creatures but only a few of us are sufficiently lucky to find PAX. Mama and Papa are L . . . O . . . S . . . T. A toast to the collapse of the world banking system. Diagolo.]*

★

I'm going in and out of the rooms now like nobody's business. It doesn't even occur to me that I'm not really allowed. I've mostly given up on Jo's, because there's not a lot of point. I do peep through the door occasionally, in case I'm missing some kind of dramatic revelation – but invariably I'm not. I've never even found her bed unmade.

I've also managed to get my hands on another of Leni's

efforts. It's not at all like the first script – I wonder what gave her the idea. It's about these women who work in a sleazy night-club.

[Ed: I'll cut out the unnecessaries rather than bore you with Leni's rather sub-standard script. The story concerns a group of nightclub hostesses who take grisly revenge on a customer. One of the hostesses – Sadie – is described as having short black hair and an intelligent face, another is 'a sluggish American', while a third is 'Hispanic, innocent-looking'. Apart from that there is little resemblance to anything like reality.

Scene I: The interior of a rather insalubrious hostess bar. The walls, sofas and carpets are a deep, blood red. The room is brightly lit and the hostesses are sitting around a table. They are fully made-up, but wearing woolly cardigans and warm jackets. The overspilling ashtrays and playing cards strewn around the tabletop tell us that they've been hanging about like this for a long time.

There is a clamouring at the doorbell and a flurry of activity. The women take off their jumpers and bundle them under the tables. Underneath they are all wearing saucy lingerie. The lights are dimmed to a bloody, reddish glow. A man enters. He stumbles, drunkenly, as **Mirabelle** leads him over to one of the booths. The hostesses go over and introduce themselves one at a time.

The man orders drinks all round, makes some rather pathetic conversation and finally seals his fate by saying:

Man 1 {to Naomi}: You look like my
daughter. She's got lovely little titties
like you.

Naomi looks worried but the others are now
red with rage. They all stare at each
other with strange recognition, as if
this last statement has a particular
resonance for each of them.

Very telling. Another man arrives, accompanied by a female escort, and asks the dark-haired, intelligent Sadie to join them. He immediately begins trying to remove her underwear. She isn't impressed, and neither is the escort, who orders him to stop and to go and splash his face with cold water.

Escort: He just needs a bit of telling,
that's all. Believe me, he gives good
tips. If you can just hold him off it's
usually worth it. He gave me £200 on top of
my fee last time!
   Sadie: Really? Have you been doing this
for a while?

Escort: No. I've got a trout farm in Epping. When my husband left me it looked like I might not be able to keep it going. But it's all I've got and I absolutely refuse to let it go without a fight.

Sadie: Gosh!

Escort: You?

Sadie: I've got a kid and I'm halfway through a degree in Modern Languages. The usual.

In the background **Man 1** is slow-dancing with **Naomi** as the others look on, arms folded. We zoom in on **Naomi's** face. Her eyes are wide open with fright.

Sadie's customers leave and she goes to find out how Naomi is getting along with the paedophile. He's fallen into a drunken stupor and the others are trying to wake him with a few swift slaps around the chops. When that fails they give him the bill, which adds up to two thousand pounds. He begins to shout.

The women look at each other, frozen. There is a long silence. Without warning **Man 1** lashes out with his fist and punches the lamp in the booth. Everyone is immediately plunged into darkness. There is another pause. We can just about make out the silhouettes of the figures. We see one of the women pick the candlestick up

off the table and smash it down on the
man's head. The others all join in. The
man is shouting and moaning. He is
helpless against the six women attacking
him with all their force. The door opens
and light floods in. It's **Ferdinando**
coming in from the kitchen. They all look
up at him, blankly. He shakes his head.
Man 1 is out cold on the floor.

Ferdinando: My poor dear ladies. Go. Go
and change. It's time we closed anyway.

They file out through the kitchen to the
dressing room, each kissing **Ferdinando** on
the cheek. Ferdinando goes over to **Man 1**.
He grabs him under the armpits and drags
him out through the exit.

Scene III: The hostesses are all saying
goodbye to each other in the street. It's
dark and there's no-one around. They have
all removed their make-up and are dressed
in jeans and sensible coats. They wave
cheerfully and disappear off in different
directions, completely ignoring **Man 1** who
is lying unconscious in the gutter only
metres away.

The street is now silent. We zoom in on **Man
1**'s face. He coughs and blood comes out of
his mouth. His eyes open momentarily and
then roll back in his head.]

★

It's such a strange script. I'm not sure about the way it ends, but perhaps she's still working on it. The dialogues are a bit cacky but I'm sure she'll catch on eventually. At least something happens and it's not about a cute kid. A fish farm, though? I think that bit should go. And there's a half-baked description of a 'strange recognition' among the women which, to be fair, might come across better in actions than in words.

The other thing I found quite interesting about it was the general kind of man-haterishness. Ever since the pub evening I'd had the impression that it was women Leni hated. But maybe it's not so simple. The more I discover about her the less I understand. I mean all those girlie pictures in the bedroom must be saying something. She likes women's faces, at least (even if it's only when they're in a bad mood). I think she likes the idea of liking women, and of thinking they're somehow superior, but in practice she's pretty impressed with guys. I wonder what type of people she goes for – apart from herself. I can't really imagine her having the hots for anybody. It's like, if someone was too charismatic or interesting, her ego couldn't handle it. But if they were too plain she wouldn't want to be seen with them either. I think she might like the *idea* of liking girls, but isn't especially into girls themselves.

I got a call from James this morning. He's off to Berkshire in a couple of days so I agreed to meet him on the South Bank tomorrow. He said they were showing one of his favorite movies at the NHS and would I like to come? Of course I said yes. In a way it's less of a stress since I decided to follow my feelings and see where they lead me. But in another way it's worse. If anything happens with James . . . I just can't imagine it. I mean I *try* to imagine it practically all the time. I picture what it would have been like if that kiss in the car had carried on. I imagine it starting off quite gently and sort of wandering about, accompanied by a bit of hair-stroking or something. Then I think of it getting gradually more full-on until it's pretty obvious we can't go much further while we're still parked in a well-lit, busy street right by Victoria station. What happens after that depends on what kind of mood I'm in. On a bad day I get suddenly embarrassed and apologize and run off. On a slightly better day, James invites me up for coffee but I tell him that I'm not ready, or that I can't cheat on Rob and we do a bit more lovey-dovey stuff before I leave. But on a good day I let myself go the whole way. We're kissing in the car and James says, 'Daisy, please come up to my apartment. I know it's difficult, but I want you and I'd do anything to have you. Can't you see I'm practically pulsating with lust?' (Or something like that, only less stupid-sounding.) And I go, 'OK James, you can have me now and we can put off thinking 'til later,' – and then we go to his house. I try not to imagine the short car journey between the station and his house. I don't like the idea of there being a gap between agreeing to go to bed with him and it actually happening – I'd keep thinking he'd gone off the idea since I said yes. So, in an ideal world

143

we'd be immediately teleported from the car to his apartment. We start off in the living room (just because it's the only room I've actually seen apart from the hall, which has a prickly carpet). We're on the couch, or maybe on the floor. We start kissing again, really gently. James is stroking me all over my body. When we really get going I start undoing the buttons of his shirt. His body is all wiry and muscular with a small patch of hair in the middle of his chest (I wonder what it's actually like). He takes my shirt off and starts sucking my nipples. When I imagine this part I really go crazy about it. In the fantasy I start coming just from having my nipples sucked although I don't think this has ever actually happened to me in real life. When the nipple orgasms have made me lose my mind completely I undo his belt and put my hand in his pants. (I can't believe I'm actually writing this down!) Then I take his pants off so he's completely naked and make him lie back on the couch (or the floor). He's pretty pleased about the whole thing. He's going, 'Oh Daisy,' (Not Daze!) 'Daisy, you're wonderful! You're exquisite! You're absolutely divine!'. I climb on top of him and start doing some stuff, wriggling around and really getting off on it. I tell him he's not allowed to come until I say so. We make love looking straight into each others eyes, as if it's really about each other and not just a meaningless bang. And when we finally come (together, although it's *my* third time) we're both practically screaming. After that we laze around in each other's arms, all happy and post-coital, but tormented by the fact that I have a boyfriend and have to leave. He can't bear to let me go and drives me back to New Cross. We kiss in the car for about half an hour before saying goodbye. And when I look back to wave at him one last time I see that he's got tears in his eyes. I cut the daydream there, before it starts getting complicated.

144

What's up with me? None of this is actually going to happen tomorrow night.

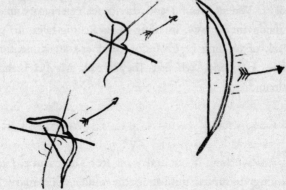

I always get confused about exactly which day Christmas is on, but I think this year it's Friday. Tomorrow's Tuesday, everybody's quitting the house on Thursday morning, which means that Rob and I are going to be left alone. I wonder whether it'll snow. The way things are going it looks more likely to rain. I can't imagine what we're going to do. Rob and I are being very civil at the moment but we haven't had sex since the night before I slept on the couch. I guess things will either improve or get worse when there's nobody around to distract us. There's always the TV. The TV seems to be the central focus of Jo's understanding of what Christmas is (she calls it the *telly*, it makes it sound so sweet). She always buys those magazines with soap stars on the front that tell you what's on. But this week she's really been yabbing about it. Yesterday – which she spent entirely in her slippers and toweling robe – she couldn't stop going on about the highs and lows of the Christmas schedule. I got stuck in a really long conversation about whether or not the *Wizard of Oz* was actually on Boxing Day and why there were no Agatha Christies this year. It wasn't fun.

Back home we tend to go see Mom's work friends on Christmas day. We eat the kind of food we normally eat, only more of it. We sit around and try to act celebratory in a slightly unconvincing way, listening to fascinating tales of Dr. Kügel's lack of funding or Professor Gardner's attachment to his lab rats. I wonder whether they'll call. Maybe I should ring them.

I was working it out today on Rob's calculator. I only have enough to survive until about the middle of February. I'd hoped I was going to manage until spring, but I don't think I was being too realistic. February is quite soon and it's making me nervous. This was meant to be the time in which I worked out what I wanted to do with myself. But I don't feel any nearer to knowing than I did four months ago. I quite like being here, but I also miss my friends. I can't imagine getting settled into any kind of career in London. But, equally, I don't see myself spending my whole life in Vegas. I guess there's always San Francisco or New York. Now that I've demystified London for myself maybe I can go live in America without feeling like I'm missing out. I definitely prefer being an English person in America than an American in England anyhow.

Rob's got to stay until the end of August to finish his course. And who knows where he'll end up after that? He could be offered a job anywhere from Moscow to Kansas. Would I want to go with him? I don't think so. Rob and I definitely don't have compatible life-plans. I guess the best thing would be to talk to him. But I can't imagine what would happen next. We'd have a miserable Christmas, after which I'd go home. In a way, I think it might be a good solution. But in another way I'd hate it to happen. It'd feel like a real failure. I'd get back, Mom would say, 'I told you so,' and I'd be forced to start looking for another job in the only industry I know.

I'd also be sad to leave London at a point when it's possible certain things might be starting to look up. And I'm not just talking about James. I really liked meeting Souazik and, even though the whole poetry thing is a bit of a schmeer, it's quite nice for me to think of being published. It feels as though I've only just scratched the surface of what it might be possible for me to do over here and I'd be sad to go back without following things through further. I could get a waitressing job, get my own place and see how things go. It's the opposite of what I imagined myself doing – I kind of imagined sorting things so that I didn't have to do adolescent-type jobs anymore. James would be impressed. It would fit perfectly with his romantic idea of who I am.

P.S. More evidence of Leni's literary talent arrived today in the form of a note especially for me. Apparently I left some hairs in the bath. Big deal. And why write a note rather than just come and tell me?

[Ed: Well, I can see why.

Dearest Living Companion,

What lovely hair you have. I had never been given the chance to appreciate its length and lustrous blackness until you left such a generous quantity of it on the sides of the bath. And what a beautiful pattern it made, a visual symphony of delicate swirls. Thank you for enlightening me, and now that we all know how divine it is you may go back to removing all trace of it from our communal washing space.

Charmed, I'm sure,

Leni.]

★

I've made a decision to lie to Rob about where I'm going tonight. I'm going to say I've gone to meet Souazik. Not because I want to cheat on him and string him along. I've decided to handle it this way because I'm going to tell him about all the other stuff on Thursday. I'd rather deal with it when we're alone. I'm going to say it's obvious things aren't really working out between us and see how he wants to deal with it. Last night we hardly spoke to each other. He got home late because it was his last chance to use the workshops at University. I'd been in the bedroom, scribbling away, as usual. I came downstairs to say hello and we ended up spending the evening watching stupid stuff on the TV and chatting with Sofia and Jo. Sofia's English is getting pretty good now. She's like another person. She's much more confident and even makes the occasional joke. Her Mom rang and she came back with all these funny stories about her brother, Diego. Apparently her Mom and Dad don't find him too hilarious. They said he went for a walk in the park at night with hardly any clothes on and was brought home by the police. The parents told the police that their son was a regular sleepwalker and apologized on his behalf. But Diego kept insisting he'd gone to look for Paxo, his pet pig, which doesn't exist. Then he ran out of the house and the police had to go after him again. Finally, they persuaded him to go back to bed. Sofia's Dad stayed awake the whole night to make sure he didn't do it again. The next day Diego woke up with a fever and couldn't stop ranting about the pig. She said she was sure he'd be OK with a bit of rest, and if their parents stopped hassling him. It seems like she's the most responsible member of her family. She told us she felt as though they were all waiting for her to get back and fix everything. Poor Sofia.

Jo was alright too. She took us through all the presents she'd got for her aunts and uncles and cousins. It was just socks and stuff, but it was nice the way she came from a really huge family and had a little piece of schlock for each of them. I imagined all thirty of them sitting round the *Eastenders* Christmas special and it warmed my heart.

Rob and I spent most of the evening on opposite sides of the room, but there was no major bad vibe or anything. I guess you could say we used Jo and Sofia to avoid each other, but it didn't feel so terrible.

Since the row, going to sleep has been a much icier experience. The first few days after my stint on the couch we both stayed up half the night, hanging around, reading and looking at the local wildlife, putting off the moment when we'd finally have to get into bed together. If it was late and we were tired it seemed natural that we should go to sleep without touching each other. But after only a few days we kind of adjusted to the new state of things and just went to bed whenever we felt like it. Now it seems normal to get under the duvet with pajamas, socks and a sweater on and say goodnight before turning over and crashing out.

I can't wait to see James this evening.

It sounds crazy but one thing I keep worrying about is what to get Rob for Christmas. Whatever I tell him on Thursday, and whatever the outcome, the chances are we're still going to spend Christmas day together. There are no decorations in the house, no signs of festivity. It would be pretty sad to ignore the whole thing altogether, so I've decided I'd better get him something – I just can't think what. I guess it's one more sign of how little I know and understand him. There's no way I'd get him anything for his course. But what else is there? Another sweater? A warmer dressing gown? It all seems so depressing and matrimonial. I can't imagine what kind of present he'll get me – if anything.

I'd hoped that last night might decide something for me, but it didn't. In fact it's made things slightly worse. I'm still going ahead with the split-up-with-Rob plan tomorrow, but not on James's account. It's all very confusing and, to cap it all, as I sit here writing, Rob is working away on the other side of the room. It's amazing how little curiosity he shows towards my stuff. After our little scuffle a few weeks back he's never mentioned wanting to read my notes again. Perhaps he thinks I'm writing poems and doesn't want to know. Fair enough. I'd hate to know about whatever it is he's working on right now too. It's only nine o'clock in the morning, but already we've drifted off into our separate worlds.

Anyhow, on to more interesting topics. I got to the NFT (not NHS) bar last night and waited a couple of minutes for James to appear. I'd got myself into a real state with all my stupid daydreaming. I was half expecting him to come straight in, tell me that he loved me, pick me up like Fay Wray and carry me off to his car. When he arrived I jumped up and went over to kiss him hello, but he leapt back and told me to watch out as he had a terrible flu. He said he'd thought about ringing to cancel because he'd hate to give me his bug, but selfishly decided that the movie was too good to miss. His eyes were all puffy and his nose was bright red. Nothing could have been further removed from my mental picture of him as a lithe Greek god with springy chest hair.

It was twenty minutes before we had to go in. We went straight away to get two triple brandies and sat down. He said New York had been a disaster. He'd arrived to find that all his meetings had been delayed. In the end it turned out he needn't have been there at all. And to make it even more annoying he'd caught 'this blasted virus' on the plane coming home. He looked pretty exhausted and miserable. I asked him whether he wouldn't rather save the movie for another day and just go to bed. (I didn't intend it as a hint and, unfortunately, he didn't take it as one.) The movie was called *The Marquise of O,* directed by a guy called Eric Rohmer. Apparently it doesn't come on in the cinema all that often so, when it does, you can't mess around. James said the last time he saw it was twenty years ago and it had made such an impression on him that he wanted to see it again. Twenty years sounded like a crazily long time. He must have been about the same age as I am now and I would have been eight years old.

He asked how things had been going with me. I didn't want to go into detail (specially not about Rob) so I just told him that it looked like a bit of waitressing might be on the agenda in the New Year. As I predicted he looked almost pleased and said, '*C'est la vie*, Daisy darling, you'll survive. Souazik's very excited about your work. Just keep going and something will come of it.' For him, news of my waitressing almost seems to bring proof of my superior intelligence and sensitivity – he'd probably be really disappointed if I told him I was going to get a proper job – whereas for me it's pretty clear that it's just more evidence of my general inadequacy. I wish I could be more like the person James sees in me.

The Marquise of O was a totally incredible movie. I wanted to like it anyway but, really, it was the best. And it was even more interesting to sit through it wondering why it had become so important to James. The story is set at the end of the eighteenth century in a small town in Italy (although it's in German). It starts with some guys in a tavern reading a notice placed in the local paper by the Marquise. She claims to have gotten pregnant without knowingly having had sex with anyone and asks the man responsible for her condition to go round to her parents' house. In the next scene it flashes back to the lead-up to the newspaper ad and shows the Marquise being rescued from a band of lecherous villains by the dashing Count F. (who's played by a really amazing actor – I don't know his name). He whisks her off to a safe place, saves her whole family from invaders, and then disappears. The next thing we hear is that he was killed in battle shortly afterwards. The Marquise starts having dizzy spells and feeling queasy. Then the Count comes back and asks her to marry him. Apparently he didn't die, he was just very ill. She'd vowed never to remarry after her first husband croaked, but says that she certainly owes the Count a favor and will give his proposal some thought. He goes travelling for a few weeks while she mulls it over and, meanwhile her bump starts to show. Her family disown her and send her into hiding. She's desperate to prove her innocence to her Mom and Dad, and puts the ad in the paper. Count F. comes back and starts hassling her to marry him again, but she tells him to go away.

The day before the mysterious rapist is due to present himself, the Marquise's mother comes to play a trick on the Marquise to see whether or not she's lying about not knowing who he is. The mother tells her daughter that the stable-hand confessed to doing the deed while she was asleep. The Marquise believes her and the mother realizes that the ad wasn't just a hustle dreamed up between her daughter and some unscrupulous scoundrel. Everybody is forced to acknowledge the Marquise's innocence. Then there's a yucky scene where her Dad drools all over her neck, just to show how sorry he is.

The big day arrives and, at the appointed hour, the Count walks in. Nobody can believe it's him (except the audience, who knew all along). Apparently, after he'd rescued her from the pack of villains, she passed out with the shock and he just couldn't help himself. She tells him to get lost, but her Dad organizes a deal whereby she marries the Count and he's obliged to pay for everything but isn't allowed to live in the same house or sleep with her. He gets himself a place down the road, is really nice to the baby and after about a year the Marquise gives in, falls in love with him and they live happily ever after.

They all have really great clothes – especially the Count who wears a lot of white and cream outfits with big hats. Apparently the costume designer won an award.

After the movie we walked across Embankment Bridge to an old-fashioned winebar in a cellar. James said it was the oldest one in London. I asked him what it was he liked so much about the movie. He said he didn't know, but that he found it really beautiful and moving. I couldn't work out whether he'd been crying in the bit when the Marquise gets kicked out by her Dad. He sniffed a lot, but it might just have been his cold. He asked whether I'd liked it and I told him I thought it was excellent. But when he asked why I didn't really know what to say. I said I liked the Count because he'd done something so wrong, but the actor who played him made him such a sympathetic character that you really wanted him to be forgiven. I told him I liked the Marquise too. She was really beautiful, in a weird, big-jawed way, and when she suffered you really felt it.

I hate discussing movies with people. I never know what to say. It's always so strange when you come out of the cinema. If the movie was good you tend to feel like you've lived through some really momentous experience. But it isn't like a *real* experience, which would probably be easier to discuss. Because it's a movie it's as though you're obliged to be critical and distant, and appreciate it at one remove, otherwise you sound like a jerk. I felt so feeble telling James I liked it because the Count seemed like a nice man. I wished I could have said something clever about the structure of the storyline, or read something into the use of pregnancy as a metaphor for Christ-knows-what (I sound like Leni) but I couldn't. It made me realize that, while I commiserate with myself over Rob's lack of interest in the arts, even if I had a boyfriend who knew everything that Kant had to say about aesthetics, and who designed stage sets for the English National Opera, still we might not have anything to say to each other at the end of a good movie.

James's nose was redder than before and his eyes were streaming. I decided that, if the flu could affect James this badly, I'd better not catch it. I was leaning so far back in my chair I could hardly hear him. I think he was saying something about the history of the winebar – maybe that it had survived the Fire of London or something. It sounded interesting, but not *that* interesting, and it wasn't a very satisfactory replacement for passionate sex on the couch.

After the wine we went out to the street. I noticed, looking at the big clock over the station entrance, that there was a train to New Cross in five minutes. We said Happy Christmas and James apologized for being such bad company. I told him he'd been charming and he spluttered. He held out his hand, saying it wouldn't be fair to kiss me goodbye (he was definitely making a big deal of it). His palm was incredibly hot. It really turned me on to feel his overheated blood. I blurted out something half-assed like, 'Oh James! You're really ill! Have you got any-one to look after you?' To which he replied, 'Unfortunately, yes. My mother, and the prospect fills me with dread'. I laughed and he gave me a look of real fondness. He touched me gently on the cheek and said he'd call when he got back. I raced up to Charing Cross and leapt through the train doors, getting my coat stuck and having to stand there like an idiot all the way to Waterloo.

I met Leni on the way up the hill to the house. She didn't even seem embarrassed about the note – it was as if it hadn't happened. She said she'd just been to a bar with some friends. I asked her about it – I was genuinely curious. I can't imagine what Leni's friends would be like. I also can't imagine what kind of bars she would choose to go to. She said the friends were just people from her course. I wondered why she said 'just'. It's quite strange that, for someone who's lived in London all her life (apart from weekends in the country), she doesn't seem to have long-term friends to hang out with. It's true that the phone rings for her quite often and that she's always going out. But no-one's ever come to visit her at home. Perhaps she's ashamed of the house. But surely that wouldn't matter with close friends. I'd have thought she'd be pleased about the 'realness' of it anyhow. She did say once that most of her friends lived in West London and found it unthinkable that they should ever be forced to cross the river. Nice people. Apparently the bar she went to was 'just' one of those bars in Soho. She seemed really down. She's generally pretty unchatty anyhow, but it really looked like something was eating her. I don't think it's romance as I'm sure she's too heartless. It can't be her family as she doesn't seem to give a shit about them so long as the checks keep coming. It can't be her work as, of course, her films are all perfect and there's nothing to worry about there. Maybe she's lonely. Well, it couldn't happen to a more deserving person.

Back home things were much calmer than the last time I went out alone – presumably in part because I'd left Rob a note saying where I was(n't). He'd spent another evening with Sofia, Jo and Jo's boyfriend (whose name I always forget). They were all in the kitchen, standing around and drinking wine when Leni and I arrived. They said 'hi' in a really friendly way, but I sort of felt like we'd interrupted something. They were laughing when we were in the hall, but when we got to the kitchen they calmed down. It felt as if all the sweet, normal, regular people in the house had been enjoying a break from the fucked-up, anxious, difficult ones and weren't too pleased to have us back. For the very first time I think I had a genuine, unmitigated feeling of empathy with Leni. I guess it had to happen at some point.

Jo suggested that we do a pre-Christmas dinner before everyone went away. I offered to make the dessert (I was pretty glad to find a way to ingratiate myself after such a bad entrance).

Sofia said she'd cook a chicken risotto. Rob offered to do the salad. The Spud said he'd bring some wine and Leni said she'd see if she could cancel a prior engagement. Great. I should have said I'd come on the condition that no-one mentioned any plans for the future. If I fainted that time in the pub I'd probably fall into a coma at this one. How could I possibly tell them that the best thing I can think of doing with my life right now is to get a waitressing job and carry on pretending to be a poet in order to make some old guy think I'm cute? It doesn't sound too impressive.

It's strange the way Lara always comes up in my mind at moments like this. Almost every time I have a crisis I think of her. It's as if she's become my replacement for God or something. She kind of hangs about in my head and makes me feel I mustn't be too crappy. Sometimes I wish she'd go away — well, not her but my own warped version of her. I mean there's no real reason why certain human beings shouldn't spend their lives working in dumb jobs if that's what they prefer. Why should I have to prove I'm special? Maybe I'm not.

I just noticed Rob sitting on the other side of the room. I'd better go get the ingredients for tonight's dessert. I wonder whether he'd like to come with me. I feel so weird about the bomb I'm about to drop on him tomorrow I think it's best if I stay out of his way as much as possible until then. There's something fucked up about acting like nothing's wrong when I know we're about to split. Maybe he'll be relieved when I actually get round to telling him. I hope so. The way he's just slouching around and ignoring me seems to suggest he knows something's up. I wonder why *he's* not saying anything about it. I guess he's just not that kind of guy. Anybody who lets you wash their socks is probably going to let you organize the break-up as well.

I'm so paranoid about my notebook now that I take it everywhere with me. I'll certainly be taking it to Sainsbury's. My old notepad is hidden between the mattress and the base of the bed. I've pushed it right to the middle in case Rob ever gets it into his head to change the sheets.

I'm seriously starting to look forward to tomorrow. I wonder when's the best time to do it. I think I should go get his stupid present in the morning and then do the other part in the afternoon.

Christmas

I'm actually in Sofia's room. Her desk is the most peaceful place to sit and catch up. Rob is in our room with his notes spread all over the floor. I haven't managed to get any writing done for *days* because so much has been happening. There was the farewell dinner, the 'splitting-up', and then everything else that came after it. I hardly know where to start. I guess I might as well do it in the order that it happened.

The dinner was good. Leni refrained from making any grand speeches. Jo didn't try to organize us. Sofia was relaxed. Rob was charming and friendly to everyone (so what's new?). The Spud couldn't make it. And I remained conscious right up until bedtime. We drank a load of wine and it all felt pretty pally and OK. In terms of research it went quite well too, although it may be a while before I can follow up certain discoveries. The main piece of fresh information came from Jo. Apparently she *does* keep some sort of journal – but Christ knows where. One day over the break, while Rob was in the bath, I had a little snoop but didn't come up with anything. It seems quite likely that she's taken it away with her. With any luck I'll have managed to get my hands on it by the end of next week. The other thing that came up, but which may take a while to come to fruition, is that Leni has found the idea for her third script. Can't wait. In the gap between the chicken and the dessert (a really excellent *Tarte au Citron*, without meaning to boast) she started acting all smug and self-satisfied, like she was freshly amazed by her own god-like super-fantasticness. She wouldn't tell us what it was – she said we'd have to wait and see – just that she was sure it was the right kind of film to be doing at the moment. What the fuck did she mean?

One annoying aspect of the evening was the teasing, mainly instigated by Jo, about what Rob and I might get up to while we had the house to ourselves. She kept making jokes about us trying out all the beds and making a mess on the living room carpet. She also warned us to watch out on the kitchen table as one of the legs was wobbly. I tried to laugh, but I didn't find it at all funny under the circumstances. I don't think Rob did either. Sofia looked embarrassed and kept telling Jo to leave us alone. Leni launched a counter-attack, suggesting we didn't have it in us to do anything so interesting as getting kicks out of humping in other people's beds. And only the day before I'd felt I might be starting to like her.

The next morning they all disappeared quite early. Sofia rushed off at dawn and the others ambled out after breakfast, leaving Rob and I alone. I told him I had to go out and he said he'd like to stay in and study. On Christmas Eve!

I caught the train downtown and found the most fantastic book of photographs of spacecraft in a bargain shop in Charing Cross Rd. It was an ideal combination of something I liked and something I thought he'd like. The photos were big and really showed how elegant and beautiful the machines were. Lately I've been so down on Rob and his studiousness that I'd half forgotten how incredible it was that human beings had worked out ways to travel through space – and that my (soon to be ex) boyfriend was one of those human beings. It was quite an impressive thought. I wanted to get him another little present too, partly because I didn't only want to give him something rocket-related, and partly because I wanted to put off going home and telling him I didn't want to sleep with him any more. I found this street full of Chinese shops and restaurants and got him some chopsticks with pictures of geishas on them, a little china bowl and a baby teapot for green tea. I thought it would help make his takeaways a more stylish experience.

Simultaneous to thinking all these seasonally appropriate, altruistic thoughts I was rehearsing the speech I'd make when I got home. I imagined myself saying stuff about how the relationship was obviously making us both unhappy and how it would be better for both of us if we let each other go. I managed to make it all sound pretty much like I was doing him a favor by offering to leave. Even as a fantasy it definitely didn't wash. The more I practiced my lines, the more shops I was forced to go into in search of something to counter-balance the mess I was about to make. I bought a clay incense burner with some oil that claimed to stimulate concentration, a Russian army hat and a keyring with a mechanized, moving barnyard scene inside. I realized that the longer I delayed going home, the more disproportionate his present was liable to become. I headed back towards the station, stopping only to spend three quarters of an hour choosing between two sheets of wrapping paper.

When I got back the bedroom was immaculate and Rob was sitting on the bed reading my graphology book. The heater must have been on for a while and the room was all warm and cozy. It wasn't what I was expecting. I asked him why he was reading that particular book and he said he felt like reading, but not for his course. He said he never knew whether he thought things like graphology and palmistry were garbage or not, but that the introduction to the book had convinced him that the differences between people's ways of writing must mean some-thing – whether or not they meant what the book's author said they did. He told me he'd decided not to start reading a novel as he was afraid it would grab him and stop him doing any work. It was all so surprising. I'd always believed Rob didn't read fiction because he wasn't interested, not because he was afraid of being *too* interested. He also said he'd been to Sainsbury's. It was as if he'd been tampered with by aliens. I didn't know what to say so I asked him if he'd like a cup of tea (clear evidence of my English blood).

All the time I was making the tea he kept creeping up behind me and kissing me on the back of the neck. I didn't know what to do. I kind of carried on making the tea and pretending I hadn't really noticed. I decided I'd better start the discussion as soon as possible before things got complicated.

We took the tea back to the room and sat down on the bed. I must have been looking tense because Rob immediately asked what was wrong. All the rehearsals counted for nothing when it came to the real thing. I couldn't tell whether his shopping, cleaning and kissing were part of a desperate attempt to retrieve a lost cause, or whether it was intended as a genuine display of love. If the second option was the case, then the, 'I'm leaving you out of kindness,' approach might not go down too well. I really wanted to do an OK job, but I was trying so hard to be elegant I ended up unable to say anything at all. Rob was looking more and more anxious. There was a super-long pause before he stepped in with, 'Daze. What's up?'. The fact that he persisted in calling me Daze was probably the thing that made it all come out. Instead of putting it nicely I just barfed up a load of clichés. I think I said, 'Rob, it's like something's really wrong between us, like we're not any good for each other. It's as if we're holding each other back. I don't know what to do, but I think it would be fairer of me to let you go.' Rob looked at me for a second, completely stunned, and went, 'WHAT?!' I carried on like, 'I just don't think I'm the right person for you. I don't know what I'm doing with my life. I don't know where I'm going. I don't want to be like some big weight on you. It just feels all wrong. I think we're all wrong for each other and I should probably let you go so you can meet the right person.' He started to look really angry. His lips went all pursed and his eyelids kind of vibrated. He banged his fist down on the mattress, spilling the rest of his tea, and practically yelled, 'Why are you trying to tell me who I should be with? I'm in love with *you*! I don't want to meet someone *else*, I love *you*! What are you trying to tell me?' I got stuck again. We looked at each other really hard in the face. I said, 'Oh! But . . .' And he went, 'But *what*, Daze? Are you telling me you don't like me? Because if that's it, I think you should just say it and stop dishing the bull and pretending to be so fucking self-sacrificing. I don't know how to discuss all this with you if I think you're talking horseshit.' We looked at each other again but I could hardly stand it and looked down. There was a silence and then a sniffing sound. When I finally dared to look up again Rob was crying. It was awful. I think I'd gotten into a habit of seeing him as a guy without strong feelings. But I was clearly wrong. He cried really strangely and noisily. It was a very disturbing sound. I found it so unsettling that my first instinct was to make it stop. I started stroking his hair, then cuddling his head, then hugging his whole body. I started crying too. It really shocked me to discover that he cared so much about me. He was going, 'Oh no! (Sob.) It's all my fault! It's because I work too hard. I'm so sorry. (Sniff.) I forgot to think of you and how it must make you feel. I'm not surprised if you're angry with me, but please let me try again. Look, Daze, I really, really adore you and I know I haven't been showing it much lately, but that's because I'm a dumb fuck sometimes. Can we just give it another month and you'll see how different it'll be? Oh Jesus.' And then he carried on crying even louder than before. I hung onto him real tight and kept running my fingers through his hair. His head was tucked under my chin and I could feel tears running down my neck. I don't think I've ever felt so appreciated in my whole life. I started kissing the top of his head and stroking him and telling him it was all going to be OK. I said I was just being stupid because I was insecure and I was sorry I'd hurt him so much. I told him I loved him too and that there was no way I seriously wanted to leave. I said he should forget I ever mentioned it. I meant it too. The way he reacted really changed the way I felt about him and made me realize how immature and superficial I can be sometimes. I can't believe I was ready to leave Rob just because of a glitch in the relationship, and that I was too self-absorbed to be able to discuss it with him before it developed into a crisis.

We carried on messing around on the bed and gradually it turned into something better than I could have imagined even in my most ambitious daydreams. It really is true that sex with love is the best. It wasn't physically painful, but the feelings it brought out were so strong they hurt. We couldn't stop. I didn't know it was possible to feel like that. The fourth time we made love that afternoon he made me come just by asking me over and over again if I still wanted to leave him. Every time I said 'no' I meant it so much that it seemed to affect my heart-rate, making my head spin and my body feel all dispersed.

After the best Christmas Eve ever we had the best Christmas Day, Boxing Day, and the day after, and the day after which is probably round about today. The kitchen was full of wines, cheeses, honey roast ham, chocolates, cakes, turkey breasts, tangerines and all sorts of other stuff. We didn't go out at all. We probably spent half the week in bed (we didn't do it in the other rooms – but only because they would have been too cold). We talked *a lot* and for the first time I felt like Rob was really letting me see some of the more obscure parts of himself.

It's cool to watch that kind of stuff seep out. It doesn't come over so much in information or confessions, it's more to do with what kinds of thing make a person really laugh, or the faces they pull when they're relaxed, or the impersonations they do of their grandparents. He did a really good one of his eighty year old grandmother asking him over dinner what the word 'fuck' meant. It was like I was finally getting to know him. Another thing that came out, giving me a new angle on Rob, was something he said about that evening when I blacked-out in the pub. I brought it up with him just because I wanted to check up on the time-travel thing. I told him I'd hate him to do it. He started laughing like a nut. He said it was just him handing out a line to see if he could get us to fall for it. Apparently human beings don't have a hope in hell of getting anything much to move even nearly fast enough to radically distort time – and certainly not while Rob and I are still around. You'd have to move at 148,800 miles per second to turn fifteen years in space into twenty five years on earth and, as it is, people would be lucky to get a rocket to move at 148, 800 miles per hour.

The only low point of the entire festive season was the inevitable phonecall from Mom. She cheerlessly wished me a happy Christmas and then did everything she could to make me feel like my Christmas could never be as happy as hers. Maybe she's angry because I'd forgotten to send her a card. But she hasn't sent me one either. She said they'd put some money in the mail, but I still haven't received it. She passed on a 'Happy Christmas' from Dad. Where was he? I hate it when Mom takes over like that. What right has she got to make the call when he's not there? She's just bitter because she knows I have a better relationship with him than I do with her and she's trying to get in the way of it.

I got an excellent phonecall from Heidi though. She said she was really missing me. I told her all about how things were going with Rob and she said she was really pleased, even though it meant I wouldn't be back for ages. She has a new boyfriend but she's not too sure about him. She said he was the only person she'd ever dated who wasn't seriously short of money, and she was finding his wealth hard to handle. She said she didn't like him paying for everything, but she couldn't afford to eat in the kinds of restaurants he took her to, or to shell out for weekends in smart hotels. I asked her whether she felt like talking to him about it and she said he wasn't the kind of person you could discuss things like that with. Sounds a bit depressing.

The other high point of Christmas was the presents. Rob loved his book and we sat around for hours looking at the pictures. He explained a lot of stuff to me and helped me to understand a little better his fascination with spacecraft. While I was listening to him and really enjoying his enthusiasm it occurred to me how strange it was that I'd shown such an excessive interest in our housemates' bits and pieces and virtually no interest at all in Rob's work. I think I imagined I'd never understand it. It was actually really interesting. I enjoyed learning about new methods of producing gravity in space and the spiralling routes astronauts have to take to get to the moon. He liked his Chinese take away kit too, but was disappointed by the fact that I'd only gotten one for him. It was horrible to remember that, when I bought it, I truly believed we were about to separate.

His present to me was excellent. He gave me a beautiful silver pen and a notebook with an amazing resin cover with real daisies embedded in it. It's the best notebook I've ever had (sorry Dad). [*Ed: I can vouch for it. It really is an extraordinary object.*]He said he hoped it would help with the poetry. I doubt I'll use it for that. This notepad's nearly finished, so I'll be able to start the new one quite soon, keeping it free from devious schemes and mean thoughts about Rob.

New Year

It's nineteen ninety nine! New Year's Eve was a kind of non-event because there weren't any parties to go to. Jo went off to one at her boyfriend's house. She asked if we'd like to come but I thought it might depress me so I said no (politely). I'd seen a clip of Trafalgar Square on the news once and thought it might be interesting to go. Rob wasn't exactly convinced, but agreed to play along. On the way there, the busses were really packed and everybody seemed pretty excitable. I couldn't decide whether the atmosphere was great or terrible. It felt like the kind of agitated excitement that can easily spill over into a fight. On the first bus there was a group of sixteen year old boys hassling a group of sixteen year old girls. The girls were encouraging them and telling them to piss off in roughly equal doses. In between the two gangs of teenagers sat a middle-aged Asian couple, looking slightly anxious. The boys started flicking their scrunched up bus tickets at the girls and one of the little balls hit the woman on the head. Her husband asked the boy if he was going to say sorry, which he did, but not very convincingly.

We arrived at Trafalgar Square at about eleven o'clock and it was already heaving with people. Most of them were mooching around, looking as though they didn't know what to do with themselves. Rob and I wandered through the crowd in pretty much the same state. An hour seemed like a long time to spend hanging about so aimlessly, so we sat on the edge of one of the fountains and just stared at passers by. We played a few rabble-watching games – like counting patchwork jester-hats (17) and Nike ticks (78, before we got bored) – but soon lapsed into silence. I thought about Jo and the party we'd turned down and asked myself how I could have been so blockheaded. Trafalgar Square on New Year's Eve is probably the most miserable place in the world. On the news it always looked pretty cool but close-up it felt more like a scrap-heap where all the least popular people in London were lumped carelessly together. There were a few optimists desperately trying to make the most of it (mainly the ones in jester-hats), squirting beer into the crowd and singing. But it didn't really work for me.

By eleven thirty the place was so packed you could hardly move. Rob and I simultaneously turned to face one another, each wearing a seriously dejected expression. We decided the only thing for it was to leave. We squeezed and elbowed our way to the edge of the square and out to Charing Cross station. The train home was full, but the general feeling was different to the bottled-up violence of the bus downtown. I don't know whether the other passengers were escaping too, or whether they were all off to parties in South London, but they seemed more relaxed. We pulled out of Charing Cross at eleven fifty two. Rob and I obviously hadn't thought about it clearly when we got on, but we soon realized that our transition into the penultimate year of the millennium was about to be spent in a carriage full of complete strangers halfway between Waterloo and New Cross.

Ten seconds before midnight a few people started a countdown and the rest of us joined in. At twelve o'clock we all cheered loudly, smiled at each other and Rob and I kissed. It was easily the most underwhelming New Year's Eve I've ever spent, but I liked it. I hate proper ones where there's a huge build up and then an anti-climax while people get used to the idea that nothing's really changed. I think next year I'll do the train trick again. I wonder where I'll be.

I try not to have resolutions as, generally, I think they're pretty dumb. But I've decided that this year I'll make it my prime purpose to find a way of making a living that I don't profoundly despise. (How many times have I heard myself say that?) It's something I have to do for myself, but I also believe I have to do it for Rob's sake. If I want to have a lasting, adult relationship I'll need to behave like an adult in other parts of my life too. I'm allowed to work over here, provided I get some kind of number from the government. But even without one I could get a job in a bar or something. This week with Rob has really cemented the relationship and probably given me a little extra courage to do the things I have to do.

Third Notebook

(resin cover with real daisies, unlined)

Jobs

I took the day off yesterday because everyone was coming home and it was too chaotic round here to start putting my resolution into practice. Jo got back from her boyfriend's, saying she'd had the best New Year's Eve in her entire life. Sofia flew in from Spain looking harassed and tired. Her Christmas had been a strain. According to her, her brother is seriously unwell, but her family can't admit it to themselves and carry on trying to act like it's just a temporary aberration. While she was home he sleepwalked almost every other night and talked about stuff that nobody could relate to about the state of the planet and all kinds of schitzi, mystical things he never used to believe in. Leni said her Christmas was 'brilliant', and New Year too. Apparently her parents always give a huge New Year's Eve party in their country house and all their friends from London come to stay in the barns and local hotels. How gross.

I had to ask Leni whether I could use her computer to do my résumé. She didn't seem too thrilled, but said yes anyway. She told me to save all my stuff on disk and not to move any of her folders around. I looked horrified and said, 'Of course I won't.' Which is true. I won't move them anywhere, I'll just open them, read them, close them and leave them in exactly the same place. I wonder when she'll start her fabulous new script.

I feel like I'm wasting time on this today. I'd better go right away and get my résumé done.

Doing my résumé was really difficult. And there's hardly even anything on it. I think I got distracted by something I found in Leni's room. It must have been there all through Christmas but, in my sentimental state, I just didn't see it. There was a sprinkling of tiny paper shreds mixed in with her other mess. I grabbed a handful and tried to make out some words. A bit of colored type on a corner scrap said 'chool' and underneath, 'ork'. On another piece it said, 'we are so' and 'est of lu'. Finally I found one saying, 'plication has been uns' and realized it was a rejection from the film school in New York. I spotted a date – 15th Dec. 1998 – which would explain why she looked so miserable that evening just before Christmas. She seems to be over it now, but I wonder how she really feels. The way she'd talked about it, it seemed like not getting in wasn't a possibility she'd ever considered. I like to think it'll be good for her, but it appears to have had the opposite effect. Ever since her thunderbolt of inspiration she's been more buttheaded than ever. I wonder whether I'm enough of a bitch to ask whether she's heard from them yet.

Anyhow, never mind Leni's life, I don't know what *my* next step should be. I guess I ought to go get a newspaper . . .

. . . I went out and got something called the *Evening Standard Classified Week*. The jobs in it are *bad*. The only things I could find worth applying for were a ticket selling job at the National Gallery, a cooking job in a pasta restaurant that offered full training, and a handful of bar jobs in the West End. The worst one I saw was as a refuse loader. The second worst one wanted 'friendly hostesses for West End night-club' – after reading Leni's script I don't think it's the sort of thing I can imagine myself doing. The best paid are probably the marketing ones, but I don't think I have the right kind of character for them. I guess what I ought to do is just go through the whole lot, picking out anything I stand some small hope of getting, and start sending my résumé to as many people as possible. Maybe I should ring a few and try to get interviews this week.

D ← No time
to mess
around!

I just spent £7.80 on envelopes and stamps! I hope something good comes from it soon. All of yesterday was taken up with putting applications together and calling people. I have an interview at a baker's shop in Chelsea this afternoon, and a try-out at an exclusive lampshade-maker's on Thursday. I thought I'd go for something other than bar work just to increase my experience and expand my skills. I didn't take a break at all – apart from a quick spell in the middle of the day which I used to have a sandwich and search for Jo's diary. The first places I looked were between the mattress and the bed frame and in her underwear drawer. After that I tried the rest of the closet – including underneath and on top – and the various compartments of the dressing table. I even squeezed the dirty linen bag hanging next to her dressing gown. After a few minutes I heard a distinct front door noise and ran into the bathroom. I can't imagine how embarrassing it would be to get caught. It turned out to be a take-away place dropping a menu through the letterbox. I sat on the toilet for a few minutes to let my pulse slow down and to think about where the diary might be. I imagined it was possible that she carried it around with her, like I do, but it seemed unlikely. I went back to her room a second time to see if any other hiding places suggested themselves. I actually looked behind a couple of the Winnie the Pooh pictures, although I could tell beforehand that it was useless. Finally, I stood in the middle of the floor and turned full circle, trying to see if there were any drawers or little nooks I might have missed. I spotted a trashcan in the corner. I picked it up to give it a shake and noticed a rectangular bump in the carpet underneath. Man, I'm practically Columbo. I folded back the corner to discover a leather-bound book held shut by a mini gold lock. My first thought was that I hadn't seen a key anywhere and I'd probably been in Jo's room for as long as my luck would allow. My second thought was that I ought at least to give it a go with a bobby pin. I found the ideal tool in the ballerina box and pulled the little rubbery bit off the end. I jiggled it about in the lock and nothing happened. I carried on in the stubborn belief that it'd give way eventually. It didn't. I wonder what the trick is. I was feeling increasingly panicked about being in her room and it must have made my hands shaky. As I fussed around with the lock frustratedly, the bobby pin slipped out and made a couple of tiny scratches by the keyhole. I hope she doesn't notice. I was meticulous about replacing everything as I found it.

The only encouraging part is that her diary must be hot stuff if she's so keen to keep it under wraps.

Souazik just rang and invited me to go for a drink with her on Friday. I said I'd love to. She asked about all the details of my Christmas. I told her I'd spent it in London with Rob. She was really amazed that I had a boyfriend. I wonder why. She said I should bring him along on Friday if I felt like. I'll ask him and see what he wants to do. If he says yes I'll have to ask Souazik not to mention James. I could explain it by saying Rob was pathologically jealous or something.

I'd better get ready for my bakery interview. What should I wear? I suppose pants and sensible shoes would go down best. And a really scraped back, non-straggly hairstyle. They said on the phone that they'd never employed a girl in the position before, but there was a first time for everything. I probably shouldn't wear too much make-up and stuff . . .

. . . Jeez! They gave me the job and I'm supposed to start tomorrow, but I realized on the way home that I have no intention of going. I suppose I should ring them to let them know. I'd have to be in Chelsea at five o'clock every morning! No chance. The way I handled it was seriously stupid. I got there so desperate to be accepted that I really enthused about the job and said I thought I'd really enjoy it. They were worried about whether I'd be able to lift the huge sacks of flour but seemed prepared to give me the benefit of the doubt. The man who interviewed me was quite nice. He was probably about fifty and came across very down-to-earth. He said I'd probably build up extra muscle quite quickly and, if I stuck at it, there was no reason why I shouldn't be able to do the job as well as anyone. I'd thought it would involve at least a little bit of cake-baking and fancy stuff, but it seemed to be more about mass-producing loaves of bread. I know for a fact that it would make me depressed, so it seems pretty pointless. It's got to be better to hold out for something more suitable.

Getting the job really gave me a confidence boost though – I got on well with the guy and he clearly thought I was an alright person. I'll ring and tell him I got another offer. The woman in the lampshade place sounded fine on the telephone so perhaps I'll have a job by the end of the week.

A letter from Spain arrived in the second mail today. I was almost tempted to steam it, but then I thought the steam trick might turn out to be just as bogus at the bobby-pin one. I ought to be able to get hold of it sometime tomorrow. Suddenly I feel very busy. What with job applications, social engagements, translations, hidden keys and a burgeoning new script on the horizon I hardly have any time to myself.

I've got two rejection letters already; one from a marketing company (I knew I wouldn't be their type) and one from an 'ambitious, rapidly expanding production company'. Bastards. Oh well. I can't let it get me down. Rob's been very supportive and thinks it's great that I'm taking my job search so seriously. Unlike stupid old James, he's really encouraging me to aim high. He's been buying copies of the *Guardian* and the *Independent* and drawing circles around all the multi-media type ads. I don't know how likely it is that I'll get one of those jobs, but at this stage it seems worthwhile to try everything. I actually feel quite angry with James for his dumb misperception of me. I don't think I want to see him any more.

On the subject of my other missions, I've managed to get hold of Sofia's letter but have had no luck so far with Jo's key. I double-checked in all the places I searched yesterday and it didn't turn up. I tried the other corners of the carpet but they were all firmly stuck down. Last night I had a quick chat with her and found myself examining her necklaces and bracelets for gold keys. I also had a cyber-rummage in Leni's computer to see if she'd got going on the script yet but found no sign of it, which was strange as she told me yesterday that she'd already started. I heard her typing away when I went up to brush my teeth last night. She must have been doing something else. Perhaps I can get her to tell me what it's called so it'll be easier to find in future. She hasn't mentioned the New York thing at all, and I still haven't managed to ask her. It feels weird to have all this background info and not be able to talk about it.

I wonder why I don't feel guilty about all this. I guess the fact that I'm considering the possibility of feeling guilty means I already do. At least as I lose my sense of morality I'm still fully in control of my sense of logic — although it isn't exactly logical to put so much energy into copying letters I can hardly even read. I guess I'm more concerned with completeness than understanding, making all this more of a collection than a study. Maybe I'm still giving it too much dignity. I should probably just come right out and call it a compulsion.

30 de Diciembre de 1998

Querida Sofía:

Fué después de la última noche cuando supuse que no querrias verme otra vez antes de tu partida. Se que tu familia está pasando dificultades y tiene que ser duro para ti. Pero por favor, considera como me siento. Todo el tiempo que has estado fuera te he estado esperando, y he querido creer que tu estarías haciendo lo mismo por mí. ¿Cómo pueden haber cambiado tanto tus sentimientos? Ya se que tu dices que no hay nadie más, pero ¿de qué otra manera puedo comprender los cambios en ti? Es verdad que podría haber escrito más, pero el sentirme tan cerca de ti no lo hacía necesario. Te llamé siempre que pude. Quizás tendría que haberlo hecho más. No dejes que ésa sea nuestra última conversación. Creí que teniamos un futuro juntos. No puedo dejarlo pasar sin implorarte una segunda oportunidad.

Sofía, te amo. No me dejes.

Joaquín.

30th Dec. 1998

Dear Sofia,

After last night I knew you would not want to see me another time before you left. I know your family are having difficulties and it must be very hard for you. But please, consider how I am feeling. I waited for you all the time you were away, and believed you were doing the same for me. How can your feelings have changed so much? I know you say that there is no one else, but in what other manner can I understand the changes in you? It is true I should have written more, but I felt close enough to you to make it unnecessary. I called you whenever I could. Maybe it should have been more. Don't let that be our last conversation. I believed we had a future together, I cannot let it go without imploring you for a second opportunity.

Sofia, I love you. Don't leave me.

Joaquín.]

Sofia's letter seemed pretty interesting. I think it's a love letter. Perhaps she met someone over the Christmas break. His name's Joaquín (actually, I think he got a mention in those letters from her Mom and sister, but I can't be bothered to check). How exciting. Strange she never said anything about it. She does appear to be pretty preoccupied with her brother's problems though. She had quite a long talk about it with Rob last night. I don't really like it when they talk Spanish together, but I think she really needs someone to discuss things with. He told me afterwards that she thought her brother was suffering some kind of psychosis but that her family didn't want to know. Her Mom and Dad seem to think it's shameful and terrible to have a crazy son and want to believe the problem will go away if they ignore it. Sofia suggested to them that he see a doctor before he does anything serious, but her parents were horrified. Poor Diego. *And* their Mom and Dad.

The lampshade shop trial is today. Rob's made me feel as though I shouldn't be bothering with stuff like that, but I think I ought to go along anyhow. It can't do any harm. The woman on the phone said they only required the most basic sewing skills and that they'd teach me the rest. Sounds like it could be OK. I think I'd rather do some kind of handicrafty thing than a dumb-ass computer job anyway.

It's twelve thirty now and I've got to be in Knightsbridge at two fifteen, which gives me just enough time to have one more go at finding that key . . .

. . . No luck. I tried all the less likely places like kitchen drawers and down the sides of the living room couch. All I found were some stained teaspoons and a load of vintage cookie crumbs. The more I looked the more I started asking myself what the fuck could be in the diary. I bet she keeps the key in her box – and I'm not talking about the one with the ballerina.

I kept asking myself whether I felt guilty this time. I kind of did and I didn't. I know that Jo wouldn't be so keen to hide her diary if she was happy for me to read it (although a more suspicious part of me supposes that, if she hides it that well, she must spend a fair amount of time fantasizing about *somebody* looking at it). But at the same time I see my nosiness as a pretty minor crime in relation to most of what goes on every day.

It's been certified that there's absolutely no fucking way I'm ever going to be a lampshade maker. Yesterday afternoon was one of the major low points of my life. And today there was another dip when I received a rejection from some pissy little production place. [*Ed: There's no sign of Daisy's own rejection letters anywhere. I presume she must have thrown them away or destroyed them.*]

I arrived at the shop and it all looked excessively pleasant. I went in and was greeted by a friendly woman in a hairband. The place was really swanky, full of crystal chandeliers and tasseled lampshades. The woman, Nikki, showed me round very proudly, telling me all about their prestigious clients, including members of the royal family. Big deal. After the first few chintzy minutes I was led out of the shop and round the corner into a dingy basement with no windows, lit by flickering fluorescent strip lights. Nikki introduced me to Vincenzo, a tiny, crabby-looking old man, and then disappeared back up to her lavish retail environment. Vincenzo then took every opportunity to bitch at me, complain and treat me like an idiot. He gave me a wire lampshade skeleton and a scrap of fabric which I was meant to stretch over the frame and stitch into place. I pulled it over and started sewing but it kept slipping off. He came over to see how I was getting on and started yelling at me for not using pins. How was I supposed to know? There were four other women there, none of whom were speaking. They didn't even look up or say hello. It's hard to describe what they looked like. Their only distinguishing feature seemed to be a communal air of depression. They were probably in their mid-forties. Two of them were white, one was Indian and one was Chinese. I wondered whether I'd been called in to replace a friend of theirs who'd been sacked or something.

I got the whole lampshade pinned together and started sewing round the edges with the smallest, most invisible stitches I could manage. It took about twenty minutes to finish the job. It looked quite neat to me, but when I showed it to Vincenzo he just scrunched his nose and told me to try doing another one without so many wrinkles. He handed over a fresh piece of fabric, tore off the one I'd just finished and passed me back the bare frame. I should have left then but I didn't. I pinned the stupid thing together and started again. The women were clearly feeling more relaxed and got to talking about the best ways to eat bananas. One said she liked to peel them and just eat them like that, another was more in favor of slicing, and another only liked them if they were blended into a milkshake. After that they fell silent again. Vincenzo started ratting on and on about a woman he'd taken out to dinner. Nobody seemed to be listening, but he wasn't bothered. He finished off the ramble with a lame punch-line about how when he took a woman out to dinner he always made sure she got her desserts. He was the only one who laughed. Listening to his repulsive cackle I lost concentration momentarily and jabbed the needle right under my left thumbnail. Three little dots of blood dripped onto the white lampshade fabric. I swore under my breath and Vincenzo came over to check up on me. He asked what was wrong and I told him it was nothing. He demanded to see how the shade was looking. For some reason I was desperate to hide the blood. I felt really embarrassed about it, like I'd farted or I had something coming out of my nose. He snatched the frame and looked at it closely, asking how on earth I'd managed to make such a disaster out of such a simple task. I didn't know whether he was seriously expecting an answer. I decided not to give him one in case it came out wavery. He went, 'Huh?'. There was no way I felt like chatting with him so I just stood up, put on my coat and left. I didn't say goodbye to Nikki, or tell her I no longer wanted the job. I just walked out the door, down to the station and came home.

What right did that stinking shit have to humiliate me? What's his problem? What the fuck was going on in that place? Rob said I should ring up to complain. But what good would it do? It would be far more productive to just go after working hours and murder the guy, but I'd hate to waste any time in prison over him. I feel like retiring to my bed.

I'm starting to wish I'd taken up the offer at that nice bakery. I never rang back to say I wouldn't be coming. He'll probably never give a job to a girl again.

Sofia was in a really bad state last night. Her brother has been put into a psychiatric hospital. Her parents are all remorseful for not having listened to her and done something sooner. Her father was crying on the phone and Sofia was trying to calm him down. Apparently it happened yesterday morning. Only the night before they'd been talking to Diego about his return to University the following week. He'd gotten very upset and angry and barricaded himself in his room. The next morning he seemed a bit vacant. He told his parents that he was going to the academic bookstore near his college and wandered out of the house. Three hours later the police called his Mom at her fabric shop to say that Diego had been arrested. He'd been picked up at the bookstore for tearing up and eating advanced mathematics textbooks. When the police asked him what he was doing he said he had to get rid of all the books to save the world from the devil, and started quoting passages from *Revelations* and Nostradamus. Why are mad people often so similar?

Sofia's parents really want her to go back home, but she's

preparing some kind of big presentation with her boss and doesn't want to miss it. She says she really feels for her brother and loves him and everything, but doesn't see why she should be called on to sort out all her family problems – especially when they don't even listen to her advice. It sounds like they're not used to her having her own life. I think she's doing the right thing by staying, but I haven't had a chance to tell her. When she gets upset she completely loses her capacity to speak English and can only talk to Rob. I think she also likes to tell him stuff because he's very calm. Sometimes it makes me anxious because I feel like she has better conversations with him than I do. I know she's suffering a lot at the moment, and I'd hate to deprive her of the one person round here she feels she can talk to, but I do find it kind of annoying. Over the break, when I had Rob all to myself, I really enjoyed being around him. But when there are other people demanding his attention it's as if he gets diluted and I start to feel much further away from him. I guess I'm just very possessive and should calm down.

Souazik just rang again to invite me for coffee tomorrow. I told her that she'd already done it, but that it was nice to feel doubly wanted.

I got four more rejections in the mail today. I also got a bank statement. I only have £191.20 left in the world. My monthly rent is £130, and it's due again in three weeks. If any bills come in I won't be able to eat. Why did I make all those unnecessary cakes? I'm going to have to start trying pubs and restaurants for waitressing work. I used to be quite good at things like this when I was younger. But now I think I might feel slightly embarrassed, like I'm too old to be begging for such dumb jobs. I'll just try to keep my mind on my poetry. Maybe I can trawl around downtown a bit before I meet Souazik. It turns out I'm going to meet her on my own. I asked Rob if he'd like to come with me, but he said he had a load of college work to do for next Monday and would rather spend the evening at home. I don't really mind, I'd quite like to get her alone anyway. I've kind of lost the urge to investigate James, but I wouldn't object to finding out a *little* bit more about him while he's not there.

I'm doing it again. I wonder where I picked up this idea that it's easier to get to know people when they're not actually present.

On the subject of my researches, Leni has been working like crazy on her script and I've been going mad trying to work out where she's saving it all. She has a huge amount of crap on her hard disk and a massive stack of floppies in a box on her table. I inquired as to how it was coming along and she looked at me mischievously and said it was 'a very interesting project'. I asked when she'd let on what it was all about and she said, 'Don't worry, you'll find out sooner or later.' I think I'll try and make it sooner. It must be in her room somewhere – you can't fit a whole disk in your fanny. Her smarmy face annoyed me so much I thought I'd ask about New York. Without pausing she said she'd *decided* not to go! What is it with Leni and perfection? Why can't she admit to being fallible? I found it nearly impossible not to say anything. I must have looked pretty puzzled because she immediately got gabby about 'real life' again and said she'd rather get funding and do the next film on her own terms, without being surrounded by 'authority figures'. She lied so convincingly I could tell she'd even managed to convince herself. Surely there must be some tiny part of her brain that looks on in horror, pleading with her to stop being such a bull artist.

I also asked Jo about her diary, using my own journal-writing as an excuse. I probed her as to why she did it and the type of subject-matter she went for. She was pretty vague. She said she liked to have a record of all the things she'd done so she could read it back to herself and remember. She said she loved reading the stuff she wrote when she was thirteen – all about who she had a crush on and which teachers had told her off. I tried to coax more out of her by telling her a bit about mine – without making it sound too exciting, as I don't have a lock on my notebooks – but I couldn't quite get her to take the bait. She didn't mention the fact that she hid her book, she just talked about it like it was the most mundane thing in the world. I wish I could believe her and stop feeling so frustrated about it. But I get the strong sense she's not telling me something.

Whatever intentions I had yesterday seemed doomed to be crushed and converted into completely opposite realities. The main one was my intention to get a job, which was floored at every turn and ultimately came to zero – less than zero, in fact, as it was so demoralizing I can't bear the thought of ever toying with that particular intention again. I'm so glad it's Saturday.

My other thwarted intention is too shameful even to discuss for the moment.

It all started off well. I had a bath and put on my most ambitious clothes. I went for black and white, with a long skirt and one of Rob's shirts. I caught the two o'clock train to Charing Cross and swore to myself that I'd try every single restaurant or pub until either I got a job, or until six o'clock when I'd have to break off to go to Earl's Court. In about the first five places I managed to come across quite cheerful and enthusiastic. They all told me do drop by with my résumé and that they'd keep it on file until something came up. It still sounded hopeless. The next five or so places I must've seemed noticeably less confident and eager. People started telling me that jobs didn't come up too often, but if I wanted to I could try giving them my résumé, although they couldn't promise anything. Feeling borderline-depressed I tried a few more places, who mostly told me that they had stacks of résumés, so there probably wasn't a lot of point in wasting my time and paper. The last place I tried, my eyes were starting to redden and I was unable to speak in anything but a monotone drawl. It was a really huge restaurant in Soho with blond wood floors and sparse arrangements of tropical flowers in giant glass vases. I went up to the booking desk and asked the man sitting there whether there was someone around for me to speak to about waitressing jobs. He was probably a few years younger than me, immaculately dressed, with cropped hair and a majorly camp voice. He looked at me really concerned and asked whether I was alright. I said, 'Sort of'. He lowered his voice and basically said it was none of his business, but that they were very fussy about the appearance of their waiting staff and I looked slightly off-color. He spoke to me like he was an old friend, saying I should go home and have a cup of tea, give myself a break and try again when I was feeling a bit better. It completely spun my head around. What was he getting at? It seemed well-meant, but I didn't quite know how to take it. I didn't want to burst into tears or anything, so I quickly went and bought myself a Coke and poured it down my throat to stop it choking up.

After my job-seeking fiasco things just kept on going wrong. I decided to go to Earl's Court, even though it was early. I bought a newspaper and headed straight for The Troubadour café. Reading about the odd major International disaster took the focus away from my own life enough for me to be reasonably placid by the time Souazik arrived. She was half an hour late and really apologetic, but said she'd imagined I'd be with my boyfriend rather than waiting all alone. I told her he was work-aholic and hard to coax away from his books. (Perhaps Sofia could invite her brother over one weekend and I could give him some of Rob's textbooks for breakfast.) She looked inex-plicably put out, but said she'd love to meet him some other time. She asked all about my Christmas and I told her it had been really excellent. I didn't go into full-on detail like I would have with older friends like Heidi and Luce, but I did tell her quite a lot of stuff about my relationship with Rob and how I felt about it. I already knew from the last time we'd met that Souazik was an extremely avid listener, but something about the way she was pursuing the topic made me feel more like I was being pumped for information than having a relaxed chat over coffee. I couldn't quite understand what was making her so keen to get to grips with the finer points of my lovelife. At the time I just put it down to her research-student type mind. But about twenty minutes into the discussion a new twist arrived in the form of James. I was horrified to see him and could hardly keep back how I felt. As he approached the table Souazik looked at me guiltily and said, 'Oh no! I'm so sorry I didn't mention it. I hope you don't mind.' I went, 'Oh no. Great. It's a really nice surprise,' by which time James was standing right beside us. He kissed me on each cheek, gave Souazik a big hug and went off to get us all a coffee. Souazik was really going overboard with the apologies and, at the same time, trying to find out why I'd looked so hacked off. I really didn't feel like telling her anything more so I just sort of clammed up, going, 'It's nothing. I just didn't expect to see him, that's all. I'm always like that when someone walks in who I'm not expecting.' She looked dubious but let it go as James was already on his way back. He sat down and said, 'It's lovely to see you, Daisy darling. I had no idea I was in for such a nice treat.' So he wasn't expecting me either. Souazik was looking all embarrassed and going, 'It was the only evening I had free for the next two weeks and I thought you'd both be pleased.' James said he was very pleased indeed. I said I was pleased too, but it came out sounding sort of limp. I thought I'd better change the subject. I started by firing off a round of questions before Souazik got there first. I asked James whether he was feeling better and how his Christmas had been. He said it was quite good, that his mother hadn't fussed around him *too* much and that it had been nice to talk to his father. I found it impossible to build up any real picture of his parents, but got the impression that his mother was a real 'mother' in the most old fashioned sense, and that his father was a real 'father'. Apparently the Mom does all the food and worrying about pathetic things, while the Dad knows about world politics and what's going on with sport.

He asked how my Christmas had been and I felt a bit stuck. I paused and Souazik said, 'I think Daisy had a slightly more exciting time than either of us,' and raised her eyebrow at James. James said, 'Oh really? I thought you were just staying in London.' I said, 'I was. It wasn't all that thrilling really.' To which Souazik responded, 'That's not what I heard earlier.' What was she up to? She'd obviously planned the meeting so that Rob and James could meet. And perhaps now that the plan had failed she was trying other strategies. What does she know about James and I? It's crazy. There's nothing to know anyway. I tried to turn it around again and asked her how her Christmas had been. She said, unfortunately for her, there'd been no family to fuss over her and no big romance to keep her entertained, so she'd carried on working. Her only break had been to go round to her married friends' house on Christmas day for lunch. She made a particular point of telling James that they had a beautiful baby.

After the first few sticky minutes we managed to chat about more general stuff, like the news and movies we'd seen on TV over the break. All of a sudden I really felt like going home. It wasn't that I was bored particularly, I just felt like getting back. I told James and Souazik I'd better be off. They both started trying to persuade me to stay for another coffee. I insisted and stood up to pull my coat on. Instead of staying put, like I'd hoped, James got up too and said he'd give me a lift to the station. I noticed Souazik's face stiffen a little before she agreed it probably *was* a good idea to get going, as she had to be up early next day for a hairdresser's appointment.

We walked out into the street and said our good-byes. I felt funny about accepting a lift from James, but Souazik seemed calm enough about the whole thing and even gave me a big hug before telling me to call her in the next few days. I looked closely as she and James said goodbye to each other, to see if I could spot any clues as to what was going on. This time there were no whispers or promises of late-night calls. From what I saw it really did seem as though they were just friends. So what was all the awkwardness about at the beginning?

As soon as I got into James's car he started saying how well I was looking, how lovely and rosy my cheeks were and all sorts of other garbage. James has never commented on my appearance before and I didn't really enjoy it. I didn't know what to say, so I just fell silent. As we got nearer to the station he started going on about this 'absolutely marvelous book of photographs' he'd bought himself for Christmas, and asked whether I had time to go to his house to see it. I didn't even wait to find out what kind of book it was. I told him I had to be back as I was expecting a call from my parents (not exactly a dynamite excuse). He looked surprised, making me feel guilty about being so ready to reject his offer. I started telling him that I hadn't spoken to them for ages, but kind of trailed off when I noticed how sapbrained I sounded.

We got to the station and he pulled up in the same place as last time. I thanked him for the lift and went to kiss him on the cheek. More ready this time, he put his hand on the back of my neck and lined up my head so that I had no choice but to kiss him full on the mouth. For what felt like a good few seconds, but was probably much shorter, I just kind of went along with it half-heartedly while my brain processed what was happening and what was the most appropriate response. First I tried pulling back but James's hand was quite firmly holding me in place. It wasn't rough or anything, just pretty unambiguous. Next I twisted my head to the side, but he just carried on kissing my neck. I finally managed to say, 'James, what are you doing?'. He kept his face close to mine and whispered, 'Do you want me to stop?'. I didn't know how to answer. I decided it was best to be honest and said, 'I don't know'. He smiled and touched me gently under the chin, saying, 'Don't look so worried. It's only a kiss.' I guess he had a point, but not a very good one. It *was* only a kiss, but it came at exactly the wrong time. A kiss from James is the last thing I need or want. I smiled back and said, 'I know'. There was a moment's silence while we looked at each other before he said, 'Run along then, Daisy darling. I'll give you a call in a couple of days.'

I climbed out and headed for the number 36 bus stop without looking back. How come *he'd* made an unwanted pass at *me* and I was the one left feeling stupid? Nice trick, James. I thought about it all the way home again – not like last time with the perve-pauses on the good bits. This time it was more with a repeating, increasing feeling of, 'Oh no! What have I done?'. I kept remembering the taste of his mouth – a cocktail of cigarettes and coffee – and the freaky feeling of having his face in my face. It wasn't so much that it was unpleasant – more that it was unwanted. How could he have got it so wrong? In a way it's lucky he didn't try anything earlier as it might have messed up my whole thing with Rob. As it is, it probably doesn't matter too much. I certainly won't mention it to Rob, but I can keep the secret with a clear conscience knowing that I made the right decision. I hated what James said about it *only* being a kiss. What kind of a person is he anyway?

When I got home Rob was sitting in here with his books and papers piled up around him. I've never been so pleased to see his face. He'd been studying so hard he'd forgotten to eat, so I made him some food, even though I wasn't hungry myself. Apparently he'd had a big breakthrough with his work and managed to sort out some major design problem he'd been struggling with since fall. He tried to explain it to me, but I found it pretty hard to follow. It had something to do with fuel consumption and gravity. I loved Rob's absolute earnestness and passion after James's nonchalance about the kiss. I much prefer people who care about things deeply to people who just fuck around.

So far my plan only to write nice things about Rob is working very well. I really do feel as though I have an excellent boyfriend. There's no doubt about it, Rob is my favorite person in the whole world.

A letter came from Sofia's sister this morning. It was a great distraction from the onslaught of rejections. I'm not altogether sure what the news is on Diego, but it does talk about Joaquín, Sofia's new boyfriend. I must remember to drop a few hints about romance and stuff to find out what's going on.

[7 de Enero de 1999

Querida Sofía:

No te puedes llegar a imaginar lo que ha pasado desde que te fuiste. Diego va de mal en peor. Ayer por la noche tuvo una pelea enorme con Mamá y Papá. Esta mañana ha salido. Parece que está mejor, aunque es difícil de decir. Estoy empezando a estar de acuerdo contigo sobre las cosas que dijiste durante Navidades, pero Mamá y Papá, tan ciegos como siempre, piensan que pueden solucionar sus problemas empujándolo a su antojo. Me gustaría que estuvieses aquí. Ya sé que tu no piensas lo mismo, pero tu eres la única la persona capaz de hacerlos escuchar. ¿De verdad que sólo por el trabajo por lo que te quieres quedar en Londres? Joaquín ha estado llamando sin cesar. Dice que no comprende tus cambios. Mamá y Papá todavía no lo saben, incluso todavía tienen la impresión de que vosotros quizás os casaréis el próximo año. Yo ya ni sé que decirles cuando preguntan porqué Joaquín está llamando tanto. ¿Qué debería decirle a Joaquín y qué a Mamá y Papá? A veces no te comprendo.

{*Ed: Aquí la tinta cambia de azul a negra*} Sofía, algo terrible está pasando. Han arrestado a Diego. Creo que tendremos que llamarte urgentemente y por lo consiguiente esta carta no te traerá ninguna noticia nueva. De todas formas la envío implorándote que reconsideres tu decisión de quedarte en Londres. Espero que estés aquí cuando la carta llegue a su destino.

Un beso enorme.

Manuela

Dear Sofia,

You can't imagine how much has been happening since you left. Diego is going from bad to worse. Last night he had an enormous fight with Mama and Papa. This morning he has gone out. He seems better, but it is difficult to say. I think I am starting to agree with the things you said over Christmas, but Mama and Papa, blind as ever, think they can solve his problems by pushing him around against his will. I wish you were still here. I know you do not think this, but you are the only person with the capacity to make them listen. Is it true that it's only your job that is making you want to stay in London? Joaquín has been ringing all the time. He says he cannot understand your changes. Mama and Papa still do not know and are under the impression that you may even marry next year. I do not know what to say to them when they ask why he calls so often. What should I say to Joaquín and what to Mama and Papa? At times I don't understand you.

{Ed: Here the pen changes from blue to black} *Sofia,*

something terrible is happening. Diego has been arrested. I think
we will have to telephone you urgently and then this letter will
be out of date. I will send it anyway and implore you to
reconsider your decision to stay in London. I hope you are here
by the time this letter reaches its destination.
  An enormous kiss,
  Manuela.]

★

Sofia's really lucky to come from the kind of family she does.
I've only spoken to my parents about three times since I got
here. Their Christmas card, the one that supposedly had some
money in it, never arrived. Diego's lucky to have so many
people around who care about him. I really can't imagine what
my family would do if I went mad. One thing's for sure, Mom'd
try to keep it secret. I hope she'd at least tell Luce and Heidi
so I'd get some visits in the hospital. Maybe I should make a
note and keep it in my wallet, saying that if I ever go crazy I'd
want my best friends to know. I wonder how Rob would handle
it. I guess the best thing would be to try to avoid it altogether
and stay as sane as possible for the rest of my life. The only
thing that worries me at the moment is something I read in a
magazine article a while ago. It was all about modern diseases
like anorexia and M.E. It said that some people chose to get ill
as a response to the unreasonable demands the world made on
them. It struck me that I was an ideal candidate. I even thought
it was totally sensible given what else is on offer. It's very
unlikely to happen though. I think my problem is that, for
reasons I'll probably never understand, I don't have it in me to
get sick. Which would be fine if I could get myself some kind
of job. As it is I'm stuck on the fence; I can't find a proper

place for myself in the real world, but equally I can't hand over all responsibility by collapsing or shooting my marbles.

My fox has been hurt! I hadn't seen her for ages and then I saw her last night dragging her back legs on the ground. It looked like she'd been hit by a car or something. I asked Jo who to call and she told me to ring the RSPCA. I spoke to a woman there this morning. She wasn't overly helpful. She just said the best thing to do would be to leave the fox alone, but to make sure she had enough to eat and drink. She said foxes like dogfood so I went and got a tin this morning and put some out near the shed. I watched for ages but she didn't come out. I hope she's still alive. Imagine getting run over and not having any medicine or painkillers. Poor fox!

Last night Sofia got another call from her family. Apparently they went all heavy on her and started insisting that she go back to Spain right away. What's the matter with them? Why can't they respect the fact that she has a life over here? I felt really sorry for her for the amount of pressure they're putting on her right now. But I couldn't help feeling annoyed about the way she kind of hogs Rob when she's having a hard time. I don't mean to be stingy about my boyfriend or anything, but I feel like she's starting to rely on him in a way that I find uncomfortable. I try sitting with them when they're talking, and speaking to her through Rob, but basically I feel pretty left out. I know it would be too expensive for her to call her friends in Spain and that she doesn't know many people here outside her work — apart from the people in her conversation class — but I wish she'd stop leaning on Rob so much. What about Joaquín? Why can't she make do with writing long, confiding letters to him? I'm annoyed with myself for being so petty, but it just gets on my nerves the way that, using her family problems, she's made herself the center of Rob's attention.

I haven't said anything to Rob about it yet as I'd be too ashamed of myself for being so picky. But I wish he'd realize without me having to tell him. Ever since Christmas Sofia and her family saga have taken up most of his time at home.

I think I should stop messing around and go get the paper. Monday is a serious job day. Fingers crossed for a super well-paid computer design vacancy for people with at least three years' experience.

P.S. The food's gone! Leni said she thinks foxes are a pest and should be hunted. All because of one pair of trainers?

The Zoo

The more I think about it the more I realize that I hate Souazik. What was she up to the other night? What did she expect to get out of it? I can't stand people who pretend to be nice. Especially when they're good at it. I would never have spotted Souazik as a backbiter at first. But last Friday she really gave it away.

I feel a tiny bit less annoyed with James now. It wasn't really his fault that he got the idea I liked him. I mean, for a while, I did. How was he supposed to know how much things had changed over Christmas? Anyhow, he doesn't seem like the kind of person who'd get embarrassed about a stupid mistake like that.

My job hunt is a big-time wipe-out. I think I've now been rejected by half the employers in London. Perhaps I should go back to that snooty restaurant to see if they'll have me this time. I bet the waiters get very good tips there.

With each rejection the possibility of finding a job seems more and more remote. What will happen if I can't get one? I can't imagine asking Rob to pay my rent. It's possible that I could pay him back quite soon after – provided I got a job.

But what if I didn't get one? It's a seriously scary thought. Every time I go out I see people working in shops, on busses, through office windows. I see them driving cars, carrying shopping bags, eating in restaurants, wearing expensive suits – all evidence that, while they might not actually be working at that precise moment, at some other point in their lives, they do. How did they get *their* jobs? Have they ever been in a situation like this? Or did they just always make sure they had a job, never leaving one until they had another lined up? I know I haven't been trying for long, but my experience so far hasn't given me even the feeblest ray of hope. It's as though people find you ridiculous for having asked for work at all. I don't think it would ever be this difficult back home. Even when I try the proper jobs, ones for which I'm fully qualified, it's hopeless. What's up with this place? When my parents hassle me about working they make getting a job sound like the easiest thing in the world. I really want to work, I really need to work, but everything's making it impossible for me to do it. I think I was given false courage by my success at the bakery. I can't help being angry with myself for being so blasé about turning it down. I realize now that I was quite lucky to get it.

I talked to Jo last night about welfare. I'd hate to do it, but she said I wouldn't be allowed anyway. Apparently if you share your bed with someone they become financially responsible for you. It's unbelievable. Maybe it's like that in America too. What Rob would think about it? Luckily for him it's not a responsibility I'd ever confront him with. Why does such a stupid rule exist anyhow? It seems pretty obvious that by making one person liable for the other you'll be likely to put a strain on their relationship, causing them to split, and forcing the government to pay for a whole room in a new house rather than half a room in the old house. If they thought a bit harder they'd see that their policy was pretty uneconomic.

I suppose there's always my parents, but I never really think of them as an option in times of crisis. I imagine Mom would just use it as an excuse to punish me. Plus I don't know how much money I'll need. It could be as much as $500. I borrowed $75 from her once to pay my gas account and she didn't stop going on about it until I'd paid her back. I don't know why. Mom can perfectly well afford it. She's practically got bank accounts coming out of her ass. She obviously has deep-rooted psychological reasons for not wanting to lend small sums of money to her only child.

Leni is a total asshole. A bitchy, pretentious, shitfaced, hairy-assed, fuckfaced, jerk-off, piece of crap. I found her script. It's just . . . Bitch! Excuse me while I throw some stuff around the room.

I was just updating my résumé to include a few more lies (I was going to say I'd been a magazine sub-editor, working with Quark X-press) and I thought I'd try again for the mysterious disk. I finally found it under the mouse pad. No wonder she's been keeping it so secret. It turns out she's been basing her script on all the characters in the house. It's a real dog – and to make it worse she's called it *Darling Daisy*. That girl has no talent for titles. How dare she use my name like that? The thing I'm most afraid of is that she's somehow been reading my stuff and knows all about James. But he calls me Daisy darling, not darling Daisy. Maybe that's Leni's idea of covering her tracks.

It's so unfair what she's done to me in it. I'm going to feel like whacking her when she comes home. The only thing hold-ing me back (apart from the fact that I'd have to admit I'd been through her stuff) is that she hasn't actually finished yet. I want to see where it's going before I kick her in the head. There's no mention of James so far, so I guess the title thing could just be a coincidence. I hope so because I'd hate Leni to have so much power over me. What if Rob found out? It'd be a disaster. But there's some heavy stuff about Rob in it too. I don't know. The only consolatory thought I can come up with is that it's so pisspoor I can be sure no public will never get an opportunity to see it. *[Ed: Not so I'm afraid. I'll let you have the first instalment now so that you'll have a better insight into the rest of Daisy's tirade. I understand that it must have been terribly hurtful and was tempted to remove certain phrases out of kindness myself. But, in the end, I felt it my professional duty to deliver it intact. Sorry Daisy (as ever). If it's any comfort I agree with you about it being a sorry effort.*

★

Darling Daisy

Cast: Daisy: Late twenties, bizarre Transatlantic accent, dresses in saggy layers of second hand clothing. Hair always slightly dirty. Exudes misery.
Bob: Mid twenties, tall, healthy, clean, American good-looks, West Coast accent. Daisy's boyfriend.
Rosa: Twenties, neat, dark-haired, Latin beauty.
Joy: Twenties, smart office girl, pastel suits. Mancunian accent.
Alina: Twenties, black Joan of Arc haircut. Laid back, stylish Londoner.

Act One
Scene One: Daisy and **Bob** arrive in a taxi
outside a scruffy house in South London.
They unload their bags and ring the
doorbell. The door is opened by **Joy**, who
greets them and shows them to their room.
The room is run-down and badly decorated.
Daisy looks dismayed and **Bob** puts his arm
around her, consolingly. **Joy** leaves the
room.

Daisy: Do you think it will ever feel like
home?
Bob: Of course it will, Daze. You'll see.
It's only a year anyway.
Daisy: That's alright for you to say,
you've come here to study. But what will I
do?

Daisy looks from the filthy mattress to the
browning walls and threadbare carpet and
begins to sob. **Bob** looks out of the window
and into the distance.

Scene two: **Bob** is at University, in a
classroom full of other students. He is
taking complex notes at high speed. We
close in on his paper and see reams of
highly elaborate algebraic calculations.
Cut to **Daisy** back in the bedroom. She is
unpacking slowly, clearly depressed. She
sits down, overwhelmed, and stares at the
ceiling. Cut to **Bob**, still writing away.
And back to **Daisy**, who is now in the living

room, in front of the television. She is watching daytime TV and sucking her thumb. *{Ed: Below the belt, Leni!}*

Scene three: Later that evening. The TV is still on and **Daisy** hasn't moved. **Joy** returns from work and joins her in the living room.

Joy: So, how was your first day in London?
Daisy (sarcastic): Just great.
Joy: Really? What did you do?
Daisy: First I went to see the Changing of the Guard, then I went to Trafalgar Square to feed the pigeons. After that I went to Selfridges and to Kensington Palace. Then I went to the National Portrait Gallery and finally I had tea at the Ritz.
Joy: Oh! Really? You must be exhausted.
Daisy: Yup.

We hear the front door slam. Enter **Rosa**. She is wearing a long red dress and looks stunning. **Joy** introduces her to **Daisy.**

Joy: Daisy this is Rosa, Rosa this is Daisy.
Rosa: Hola, I am Rosa, Rosa Perez. Are you settle yet? Eeet eez bery deefeecult to feel a home abroad, no? Nevermine – I make paella and we weell ol be friends. There eez one more you will mit, she Alina. She very nice.
Daisy: Yeah, right.

Daisy is looking enviously at **Rosa**. The front door slams again. Enter **Bob**. **Bob** only has eyes for the beautiful stranger and **Rosa** too lights up as he introduces himself to her.

Bob: Hi, I'm Bob, your new flatmate. Lovely to meet you.
Rosa: I am Rosa, Rosa Perez.
Bob: That's a lovely name, where are you from?
Rosa: Espain.
Bob: Aaah. Usted es española. ¡Qué bueno! Hablo muy poco español pero sí habla muy despacio tal vez entiendo.
Rosa: ¡Pero hablas muy bien! El solo error es qué dices 'Ud'. Llamame 'tú', por favor. *(Note: check Spanish with Enrique.)*
Daisy: Come and see the room, Bob. I made it all nice.
Bob: Jeez Daze, I didn't see you there. How are ya?
Daisy: Cool. Will you come to the bedroom with me? Now.

Bob shrugs his shoulders, rolls his eyes at the others and leaves the room with **Daisy**.

Scene four: The flatmates are in the kitchen, about to eat dinner. There are five places set at the table but, so far, only **Joy, Rosa, Bob** and **Daisy** are there.

Rosa puts a steaming dish of paella in the middle of the table and, just at that moment, the front door bangs particularly loudly and in bursts **Alina**, wearing light-reflective combats and modern, sculptural jacket. She looks incongruous in the mundane, domestic setting.

Alina: You must be Daisy and Bob. Nice to meet you. I'm sorry I wasn't home sooner but I had to go to the most boring conference on Gender Politics and the Virtual Body – just a load of ageing professors trying to be hip, when it's obvious they aren't even halfway keeping up with what people of my generation already take for granted. Did you have a good flight?
Bob: Yeah, thanks.
Alina: Sorry about the decor, but we divided up the rooms on a first-come-first-served basis and I'm afraid you lost out.

Alina turns to look directly into the camera and shrugs.

Daisy: But I made a real effort with it. I even put up some pictures of flowers.
Alina: Great. I bet it looks like Eden. Hey, Rosa, can we try this stuff? I can't believe you cooked it. *{To camera again.}* I'm starting to love this house, it's like stepping back in time. We've got a

blooming rural idyll in the ground floor bedroom and a resuscitated Mrs. Beeton in the kitchen. Who knows where it will end? Shall we start paying visits to the local peasants in the afternoons? Get a piano for the long winter evenings?

Daisy is sitting looking glum.

Bob: What's up, Daze?
Daisy: Nothing. And, for everyone's benefit, my name's Daisy, *not* Daze.

Daisy, embarrassed by her outburst, goes back to looking gloomily into her lap as the others chat amongst themselves.

Joy: It's great that we're all here at last. This paella's gorgeous, by the way.
Rosa: Eez the recipe of my mama.
Joy: Delicioso. Let's have a toast. Here's to Rosa's cooking!
Everybody: Cheers!
Rosa: De nada.
Alina: And here's to our year of domestic bliss!
Everybody (except Daisy): Hooray!
Joy: It almost feels like we're old friends already. I know – let's go round the table and find out a bit about each other, like in *Shallow Grave*, only we all live together already. Starting with you, Bob. What do you want to get out of life?
Bob: Now you're asking, Joy. I don't know.

I'm studying aeronautical design and
technology. And . . .

Rosa: You mean you makin' espacesheep?

Bob: Space sheep?

Rosa: Ha ha ha ha ha ha ha ha ha . . .

Daisy: I don't see what's so funny about
that.

Joy: You mean you makin' knob extension.

Alina: {Rolls eyes at **Bob**.}

Bob: Order, order. I think the main thing
I'd like to get involved with is
experimenting with time travel. There's
this cool thing that Einstein worked out.
If you travel through space faster than
the speed of light, you can distort time.
You could fly around the solar system for a
year of your life but, when you got back,
ten years would have elapsed on earth.
It's awesome!

Daisy: Oh.

Everybody else: Wow!

Joy: What about you, Rosa? What would you
like to do?

Rosa: I like learn many languages and go
around world. I weell work weeth Amnesty.
And you Choy? What weell you do?

Joy: I think I'm quite traditional at
heart. I'd like to work in TV, but I'd also
like to have kids. My boyfriend's into
having babies too, but I'd rather wait
until my career's more sorted. I think
it's better for them if both parents are
happy with their own lives – kids can tell

if you resent them for holding you back.
I'll make sure their nanny's really nice.
Alina: What are you talking about nannies
for? You still haven't got enough cash to
pay your share of the TV licence.
Joy: Yeah, well, keep reading the Jobs
section, eh? What about you, Leenz? In
those trousers you look more than a
spaceman than Bob. Thinking of a career in
the rocket industry yourself?
Alina: No way. I'm gonna be a famous
writer. I've got three novels lined up in
my head already. The first one's just about
finished. I've got two agents interested
and they both say it could be *big*.
Rosa: What eez the story?
Alina: It's too hot, I can't tell anyone,
y'know? Just watch this space. {Winks at
camera.}
Rosa: Eez about space?
Alina: Yeah. Martians, lazer warfare,
cyborg love-scenes and everything. Nah,
only joking. Just everyday life, only
hot.
Joy: What about you Daisy? You've been
very quiet. Got any plans up your sleeve?
   Daisy:I . . . er . . . mmmm . . . I . . .
{stands up}.I . . . think . . . I . . . oh
. . . {klunk}.

Daisy faints face-first into her paella.
The others look at one another,
uncomprehendingly. **Joy**, who is sitting

next to **Daisy**, pulls her head back and makes her sit up. Her face is covered in food. **Bob** looks at her, repulsed, and then turns his eyes towards **Rosa's** cleavage. **Rosa** sees him look at her and coyly covers her chest with her hand. **Joy** fetches some wet kitchen towel and mops **Daisy**'s face. **Daisy** starts to come round, but seems to be slightly delirious.

Daisy: I . . . just . . . want to . . . be . . . loved . . . {klunk}.]

★

I wonder whether Rob really did act like Leni says he did when I fainted in the pub. What an asswipe. I doubt it though. I remember him being really nice to me. And what's this thing she seems to have about him liking Sofia? He doesn't *like* her, he's just kind. Leni knows nothing about people and what motivates them. She also knows nothing about Einstein. 'Faster than the speed of light'! I don't think so. She should make films about tables or plates. As for her dialogues! I've seen less wood in a fucking forest. There's one character that's obviously based on her (it's called *Alina*, pardon the puking noises) who gets all the 'best' lines. But Leni's idea of a good line is like, 'yah, it's just like they can't even hope to keep up with what people like me have known since the day we were born, yah.' And all that shit about looking at the camera? Is that supposed to make it postmodern? That girl has got less than no talent. She's got minus talent. If I had any myself I'd steer clear of her for fear of it being deducted.

I don't like reading about Rob and Sofia though. Why does Leni have to make such a big deal out of it? I've been feeling pretty pissed at Sofia, but just about managing to keep myself under control. Now I'm not sure I'll be able to. Is it obvious to everyone except me that Rob likes her? Maybe I should ask Jo what she thinks. She'd probably just try to reassure me in her usual Momsy way. Rob's the only one I can imagine asking. I know he'll say he doesn't – even if he does. I suppose it's possible that he finds her attractive, but has no intention of doing anything about it. That's even worse. It makes me mad to think he might like Sofia but is too honorable to act on it.

I wonder whether I'm worrying partly because of my thing with James (who *still* hasn't been in touch). I know I didn't exactly kiss him properly but, whatever it was, if Rob found out he'd probably blow up. It makes sense that if I can meet up with James, go for lunch with him, drive around in his car, fantasize about him, promise myself I won't go to bed with him, all without Rob catching on, it has to be possible that Rob could be doing the same things with Sofia (excluding the driving around). I do think it's a bit dangerous that she's in such an emotional state and that he seems to feel a lot of sympathy for her. But what can I do? The first thing that occurs to me is that we should move out. This house is a shithole anyway. It might be easier to look for somewhere when I've got my job. But right now I've got all this free time. I could go find the place and, once I'd got it, Rob could come and check it out. If he liked it we could move in. Maybe it's better if we do it *before* I get my job, so I've got time to hunt around. As long as we go before next month's rent is due, I'll be able to afford it (just about). Perhaps if we have our own place it'll give me the incentive I need to push myself to get a good job. I don't really care about this house, so I have no urge to go out and get things to make it better. But if we had a place of our own

I'd love to go out and earn money to make a real home for myself. Even if it would only be until August. The only thing I'd miss is the fox. But I don't even see her anymore, I just put out the food and it's gone by next day. I'm sure Jo would take over for me.

I'll try the idea out on Rob later. I'm sure he'll go for it. He could probably do without Sofia's moaning in the evenings too – although he's much too nice ever to say so.

It comes as a shock sometimes to realize how little I know my own boyfriend. I got really over-excited about the whole house-move thing and suggested it to Rob last night. I explained all the stuff about how I'd contact the estate agents and do all the boring, time-consuming bits and he could just move in – which doesn't take more than a weekend, at most. But he wasn't interested in any of it. All he could think of were problems and reasons why it wasn't a good idea. He said he had loads of college work at the moment and couldn't afford the time. So I offered to do all his packing and unpacking. Next he said we had to give a month's notice in order to leave this house. I told him that, if we could get someone else to take the room, we could leave whenever we wanted. I offered to make myself responsible for finding somebody. He said he was just starting to enjoy living there now we were getting to know the others better and that he didn't want another upheaval. This was the last thing I wanted to hear. I said I quite liked them, but not nearly as much as I liked him and that we could stay in touch with them, but I wanted to have him to myself a bit more –

216

like at Christmas. I thought that ought to work. He acted flattered, briefly, and then threw another technical obstacle in the way. He said that having a place just to ourselves was bound to be more expensive and, although he might just about be able to afford it, he couldn't see how I would. What does he know about my economic capabilities? Just because I've been taking time off since we've been together doesn't mean I can't look after myself. I had a full time professional job for four years before I met him (although I think I'm starting to notice I'm repeating this to myself slightly too often, like I hardly believe it any more either).

It all makes me very suspicious. What is his big attachment to this house? I did suggest to him it was a bit odd that he was so reluctant to leave, and asked whether it had anything to do with a certain person he'd been getting very close to lately. At that point he just shut down. He told me not to be so stupid and to stop trying such pitiful strategies for blackmailing him into doing something he didn't want to do. When I tried to push it he said that if I wasn't so unnecessarily jealous it would be perfectly obvious to me that staying put was a far better idea. He told me it was my perverse imagination that made me want to leave, and that it had nothing to do with him. Who taught him to say perverse imagination? It sounded totally un-Roblike.

I didn't like the way he flatly denied any interest in Sofia and turned it all onto me. It made it very hard to take what he was saying seriously. The way he denied it came across more as a confirmation.

Jo got a job. She screamed so much when she opened the letter I thought I'd better go find out what was up. She's going to be a fashion buyer's assistant and get paid £25,000 a year. Realistically, it's the last thing in the world I'd like to do, but I can't help feeling super-jealous. Why can't I get one? Without meaning to sound bitter, I guess it must have something to do with Jo's hyper-averageness. Most people with jobs are like Jo.

After Rob left I caught the train into Charing Cross and just started walking. I walked all the way up Regent Street, across Oxford Street, round this crescent of big, white houses and into a park. In the park I carried on in pretty much of a straight line until I came to a zoo. I hate zoos and felt no desire to go inside. Especially given my financial situation. The only thing that made me go was noticing I could get away with it for free. There was a little row of booths which were all empty, maybe because it was early in the day and out of season. The ticket people must have thought it wouldn't matter too much if they chose that particular moment to go to the toilet or to get a cup of coffee. So I strolled through without paying and ambled aimlessly about. It's always the same in zoos. Half the animals are either hiding inside their hutches or buried under piles of straw. You can walk around for ages without seeing a single creature. I saw a really frustrated-looking leopard pacing up and down and a lioness just standing still, as if she'd lost whatever the point was meant to be. It was pretty horrible to look at. I know these days that zoos are supposedly no longer just places where animals are cruelly caged but are now seen as vital centers for research and for the protection of diminishing species. But they still suck. The animals don't know they're being detained so that their grandchildren's grandchildren can skip around freely in a forest somewhere. Who knows what they think is up? They mostly look pretty miserable. Zoos remind me of those pills people take to counteract the side-effect of another pill which, in turn is supposedly the antidote to the pill that they take for the thing that's actually the problem. I know some animal species die out because they just do, but mostly it happens because people either kill them or burn their homes or fence off their migration routes in order to make farmland. It's all very well to say at it's OK to lock a few of the poor creatures up for their own good, but it's hardly their fault they couldn't get on with their lives in the first place. Things like that can make me pretty furious when they get me on the wrong day. The zoo reminded me that it isn't *me* that's fucked up, it's the entire planet.

I just phoned James in tears. Luckily he was in. He was really sympathetic. He asked what it was but I couldn't even tell him. I just kept crying and crying. He said he had to go see some people, but he should be free by three o'clock if I wanted to come over to his house and talk about it. I really feel like talking to someone, but I'm not sure James is the right person. I can't be too picky though. It's impossible to talk to anyone round here as they're all either too stupid, too self-obsessed or too untrustworthy. Souazik is a total write-off. I've already tried Heidi and Luce, even though I can't afford it, and neither of them are answering. And I'm not ready to start talking to lamp-posts just yet.

Last night stank. Rob seemed to think that everything was back to normal and suggested to the others that we all get a take-away together without even consulting me. Unfortunately my problems aren't so easy to sweep under the table. I've had no luck getting a job, a gas bill has just arrived, meaning that I'm down to my very last pennies, and Rob is doing less than nothing to reassure me that I am more important to him than certain of our housemates. When I asked him what he thought I should do he advised me to extend my overdraft and keep on trying to get work. Great. So in a couple of weeks' time I'll be unemployed *and* in debt. I don't feel like he cares about me at all any more. It's amazing how much someone can change their mind in the space of a fortnight. I was really affected by what happened between Rob and me over Christmas, but now it's as if I might have imagined it. Whatever declarations he made back then seem pretty meaningless in the face of what's going on today. I'm sure nothing's actually happening between Sofia and him, but it's obvious – even to someone with as little insight into human behavior as Leni – that they're completely infatuated with each other. It's pretty sickening to see. That stupid bit in the script when it says she 'lights up when he enters the room,' is totally true (even if it *is* the most moronic way of putting it). I don't want to use James to make myself feel better, or to get him mixed up in something that doesn't really have anything to do with him, but if anything happens between us I certainly won't hold back on Rob's account. I wonder if it will. I can't tell whether I did exactly the wrong thing by calling him. It's not as if I know him, or can really talk to him. He probably understands me even less than Rob does. He just has a handful of hokey ideas about me from a conversation we had a few months ago which he's built into something I can hardly even relate to myself.

I got to James's house exactly on time and he wasn't quite ready for me to arrive. He'd just run himself a bath and was walking around in a faded blue t-shirt and some slobby-looking brown denim trousers. It was great to see him dressed a little more casual than usual. Without his work shirt and blazer he seemed more approachable. He asked if I didn't mind waiting while he bathed, so I sat in the living room looking at his book collection as he splashed around in the bathroom singing all-out uninhibitedly. At the time I was pretty psyched-up and just about ready to walk out the door. I was having some kind of two-way crisis around both my personal morality and my desperate insecurity. On the one hand I was worried about the low-down thing I might be about to do, and on the other I got kind of anxious about whether or not James was interested in doing it with me. I imagined one more rejection might just about finish me off. The thing that made me not leave in the end was the way he sounded so harmless singing to himself in the bathtub. I felt like nothing terrible would happen if I hung around, and that, as things were generally pretty terrible anyhow, it wouldn't be too different if they got a little worse.

James came out wearing a big purple robe and with his hair all wet. People look so great when they're clean. He smelt good too. It was a bizarre mix of stuff – aftershave mostly, but with competition from a blend of shampoos, conditioners, soaps and deodorants. Then there was also an undertone of warm, damp body smell trying to break through, probably made more appealing by the difficulty of the job. He asked if I wouldn't mind if he stayed in his dressing gown. I told him I didn't mind at all. He said he had loads of interesting things to show me and offered me a glass of wine. He went to the kitchen to fetch the glasses and the bottle. It was a dusty thing that said 1988 on the label, and he'd obviously un-corked it before I came. It made me realize that the moral crisis was the one I ought to have focused on, as James was virtually in the bag.

We sat on the couch drinking the wine (which tasted like any old wine to me, but James insisted it was really special) and looking at a book he'd just bought – a fold-out book of Bauhaus furniture and architecture. It was really well done and showed how the insides of the buildings related to the outsides. Apparently the book was designed according to Bauhausian principles, but I was too embarrassed to admit that I didn't know what these were, so I just let it go. From what I could see, their main principle was that everything ought to be black and white with little geometric flashes of primary color. But I guess they must have been up to something more radical than that. In any case, the book conformed.

Next James asked whether I'd like to see his collection of African artifacts. He had a load of masks. One was a woman's head with tiny eyes, huge black lips and a hairstyle like two Big Macs stuck on either side of her head. It was really beautiful. He also had some contemporary masks made from soap packets, soda cans and squished up petrol containers. They were cool too. The last one he showed me was a huge mask about the size of a whole torso with big clumps of wool, feathers and dried grass streaming out at the top. The face was truly ferocious, like if you saw it running towards you, you probably wouldn't wait around to see whether it was just a little guy underneath. I think the most interesting thing about this particular mask though, was that it was just above his bed. As I stood there admiring it James told me to wait while he went to fetch something else. He said he'd just be a minute if I wanted to sit down. The only places to sit were either the bed or the floor. I knew I'd look like an idiot if I sat on the floor, so I perched myself awkwardly on the edge of the bed.

James's bed was the kind of bed that only a person who was

serious about comfort could choose. It was a kingsize double. The mattress was soft but not flabby. It had a thick, lightweight duvet and the kind of clean, ironed, fabric-conditioned sheets which you know straightaway must be maintained by a professional house cleaner. I was impressed.

James came back with another book – a fat Van Gogh monograph with a freaky blue self-portrait on the cover. He asked whether I liked Van Gogh and I said I did, although I couldn't understand how any artist could have treated his own paintings so badly. James asked what I meant and I told him about the criss-crosses in the paint. He gave me a kind of funny look that might have meant, 'How facile,' or could have been intended to mean, 'How observant'. (A slight widening of the eyes and tipping back of the head, in case I ever re-read this and suddenly understand). The illustrations were great. Without surface details to distract me I could see better what excellent paintings they were. The portraits best of all. I love it when portraits – which must take quite a while to do – manage to seem as though they've used up only a split second of the sitter's life. Van Gogh's paintings show people looking like they've been caught off-guard. Although they must have sat still in front of the guy for hours, with full knowledge of the fact that he was painting them, Van Gogh manages to make you feel as if you're catching them unawares – like you're walking past their window, or spotting them through a half-open door. It was nice finally to understand a little bit why people make such a fuss about his work. James told me some stuff about Van Gogh's life-history. It was all things I knew already about his brother and his ear and everything. I don't ever remember being told about it specifically before – but I guess that's fame for you.

It didn't feel at all awkward to be sitting on James's bed with him – or at least not too much anyway. We went right through the book and when we got to the end he yawned and apologized for feeling sleepy. He said he'd been in his office until midnight the night before, finishing off a project, and had gone to bed feeling so tense he couldn't sleep. He said there was a little café nearby that he really wanted to take me to, but that if he was going to manage to stay upright on his chair he'd have to take a nap first. He said I could make myself at home – watch the TV, make tea, read his books or do whatever I felt like doing. It felt like we'd been friends for ages. The wine had made me kind of sleepy too, so I said I'd snooze on his couch. He told me not to be so silly, and that if I didn't mind sleeping in his bed, then he wouldn't make a fuss about it either. I said I wouldn't mind at all. I kicked off my shoes and climbed under the covers. James laughed and got back out of bed. He went to his drawers, pulled out a huge navy t-shirt and gave it to me saying, 'Daisy darling, for goodness' sake, if you want to have a rest at least make yourself comfortable.' I felt pretty stupid, but what did he expect me to do? Strip off right there in front of him? I took his invitation to sleep at face value and it would never have occurred to me to take my clothes off. I needed to pee anyway so I disappeared into the bathroom to change and when I came back he was already out cold.

I must have lain there for about fifteen minutes before I finally drifted off. It suddenly felt so strange to be in James's t-shirt, in James's bed, with him sleeping right there next to me making little snuffling noises. (He didn't snore – thank God – he just make these adorable sounds that showed he really was asleep and wasn't just pretending so that he didn't have to talk anymore.) I'm not sure how long we slept for, but the next thing I knew it was already dark. I was barely awake when I felt James's hand stroking the front of my thigh and then feeling its way under the t-shirt and up to my stomach. It felt really, really good. Each time he stroked me my body felt more and more relaxed until it was almost as if I was dissolving. He

224

touched my throat and my breasts and my hips. When I felt as though my whole human existence had seeped away into the mattress leaving me suspended between the sheets like a bubble of immaterial bliss, he slipped his fingers inside my panties before easing himself down on top of me and making love to me in the most natural and beautiful way. (Mom, in case you ever read this – although I hope and pray you never do – that *doesn't* mean we didn't use a condom.) It almost felt as though we'd done it a thousand times before – only without it ever having gotten boring. After we made love we went back to sleep.

I woke up before James did. I noticed that the bedside clock said six o'clock. I had no idea whether it was morning or night, but I felt like I'd better get going.

There were so many cars in the street below I realized it must be evening. If I got to the bus stop fast enough, Rob need never know I'd been away. I pulled on my clothes really fast and kissed James right on the lips to wake him up. It was a truly gorgeous kiss. After a while he half-opened his eyes and I told him I was leaving. He seemed sleepy and confused. He said, 'OK then darling, I'll call you.' Then he did the sweetest thing. He took my left hand and gave each one of my fingertips a little suck. In terms of understanding what turns me on the guy is a total genius. I kissed him all over his face, ears and neck before racing downstairs and halfway over Vauxhall Bridge to the bus-stop. I wondered whether all the people who saw me could tell how happy I was.

Rob didn't notice anything (of course). I think I might be really beginning to hate him. He just asked how the job-search was going before suggesting we go get some noodles and see what the others were up to. I guess it suits me now if that's the way he wants to play it. At least if he's not on my back all the time it gives me room to work out what my next move ought to be.

When I started writing I thought I might be in love with James. But now I've given myself time to consider it, I can state it as an undeniable fact. It's dark again and everybody must be about to arrive home. I've survived a whole day without James. Thank you Dad for getting me started with this journal.

J J J J
J J
J J
J J J

Last night I got it into my head that I'd like to see my fox. I just wanted to know how she was getting along legwise. After I put out her food I crouched down at the opposite end of the garden and waited. It was all dark and whispery like the middle of the countryside. She popped out pretty quick, as if she'd been waiting for her dinner. Her back legs still looked unstable, but she was walking rather than wriggling along the ground. It made me really proud of her. The best thing was that she kept staring right at me, but it didn't put her off her food. When she'd finished she looked me straight in the eye and gave a weird kind of nod before limping off under the shed. From a wild animal that's got to be about the best compliment you can get. It really made my eyes water. After that I must have stayed outside for another hour or so just listening to the breeze and watching the clouds smooching around in the sky.

Then this morning I got a bank statement. After paying the rent I have exactly FIFTEEN POUNDS left! What in hell I am supposed to do? I've been looking at the newspapers every day and sending off my résumé. And in return for my efforts what have I got? Absolutely fucking nothing!!! Maybe I should put on a wig and false nose and go around all the same restaurants to see if they'll have me. Rob suggested that I try local places. What local places? He lives here too. Howcome he hasn't noticed that there aren't any? What a wethead.

As far as I can see the choices I have at the moment are either to get an overdraft and keep my fingers crossed that something comes up (provided the bank agrees to give me one), to ask Mom and Dad for a loan or, even worse, to ask Rob for one. Asking James is, of course, 100% out of the question. The other option is to leave the house and not allow myself to come back until I have a job. The only good thing about this last option is that, at least if I fail to get a job I won't have to pay rent anymore either.

One thing's for sure − I'm not going back to Vegas. The longer I've been away the more I understand what a horrible, lurky place it is. I also refuse to leave London just at the moment when it seems like I might have a real chance of finding some kind of happiness. James is exactly the guy I've waited all my life to meet. Whatever happens, I'm going to make certain the relationship doesn't hang on the present state of my finances. In fact I think I'll go get myself a job right now.

(Same day.) I just had the worst dream I've ever had in my whole life. I woke up feeling sick and I still do.

After I decided to get a job this morning I got myself all ready and went out the door. I caught the bus to Camberwell to see if I could do some waitressing in one of the cafés there.

I tried every single place in the whole fucking neighborhood without one single bit of encouragement from anyone. I guess because there are so many students around, all the shitty jobs get snapped up straight away. After that I tried Brixton and it was the same story. I was much more persistent than the last time, but it made zip all difference.

It's pretty hard to know when to give up when you're this desperate, but I started to feel really exhausted and hungry, so I thought it was best to come home for some food and a lie down before carrying on. I usually hate sleeping in the afternoons anyway (except when it's next to James) but this was the worst. I think daytime nightmares have a vividness that makes them even scarier than nighttime ones. I dreamt about Lara. I was going to a party on my own. The light in the streets was really bright but gray. When I arrived at the place where the party was supposed to be there was a huge crowd of people standing outside the door. I tried to get through to go into the house, but no one would let me past. I noticed small splashes of blood on the sidewalk and realized that something must have happened just before I arrived. I managed to push through the people and get inside. It was decorated like a swimming pool with white tiles everywhere and bright fluorescent lighting. On the walls there were a few smeared, bloody handprints. I had the feeling I'd known that something like this was going to happen. I went upstairs in the house to see if I could find my friend (in real life I have no idea who this friend was meant to be). I found him in his bedroom. I looked around and saw that one of the walls had a big block of ice embedded in it and inside you could see a girl's body. I understood straight away that it was Lara and asked what had happened. My friend said he was keeping the body on ice while the police went ahead with their investigations. He told me that the police had found a piece of paper with all these shitty

228

things I had written about her. I remembered writing them and felt really guilty. I was terrified that they'd think I'd killed her. I wanted to tell them that I hadn't meant any of it, but I didn't want them to find me in case they arrested me. I felt so bad it was as if I was actually somehow responsible for her death. I started really panicking and then I woke up. As soon as I realized it had been a dream I felt relieved, but at the same time I couldn't get rid of the feeling that I'd done something really, really wrong.

I don't understand dreams and how they work. What could make me dream that I might have killed Lara? I know Freud said some stuff about wish-fulfillment and dreaming. But I definitely don't think I ever wished I'd killed her. Exactly the opposite in fact. I wish more that anything that she was still here. Maybe I feel guilty because I'm alive and she isn't. She'd known all her life that she wanted to act and just as it was about to become a reality she was killed. I don't know what in hell I'm up to and I'm still here. It's so unfair. But I wonder if there's some weird connection with the James thing. Just when Lara got what she wanted she died. Now that I feel just on the verge of getting something I want my whole life collapses. But why would that make me wish I'd killed her? And if I really wished I'd done it, why do I feel so terrible now? I wonder why I dreamt I'd written nasty things about her. Lara is one of the few people I would never, ever have anything bad to say about ever. If I did, here is the place I would say it and I haven't. Maybe I do feel a bit incriminated by this journal – but more because of the things I've said about my mother and the way I've talked about my relationship with Rob. It was odd the way that, in the dream, it was the police who were accusing me, whereas in reality it was them who killed her. The block of ice was funny. It was spooky, but beautiful. Maybe that was the wish part. It was a load better than the picture I have of Lara's body when I'm awake. I wonder who the friend was. He doesn't seem to be anyone I know, although he felt totally familiar at the time. It was like he was an ex-boyfriend or something – only he was much too nice to have been any of my actual ex-boyfriends.

I can definitely see how a shrink could get a lot of mileage out of this dream. That's the other thing I gathered from Freud – if you're going to get anywhere with a dream, you'd better follow all the threads as you don't know which ones are going to lead where. I'd love to understand this sort of thing better. I guess you can't do it all by yourself or you'll probably only tell yourself what you want to hear – although that can sometimes be good too. I definitely feel a whole lot better than when I just woke up.

Maybe I could go back to my original childhood plan of being a shrink. I wonder how it'd be. Would I be a full-on Freudian or a hippy humanist or one of those guys that cures you in six sessions so you can get your insurance company to pay for it? You probably have to study for a long time, but I'm sure it's worth it in the end. It sounds like a good idea – even though, in the short term, it does nothing to alter the fact that I only have fifteen pounds in the bank.

Rob's going to be home in about an hour and I really don't feel like seeing him. I remember when I used to look forward to him coming home. I still sometimes find myself visualizing his journey. Only now I do it with a feeling of dread. I'd much rather leave a note saying I've gone to meet Souazik (Rob doesn't know that I hate her) and then go drop in on James. But I don't feel like seeing James until I've sorted out better what I'm going to do next. I'm glad he didn't ring today – or, if he did, that he didn't leave a message. Next time I see him I want to have a good idea of where I'm going. I'm sure I could talk to him about it if I felt like it, but I don't want to hit him with a pile of problems right at the start. The thing I loved about going round to his house the other day was the way it felt so relaxed. When I rang him in tears he really calmed me down. By the time I arrived at his apartment I didn't feel like I needed to start going on and on about how awful my life was. I was so happy to be there, looking at his books and being next to him in his bed that I forgot my problems for a while. Just knowing that James is there if I need him is enough right now. It makes me feel so much better to think that there's someone else in the world who cares about me. It gives me courage. I feel like I can do the stuff I need to (if only I could work out what it was).

The shrink idea has inspired me though. I think I have exactly the right kind of mind (with the correct training). I'd hate to do another crappy job without some kind of master plan to back it up. If I was studying I guess it could work out OK. I wonder what I'd say to James about my lack of poetic output. Maybe if I have my studies to distract me it'll seem natural that I have less time to write poems. I'd love to know what James thinks about psychoanalysis.

Sometimes a cigar is just a cigar

P.S. I found the key to Jo's diary! I haven't looked at it yet as she might get home any minute and I'd feel too nervous. But

231

first thing tomorrow morning I'll be in there. At last! I hold the key to the mysteries of Jo's mind. I can't wait to open it and see what's inside.

I think, now that I'm not sure what's going to happen over the next few weeks, I feel urgent about following up the stuff I started while I've been in this house. It's great when you really set your mind on things. I knew that Jo would be back soon, so I just went into her room and said to myself I'd find the key within five minutes. Two minutes later it was in my hand (one of the bears had a pair of mini y-fronts on and the key was tucked into the back – so my earlier theory wasn't altogether out of line). I'm also going to get back on the case with Leni's magnum opus. Now I couldn't care less what she writes about Rob and Sofia. Or about me for that matter. Why should I give a rip about what Leni thinks? She's far too self-centered to have a real clue about who I am.

PPS. I think I may just have realized something about the dream. Maybe because I went to bed feeling so bad about my life I dreamt about killing Lara as it was slightly preferable to killing myself (plus she's dead already, so I could allow myself to do it more easily as I've already started to deal with the loss). But perhaps it was more that I'm angry with my memory of her and the way I use it to torment myself. Maybe I wanted to murder *it* so I could start dealing with life on my own terms. I guess that makes it seem less evil. Is this the sort of thing a shrink might say? I imagine it has to be more complicated than that.

I don't believe in heaven, or any kind of life after death but – just in case I'm wrong – Lara, if you can hear me, I never, ever wished you any harm. I love you and hope that, if there is something after all this, it's fairer and better.

★

Last night, when I went to put the foxfood out, I decided to lie on the ground a few yards away. I took an old brown blanket and wrapped myself up like a giant pupa in the hope it'd help me blend in with nature. The fox appeared the same as last time. She looked a little suspicious, but edged up to her bowl and started eating anyhow. Our faces were at the same height and I could see all her individual hairs and whiskers. I shut my eyes a few times to show that I trusted her (I know this works with cats).

As she was gobbling down her dinner she kept looking up at me, but it felt more like curiosity than mistrust. When she'd finished, instead of disappearing straight back under the shed, she came a little closer and started to sniff the air. Her pointy nose was sticking out as far forward as it would go and her nostrils were opening and closing like crazy. She stayed like that for about a minute and then backed off slowly and disappeared into her hiding place. My heart was beating so hard I could almost hear it. I can't believe she trusted me like that. I wouldn't pretend to know what goes on inside a fox's mind, but I think she realizes I'm on her side.

I can't decide whether to feel disappointed, touched, horrified or encouraged by Jo's diary. I suppose I'll go for a bit of each. I feel disappointed by the fact that it wasn't full of blinding insights and embarrassingly truthful revelations. I feel touched by the way it seems quite private and genuine (while my journal, although private, would probably come over a bit show-offy to someone like Jo if she saw it). I feel horrified by the fact that it shows so little evidence of intelligent thought – can Jo really be as braindead as she seems, or is she just too paranoid to record her more risqué ideas (in case of people like me)? And I feel encouraged by the fact that I think my journal might be OK and of great potential interest to future generations due to my small inheritance of literary talent. I think even if someone came across Jo's diary in five hundred years' time they would be more impressed that the paper had survived than by its contents. Jo should definitely marry the old potato, though. She's obviously totally into him. There's not one place in the whole book where she expresses any doubt about her feelings for him. It's true that she's not exactly articulate on the subject of why she likes him either. She just writes his name really big on almost every other page and fills the letters up with hearts and shit. Some of them are even in color. I'm tempted to keep a print of it, but I couldn't afford the photocopies and I'm nervous about taking it out of the house in case she comes back by surprise or I get shot on the way to the shop and they find it in my bag. Maybe I could use Leni's scanner. I could pretend it was for some other reason – although I'm not sure what. I'd have to give her some advanced warning to give her time to hide her script under the mouse pad. Her printer might even be a color one – and if it isn't I'll ring her father to complain on her behalf. Everything's really coming together again. My life is just so great.

The weekend starts tomorrow. I feel really nervous about it. So much has happened this week. With any luck Rob will spend most of it in the library like he has the last two or three times.

I don't really know what to do with myself at weekends. They're generally the most boring part of my life here.

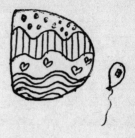

Altogether Now

I have to keep writing to stop crying. I guess it's going to be OK. Or at least that's what I have to keep telling myself. Only two and a half days until I'm out of here. I can't wait. Now that I've decided to leave (not that I had a lot of choice) I'm 100% looking forward to it. These last sixty hours are going to be a drag but, if I can survive them, this whole ordeal is over.

What a weekend! Some moments I thought I was going to burst just from the pure, total difficulty of being alive. I didn't though. Or go mad either – further proof of Leni's minimal understanding of the world.

I guess the thing that set it all off was a major error of judgement on my part. I decided to go to Leni's room to copy the diary without waiting to ask for her permission to use the computer. I figured that, as she knows I borrow it from time to time, she wouldn't mind my going in there, provided I apologized and majorly thanked her afterwards. I don't know why I wanted to copy Jo's stupid diary so much in the first place. It wasn't even interesting. Maybe I just wanted to do *something* – other than look for a waitressing job or write my own journal.

It must have been about four o'clock when I went in to Leni's room with the diary – usually a safe enough time for research. The scanner was pretty much like the one I'd used in my old job, so it didn't take long to get it done – especially given the fact that Jo's diary is excessively free of page-consuming information. The prints came out really great – proving it's not just Monet whose work is improved in the act of reproduction. Shame I lost the whole lot before I had a chance to appreciate it. I must have finished with Jo's stuff at about a quarter to five. I decided I probably had time to see how Leni's script was coming along. The disk was still in its original hiding place. I slipped it into the slot and printed it out, skimming the pages a little just to catch the general drift – which was actually the only time I read it in the end. It was just as ropey as the first half and, from what I gathered she has me go nuts – the last thing I have any intention of doing. The whole thing was more like a very bad pop video than an insightful treatise on human nature. It was pretty offensive to me though. I wonder whether Leni's room is locked now – like Sofia's is. Perhaps if it's open I could go stick a few fridge magnets onto the floppy, just to make absolutely certain it never sees the light of day.

Anyhow, I'd just finished printing out and was putting the pieces of paper back in the right order when I heard the door slam. It was probably about five by then so I figured it could have been anyone – except Rob. I switched off the computer without doing the proper shut-down ritual, flicked the disk under the mouse pad and grabbed the prints and the diary. What I probably should have done next was to duck into the bathroom and wait until I knew who it was before trying to put things back in place. If it'd been Jo, she would have switched on the TV, giving me plenty of time to replace her precious journal. If it had been Leni or Sofia I could have waited in the toilet until they went to their rooms and then slipped downstairs, dropping the diary off on the way. It pisses me off now to think that the whole drama could have been completely avoided if I'd thought to do either of these things. What I did instead was to tip-toe down the hallway to see if I could see who'd just arrived. At first I thought it must be Jo, as whoever it was seemed to be disappearing off towards the living room. I twisted her bedroom doorknob and tried to open the door without making a noise – at which point the person turned around and started to come upstairs. Still believing it was Jo, I ducked back quickly into Sofia's room. The person went into the bathroom and turned on the tap. As far as I could tell they hadn't shut the door behind them so I didn't dare go out. At that point it hit me that the person might be Sofia. As if I wasn't freaking out enough already, I started really freaking out properly to the point where I could hardly breathe. The only thing I could think of doing was to get under the bed, just in case it was her, and to hope to hell it was Leni. At this point I did the only sensible thing I'd done all day. I slipped the copies down the back of Sofia's bedside cabinet, figuring I could always retrieve them at a later date and, meanwhile, the diary was the main thing I'd better sort out.

I lay under the bed going, 'Oh no, oh no, oh no,' over and over again. The water stopped running and I crossed my fingers so viciously I've actually still got a pain there. The person left the bathroom, walked along the hallway, opened the door and came into the room. It was Sofia. I stayed really still. She went over to her desk and started writing a letter. I knew already that Sofia's letters could sometimes get pretty long, but I had no idea she thought so much in between words. She seemed to be writing for hours. Meanwhile Leni came home, but Sofia didn't even put her head out the door to say hello.

It was seriously uncomfortable under the bed. I wished that, when I'd first ducked under there, I'd had some idea how long I was going to have to stay so I could have chosen a more comfortable position. As it was I was on my back with my knees bent up and twisted off to the side. My spine felt really tense and my right hip-bone was digging into the floor. I didn't dare move in case the boards creaked, so I just stayed still, getting more and more panicked about what was going to happen next. To make it worse it was really dusty under the bed and I was having to concentrate the whole time on not sneezing. The only thing that kept me going was the idea that, at some point Sofia would surely have to eat or at least have a coffee.

I guess it was about an hour before I heard the front door slam again. I prayed it wasn't Jo. She often stays with Ian on Fridays, so I imagined I might be lucky. As it turned out, it was Rob. He must have checked around the house first to see whether or not I was there. When he was satisfied that I wasn't, he came and tapped on Sofia's door. I couldn't tell whether she'd been expecting him or whether she was surprised. I didn't have a clue what was going on at all most of the time as they were both speaking Spanish. They were whispering too, like they didn't want Leni to know they were there. They mentioned my name a few times quite early on, so maybe they were discussing where I might be. After that they sat down on the bed and carried on chatting. From what I could gather they weren't touching or anything, but they were certainly acting pretty friendly. The whole scene really turned my guts over. At that point it did actually occur to me that this might be the moment to announce myself. I could almost have justified it on the grounds that they were clearly up to no good themselves. But then I thought about it and decided it might just be a friendly conversation and that they would think I was a total loon if I suddenly popped out from under the bed to interrupt it. I was also nervous about rocking the boat with Rob when my whole life seemed to be in such a fragile state. I briefly imagined he might be able to be happier with Sofia too (although I tried to wipe this thought before I had time to think

240

it fully). Basically, I was having a load of imbecilic ideas. But it was just so yucky to be underneath the bed with Rob up there acting like a completely different person to the one I thought I knew.

The worst thing about them being on the bed together was the way it made the whole frame sag in the middle and forced me to twist my knees even further off to the side. The sneezing wasn't getting any easier to control either. My nose kind of decided that, as I wouldn't let it flush the tickly particles out with a major blow, it would try to wash them away with a slow trickle of water. It's hard not to sniff when you really want to. I came so close to sniffing noisily so many times but, miraculously didn't. Instead I had a stream of wet stuff beginning at the base of my nostril, following the upper edge of my lip, trailing down the side of my chin before dropping onto my collarbone. As much as I was pissed at Rob and Sofia, I also felt totally mad about the indignity of not being allowed to clear my own nose.

The next thing I knew, all sorts of stuff started to happen simultaneously and, apart from the fact that it eventually enabled me to sniff, none of it was good. The first part was that Sofia and Rob stopped talking for a few seconds. At the time I couldn't understand why, probably because I had no idea what they'd been saying just before. But then I heard a little slurp which made me realize that they were kissing. Although I see now that I was being pretty naïve, I hadn't expected them to do that. I'd been just about getting used to the whole thing of them sitting up there talking away in Spanish while I lay underneath struggling with my nose. But when they started up the spit-exchange I couldn't stay so relaxed. I felt all cold and strange and like if I'd been on my feet I would have fallen over. As it was I didn't have anywhere to fall, but I had the strong sensation of being unsupported by the floor. It didn't even occur to me at that point to announce myself. I felt totally incapable of moving or speaking.

I don't know what would have happened next if what actually happened hadn't happened. But, luckily or unluckily, it did. I'd like to think that, Sofia being Catholic, things wouldn't have gone much further. Who knows? Anyhow, just at that moment, there was a yell from Jo's room followed by a bang – which must have been her door flying open – and then a loud, 'Where's my fucking diary?'. I had no idea Jo was home. I guess she must have come in quietly. Sofia and Rob cut out kissing and started whispering and giggling nervously. They jumped off the bed and stood there, listening out to see what was coming next. Jo knocked loudly on Leni's door and Leni shouted back, 'What?' Jo yelled, 'My fucking diary's disappeared, that's what!'. To which Leni replied, 'So? What are you fucking screaming at me for?' Rob was speaking really fast to Sofia, like he was doing a simultaneous translation. They started giggling again and Sofia ran over to the closet to open it. Rob tried to get inside, but Sofia's closet is pretty small and wouldn't close. They were sniggering like mad when Jo banged on the door and carried on screeching about her stupid diary – which doesn't even have anything interesting in it anyway. Sofia was going, 'Un momento! Un momento!', and dithering around the room. Jo started getting really nasty and going 'I don't care what you're doing I just want my fucking diary back NOW!' She was acting like she thought Sofia had it, maybe because Sofia was trying to stop her coming in. I could hear Leni telling Jo to calm down. She was totally hysterical, like it was the worst thing that had ever happened in her life. She was going, 'Don't fucking tell me what to do when someone's just fucking come and stolen my diary! OK? Now open the fucking door!'.

I didn't know what to do, but at least Jo's shouting had woken me up. I didn't feel dizzy at all any more. The only constructive thing I could think of was to try and jam the diary down the back of the cabinet where I'd hidden the print-outs. I started to twist around as quietly as I could. It was all going quite well. Nothing squeaked or creaked or crunched. The plan looked like it might just about work when a bright shaft of light hit me right between the eyes. Rob had lifted up the bedspread and was just about to crawl under the bed. I think at first he must have thought I was a suitcase or something. He reached out his hand and gave me a shove. His reaction was pretty extreme. He yelled like he'd found a corpse and jerked his head back, banging it really hard on the side of the bed. I couldn't stop myself whispering, 'Are you alright?'. And just as I said it the door flew open.

Jo and Leni must both have been standing in the hall, Rob was lying on his belly on the floor with his head under the bed, groaning, Sofia seemed to be bending down trying to work out what was going on and I just lay there, wiping my nose and thinking what the fuck.

Rob backed out and stood up. I guess Jo was so surprised at what she was seeing she couldn't decide whether to carry on being angry or not. She asked him what he was doing, but he didn't answer. Then she asked him if her diary was under the bed and he said he didn't know. She went, 'Well, is it or isn't it?'. Rob isn't good at stuff like that and went, 'Um, I don't think so.' So Jo got straight down on her hands and knees to check it out for herself.

I decided at that point that the only thing to do was to come clean. I wasn't going to mention the copies or that I'd read the script or the letters or anything. But I was pretty sure they'd realize it was me who'd got the diary, so I thought it would be better to be honest and to give it back in the hope it would make everyone more inclined to forgive me. Jo lifted up the bedspread and I handed the diary over before she had a chance to go nuts again. She looked back at me really shocked and just said, 'Bloody hell'.

At that point it must have dawned on Sofia exactly what was going on. She put her hands over her mouth and started crying. I took a quick look at everyone, just to check their reactions, and then looked away. I don't think anybody knew what to say. The person I felt the most sorry for (apart from myself) was Jo. Most of what she'd written in her diary was totally harmless. She's really the only person around here who wasn't up to any bullshit.

I crawled out from under the bed because it seemed like what I ought to do, but I felt so ashamed of myself I just sat back down on the mattress and looked into my lap. After that there was a pretty long and painful pause while everyone tried to work out what to say next. I really wanted to know what they were all thinking. I guess Sophia was feeling all cut up and guilty. Rob was most likely embarrassed both for himself and for me. He probably felt sorry for Sofia too. Jo must have been relieved to get her diary back and was probably trying to remember whether she'd said anything too embarrassing in it. And Leni was undoubtedly congratulating herself on being so right about everything. But then again, what do I know? Maybe everyone was wondering about what each other was thinking and not actually thinking anything for themselves.

Leni suggested that we all go downstairs for a coffee. We definitely needed to get out of Sofia's room and I don't think any of us felt like going back to our own – specially not Rob and me. So we all went to the living room – apart from Sofia, who stayed in the bathroom splashing her face and blowing her nose for about ten minutes before coming to join us.

I still couldn't really speak or look at anyone, so I shut up while they started talking. Jo was saying that since she'd got her job she and Ian had been thinking about moving in together. She said she'd had enough of communal living and wanted to have a place just for the two of them, where they could deal with their own problems on their own terms and not worry about anyone else's. I wonder whether Jo actually worries about any of our problems and, if so, whether she comes up with any solutions. I decided it probably wasn't the moment to ask. She was looking all smug and creamy and as if she had something more to say. It was pretty obvious what it was going to be, but everyone still pretended to be surprised when she announced her engagement. (Engagement!? Like, who does *that* anymore?). Sofia went over and gave her a stiff, soggy hug, Rob went, 'That's great news!' and Leni said she'd been thinking about moving too, just because the house is on the wrong side of the river according to her friends and she'd rather travel a long way to college than be a social outcast. Apparently the wedding date is set for August 2001. What spontaneity!

Sofia was sniffing and having a hard time speaking but, as usual, everyone was very helpful and gave her time to talk and suggested useful words to her. It makes me sick the way she manages to persuade everybody that she's so soft and fragile and in need of their support. I'm sure that if Leni had just slopped all over Rob Jo, at least, would be sitting there thinking what a poisonous piece of shit she was. But Sofia's apparently so vulnerable she's above the law. She said her family were still trying to persuade her to go back but she didn't want to. It made me so mad. It's obvious the only reason she wants to stay is her crush on Rob. What would her family think if they knew? I can't believe she thinks it's OK to stay in London while her brother is so ill, just in order to steal my boyfriend. She might pretend to be full of feelings and stuff, but I don't think they go too deep. Sofia's just one of these people who has a sensitive face but is actually pretty superficial. The others started asking her questions and making suggestions – like whether there was anyone at work she could stay with while she looked for a new room. It was obvious they were all agreeing that the house arrangement wasn't exactly working and that they wanted out. Even Rob, who'd been so keen to hang on to the place last week, said – without acknowledging my presence – that he could easily go stay with his cousin in an emergency. That was the moment that I realized we'd officially split up. I started to cry, but nobody asked whether I was alright or showed anything like the concern they'd shown Sofia. In fact they just ignored my existence altogether. I made sure I cried really quietly as I thought that making a stupid noise would make things even worse. I should have left the room, but I was so scared of what they'd say about me I couldn't bring myself to do it.

They all agreed that it was better to get out sooner than later. The deposits here are only half a month's rent in advance so they all decided it was cheaper and better to bail out without giving any notice. They'd leave the deposits to cover the household bills rather than to risk losing them *and* end up having to pay for the gas and the phone as well. They decided to do it next Saturday to give themselves time to get organized. I'll be gone well before then, not that anybody's bothered to check what *I'm* doing.

They all stayed up talking about pretty general stuff like their families, their work and some crappy-sounding documentary about female boxers. I was still crying and preparing my apology – although I could never quite make myself say it because I felt so much more like telling them to go boil their heads. Jo was the first one to claim to feel sleepy. She said goodnight and went off to her room. After she left there was another long silence. I noticed how much Jo keeps the rest of us together. I might have been a bit disparaging about the way she tries to make us get along, but actually she's pretty good at it. Without her there, there wasn't much to say. Leni was the next one to say she felt tired – which would have left Rob, Sofia and me if those two hadn't been cowardly enough to say they were

246

exhausted too. Leni went to put the gas heater off, but Rob asked her to leave it on as he was going to sleep on the couch. Leni said we should all use the phone and heaters as much as possible before next Saturday. I said under my breath that I hoped they'd die of carbon monoxide poisoning, but they either didn't hear or decided to ignore me.

I went to the bedroom and listened out to see whether Rob really was going to sleep on the couch, or whether he was actually going to sneak up to Sofia's room. I didn't hear any sounds on the stairs so I supposed he was telling the truth. I thought about going to talk to him, but I wanted to see if he had the courage to come to me. What a total cocksucker not speaking to me in all that time! It was like he was too ashamed to face me and he used the others' disapproval of me to get him off the hook. Like, of course you'd have an affair if you were going out with someone who read other people's diaries. I don't think I'll talk to him ever again – even if he really wants to.

He may even be in the house right now for all I know. I could hear the TV up until an hour or so ago and I know that there are at least two other people around, although I think they might be Leni and Jo. Perhaps Sofia and Rob are staying in a cheap hotel or at a friend's house. It's totally vile, but it's better than them coming back here.

It's really late. I think I'll go say goodbye to my fox.

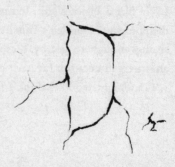

P.S. I'm so happy I hardly feel human. I went down to the garden the same as before, put the food on the ground and lay there wrapped up in the bug blanket. The grass was damp and it was real windy. Without the fox I guess it would have been creepy, but she popped out pretty sharpish before I had a chance to get spooked. All the while she was eating her food she kept a close eye on me. The same as last time, after she finished, she stuck her nose out and smelt the air like mad. She took a couple of steps forward, then changed her mind and started limping backwards in the direction of the shed. It made me so miserable to think I wouldn't be seeing her again.

I could hardly bear to make myself come back inside, partly because of the fox, and partly because I associate this house with everything sad and bad about existence. It was pretty snug inside the blanket, so I just lay there listening to the wind in the leaves and seeing if I could work out which was the Big Dipper. I didn't hear the fox re-appear, but suddenly there she was. She came right up and sniffed my face! I smelt her doggy breath! I felt total, unadulterated love. I just lay there in my woolly cocoon enjoying her warm, damp, stinky panting on my forehead and my cheek, feeling like I didn't deserve to be this happy, ever. Anything good that happens in the rest of my life is just an unnecessary bonus after that. I know now that I'm ready for anything. I hope she'll be OK without me though. I feel like a bit of a shit, letting her depend on me and then disappearing. Her leg's much better though. I'm sure she's strong enough to get by. Perhaps the person who moves in after us will be a fox lover.

Goodnight world. I think I love you after all.

★

Only thirty six hours more. I hope I can get all this down before I disappear. I think that, after I've left, I won't want to keep going on and on about it, so I'd better round everything off beforehand. It sounds corny, but I'm about to start a new chapter in my life and I don't want to be stuck writing up the old one at the same time.

So, back to where I left off yesterday. I was on my own in bed and all I could think about was James. As soon as the others weren't there and I didn't have to worry about what they thought of me, I started to feel really glad about getting out of a situation which I wasn't even happy in anyway. I guess I'd exhausted my supply of misery, leaving room for an influx of sloppy-feely stuff. I thought it'd be too late to ring, so I decided to do it first thing the next morning. I remember, as I was drifting off, totally forgetting what had just happened and imagining my future as a shrink with a cool apartment in London, looking at art and eating in candlelit places with James.

I woke up Saturday morning and the house was all quiet. It was sunny outside with a crunchy layer of frost stuck all over everything. I went to the bathroom to get cleaned up. There wasn't a single sound coming from anybody's room. I got dressed real quick and went into the kitchen to use the phone. The door to the living room wasn't properly closed. I glimpsed through to see whether or not Rob was there. He was – not that I care *that* much about what he does any more, but I was still a little bit pleased to think that he'd at least have a few major back pains when he woke up. (It also occurred to me that it would be very easy to bash him with a frypan if I felt like it, only I didn't.)

I dialed James's number and, after about seven rings, the

ansaphone picked up. I felt disappointed, but decided to leave a message saying I'd call him later and that I needed to see him as soon as possible. I started to speak, but before I'd said ten words he answered the phone, all out of breath, like he'd run to get it. I was so happy to hear his voice, but kind of nervous too. It was funny to be speaking to him after having thought so much about him. I was talking super fast, trying to tell him that all sorts of things had been happening (although I was probably too excited to have made any sense). He sounded distracted, like he wasn't all there. Suddenly he butted in with, 'Daisy darling, it's seven thirty in the morning. Can I call you back?' I went, 'Oh, sorry, yes of course. Speak to you in a bit,' and hung up. At that point I started zeeking out again. I felt like I really, really *needed* to see James. It wasn't like the normal feeling of wanting to see a person, but more like every split-second that separated me from him was the temporal equivalent of a pin in the ass. I couldn't handle waiting around until he had his beauty sleep, breakfast and shower before calling me to make some kind of appointment that would be even more unbearable hours into the future. I decided the only thing to do was to get on a bus to see him direct. I figured that if I brought along a few croissants I'd arrive in time for breakfast and everything would work out OK.

I felt much better once I'd got myself moving. In fact the whole bus ride was a pretty ecstatic experience – the further away from New Cross and the nearer to Pimlico I got, the happier I became, until I actually arrived at Vauxhall Bridge and literally felt about as happy as I ever remember feeling. I can't imagine what I thought was going to happen but, what-ever, it was sure to be just great. I started skipping about in the street and acting like a total spoon, all because I was in such a hurry to see James.

A youngish lady dressed like an old lady in a tweedy suit

with pearls was walking out the main front door of James's apartment block just as I arrived and, surprisingly, she let me into the lobby without a fuss. I raced up the stairs and rang on the bell. After what felt like about ten billion more split-seconds he came to the door. He was in his bathrobe and looked almost exactly the same as the last time I saw him. I didn't give him a chance to say a word. I threw my arms around his neck and just kind of hung onto him. I think he must have been pretty shocked, which is why he took such a long time to react. But after a few seconds' standing there and taking it he got a hold of my wrists and gently put my arms back by my sides. He asked me really quietly what I was doing there. I took his soft tone for a sign of concern and started to tell him that I'd split up with Rob and I was going to leave the house in New Cross. He looked pretty worried and went, 'Shhh'. I didn't click at all and just carried on talking only quieter. I was just telling him all about the shrink thing when a woman's voice from inside his apartment called out, 'Who's there?'. James put his finger to his lips and pulled a really desperate face. The woman went, 'Jamie, who is it?', and he called back, 'Oh, just someone from downstairs.'

The first thing that came into my mind was that it must be Souazik. I was pretty repulsed, but it kind of made sense. I went, 'What's going on? Is that Souazik?' James looked confused but didn't say anything. I assumed I must have been right. I began trying to process the information when a blonde woman in about her mid-to-late thirties poked her head out from James's bedroom door and called, 'Is there a problem?' James didn't even flinch, he just turned around really calmly and said, 'No, everything's fine, darling. Apparently there's a leak but I'm sure it can't be us,' to which she replied, 'No, it can't be. We haven't used any water all morning.' I looked at James and he looked back. I realized then that I *never* know what any of his facial expressions mean. He might as well have had an egg for a head for all the clues his features gave me as to what he was feeling. I imagine my face made it pretty clear to him that I was upset. He whispered, 'I'll speak to you later. Give me a couple of hours, OK?' I looked at him with a bit more purpose in my face this time, as if to say, 'You make me barf, mother-fucker' – which I really hope he understood.

Now that I'd stopped feeling all deluded and happy I started feeling seriously tired and fucked up. I got out into the street and looked around, noting how dumb the whole world was. I stood on the sidewalk watching the cars, thinking what assholes the drivers were. I crossed the road, making no concessions, and forcing one of them to break so hard it left a burning rubber smell. There were a few people walking along the Thames, some of them actually braindead enough to look happy. (I don't really feel this bad anymore – I'm just putting it on for effect.) I looked down at the putrid water and noticed myself deciding against suicide. It wasn't like a conscious thing – more as if my real self had floated halfway out of my body, leaving another, simpler version of me down there making the pragmatic decisions while I had a quick break from the agony of my dumb little life.

In this state I managed to maneuver my body along to the subway station and onto a couple of different trains until I arrived at Earls' Court. I kept thinking all the way that I didn't even want to go there, that Souazik was the last person I wanted to see and that I didn't have her address anyway. But my body kept on moving and I didn't put up too much of a fight. I went to the Troubadour café and looked through the window, but Souazik wasn't there. I couldn't even tell whether the café was open or not because I was temporarily unable to understand normal stuff. I think, if I'm honest, it was the nearest I've ever gone to being crazy. It wasn't as if I was going to start eating any books or anything, but the feeling of not being completely inside my body was carrying on, as if my mind was sticking up out of me like the headrest of a car-seat. I also felt like there was some kind of electricky stuff all around me, but I can't remember now what I thought it meant.

I started to walk in the direction I'd seen Souazik go the times I'd said goodbye to her with James. She'd said her house was two minutes away, so I figured that if I walked at round about average speed for two minutes in the right direction, the chances were I'd arrive somewhere near her house. I imagined Souazik was more the type of person to live on a quiet road than a noisy one, so I turned left into the first quiet street. On a normal day I never would have done this next part but, when I guessed that I must be in roughly the right place, I started calling out for Souazik. I was totally uninhibited, like it was a really normal thing to do. I stood still and kept yelling out the name for a couple of minutes. Nothing happened. But I had such a strong belief in the infallibility of my scheme that I started walking along the street, turning left into a square of houses with a fenced off garden in the middle, still calling out over and over again. A genuinely old lady came up to me and asked whether I had lost my dog. I said no, but she carried on as if I had said yes, and told me I could try putting an ad in the paper. I thanked her and carried on walking around the square. I'd gotten about three quarters of the way when I heard a voice behind me go, 'Daisy, is that you?'

I turned around and saw Souazik standing on the sidewalk with a towel on her head. I didn't feel at all surprised or anything but she was looking at me as if I'd just come down from a spaceship. I told her that her house was much more than two minutes away. She started with the questions again, like, 'What are you doing? Is something wrong? How did you work out where to come? Would you like a cup of tea? Do you mind if

I get dressed first?' and all that type of stuff. She looked pretty pleased to see me though, as far as I could tell, so I said I'd like a coffee.

Souazik's apartment was seriously out of this world. She lives in the basement of the house of a rich old man who likes to have someone around to water the plants while he's away (which is most of the time). She had a load of plants of her own, but mostly her place was full of books. All the books had little flappy scraps of paper sticking out the tops where she'd marked the pages, like she was really using them for something more than just to look smart.

I sat on the couch while she went into the kitchen to make coffee. I guess I must have been so relieved to be in a place where no-one hated me or thought I was an idiot that I relaxed enough to fall asleep before the drinks even arrived. I woke up about one o'clock and Souazik was working at her desk, taking notes from some really fat book. She must have heard me move because she turned around straightaway.

Souazik must be about the easiest person in the world to talk to. Whatever mean things I said about her before were totally and absolutely wrong. Sometimes I think, because I'm so screwed up myself, I can't believe in real goodness when I come across it. I don't want to go overboard, but Souazik is like my new heroine. I told her everything (except the diary-stealing part – I think a shrink is the only person I would ever discuss that sort of thing with). I said I'd spied on Rob to catch him cheating on me and that everyone at home was on his and Sofia's side. I told her about the money thing, the job thing, my parents attitude towards my trip and, in the end I got around to telling her about James. She seemed so upset, like it had somehow been her fault. I asked her about the time she'd arranged the meeting that Rob was meant to come along to, and whether she'd set it all up. She admitted that, although she hadn't done it fully on purpose, when she realized that she'd double-booked us, she'd thought it was probably a good thing for my sake. I asked her, without having to be sneaky, what the deal was with her and James. She told me they'd had an affair that had lasted a year and which finished about eighteen months ago. She said she'd been pretty lonely when she came here to study. The way she'd met him was similar to the way I'd met him (only she didn't have to lie about what she was writing). She told me she'd really believed at the time that they were totally in love with each other and that it was a big deal. She got pregnant and he went crazy because she wasn't sure whether or not she wanted to have an abortion. He kept insisting that she had to have one, and being really shitty about it. She said, in the end, she was so mad at him she didn't want to have his baby anyway, but that she wished she could have made the decision on better terms. After that she didn't feel like seeing him anymore, but he called her from time to time to ask her out to dinner and stuff.

As if that wasn't bad enough, she found out later through someone she met by chance at a party, that James had been dating some other woman for ten years (even while he was married) and that the woman was desperate to marry him, but that he kept putting her off. Souazik had never seen her, so we don't know whether she was the one in the flat, but I don't suppose it makes too much difference. He's such a good pretender he could probably have ten girlfriends and none of them would ever catch on.

That time in *The Troubadour* when I first met Souazik was the second time she'd seen James since they split. He hadn't told her I was coming until just before I arrived (which doubly justifies why she might have tried out a trick of her own). She said she'd been completely mad at him, but that when she'd seen me and realized that I didn't have a clue what was going

255

on, she'd decided it was better to be nice to me as it wasn't my fault and because it was the thing most likely to piss James off. Then – and this was the really sweet part – she said that she couldn't help liking me, especially when she saw my work. She said this thing again about it not being often that she met people on the same wavelength. I felt so confused when she said it that I burst into tears. She asked why I was crying and I could hardly bear to tell her. But she'd been so generous with me I couldn't keep up the lie about the poems. I told her that they weren't real poems and that I'd just gotten them out of a book on shoes and mixed the words around. She laughed at me for about five minutes and then gave me a hug and carried on laughing. I kept asking her what was so funny, but she couldn't even speak. It turned out that my way of doing poetry was a respectable method, used by the Surrealists, and that she'd even written a section about it in her thesis. What a fucking freaky world we live in. I didn't know what to think about it really, but I guess the bottom line is that, whether they're real poems or not, as I only wrote them as a joke and they didn't mean that much to me, there's not a lot of point in my writing any more. Especially as poets generally don't get paid.

At that point I told her I was going to be a shrink and she said she thought it would suit me perfectly. The person who should probably be one most of all is her, but she's got other plans. We talked for ages about what I should do and decided in the end that the best move was probably to go back to America. I didn't like it at first, but the idea started to grow on me. I know enough people to be able to get some kind of job pretty quickly. I could go to night school to get the grades I need. I imagined getting into the University of San Francisco and gradually coming to feel that my life might actually have a point. Like, not only might I find it interesting, but I might also eventually be able to help other people – and get paid!

I called collect to Mom and Dad from Souazik's phone. Luckily Dad picked up. He sounded so pleased to hear my voice. When I told him what I was thinking of doing he practically cheered. My Dad has a bizarre faith in my intelligence (and it really is faith as, according to my high school grades, there's very little actual proof of it). He said I'd make an excellent shrink and that he thought it would make me very happy to use my brain to do something worthwhile. I'd never have thought of it that way, but I guess he had a point. Human brains are pretty complex and if you don't give them something serious to keep them occupied they're bound to give you a pain in the ass.

Dad said he'd transferred his typewriter and desk to my old room as he found it a good place to concentrate, but that he'd be happy to give me my bed back while I found my feet. I asked him how the book was going – expecting the same old answer – but instead he said it was pretty good. He hasn't finished it or anything but he told me that, for the first time in years, he was really starting to believe there might be something in it. I wonder what it could be. I asked him if I'd be able to read it and he laughed in a kind of 'we'll see' way, but didn't answer. Maybe I understand more now what makes him so clammy. There's no way I'm going to show him this either. But it's different because I don't call myself a writer. Maybe I'll be able to discuss *his* career with him when I get back. I wonder how that would go down.

Mom got on the phone straight afterwards. She'd obviously been listening and knew what was going on. She wasn't exactly as grooved-out about it as Dad, but I think she was still pleased in her own way. I wonder how she'll act when I get back. I doubt I'll stay at their place for more than a couple of weeks. But perhaps the fact that I have a plan will ease up my relationship with her. I'd like to like her more, I think.

Mom got in a fuss about the ticket thing when I told her that, ideally, I'd like to fly the following morning. She said if I was about to start getting real about the rest of my life I might as well begin by getting real about air travel. She asked whether I could afford to change the date of my flight and I had to admit I couldn't. I had no idea it was so expensive to do stuff like that. She gave me her credit card number so I could sort it out, which I guess was pretty kind. But it pissed me off to think she might believe I was just coming back because I'd run out of money. I'm going back because I want to and that's that. If I wanted to stay here I know I could find a way, but there's no point busting a gut to do something you don't even feel strongly about. I'm sure we'll talk about it when I arrive. I hope I manage to stay calm. The more I think about it the more I start to get annoyed in advance, but perhaps it'll be OK.

The question of how I was expecting to finance myself through college never came up, but I predict it'll be an issue. I'm not going to rely on Mom to do it. I'll get twenty cleaning jobs if I have to.

After I hung up, Souazik and I talked for ages about our parents, our lives and ambitions and everything. Her father is a surgeon and her mother works in hospital administration. She said they always hassled her about the comforting safety of campus life and asked when she was going to stop living off grants and start dealing with the world properly. Mom would love me to be an academic (so long as I received grants, of course). Life can be so mean the way it makes practically everyone feel like they're living it wrong.

I stayed at Souazik's house on Saturday and Sunday, and then came back here. I finally managed to book a seat on an airplane for Wednesday night. Which brings us up to round about yesterday morning when I started writing everything down.

Someone came in the front door a couple of minutes ago. I wonder who it was. I wish I'd made myself some coffee and toast earlier. I hate going into the rest of the house when the others are here. I feel like I ought to say something to at least one of them before I go, but I can't think what. I'd like to tell Rob to go fall on a spike, but then again I'd like never to see him again – even for the three seconds it would take to get the message over. Actually I'm going to write him a note. I'll do it tomorrow and leave it behind. If I try to think of an appropriate farewell for Sofia, all I can imagine doing is nutting her as it's the only thing I could be certain she'd understand. I don't think either of them have been here since I last saw Rob asleep on Saturday morning though, so it's perfectly possible I'll never see them again. I'd love to tell Leni what I thought about her screenwriting skills and to say I know she lied about New York. But then she might tell me what she thinks about *me* and, as I already know, it isn't very complimentary. Maybe a plain whump on the forehead could be good for her too. I don't know about Jo. Basically, I think she overreacted about the diary thing, but I feel sorry for her for not realizing how dopey all her stuff is. She could leave it on the kitchen table and, after the first peek, nobody would bother to read it anymore.

Whoever it was just went upstairs. I might sneak out and go visit Souazik one more time before I get out of here. I don't have to be at the airport until eight o'clock tomorrow night. It'll only take a short while to pack, so I might as well try to enjoy my last twenty four hours.

I wonder whether I'll ever come back to London. Maybe if it's for a really good reason, but not just for the hell of it. I don't think I'll even call myself English any more – only I still don't see myself as American either. I guess it doesn't matter too much. I might as well claim to be Slovenian for all the difference it'll make to my life.

Fuck it. I'm bored with my own brain. I'm going to go and see Souazik before anyone else gets home.

It's my last day! I've packed already and it's only eleven o'clock in the morning. I spent my last 39p on foxfood and cried in front of the shed for a few minutes. I stayed at Souazik's house last night. She's such an incredible person. I know we'll stay in touch. She said she had some kind of poetry event coming up at the University of Santa Cruz and that she'd love to visit Las Vegas afterwards. I hope it happens. She has an e-mail address anyhow, so it'll be easy to keep up.

We talked some more about James. She said she thought he was drawn to girls who seemed to be doing whatever they felt like, but then he got jealous and started wanting to punish them and show them that he was the one with all the power. I said I thought he needed to be around people who'd been able to do what he hadn't, but that he'd made a mistake with me because I wasn't even doing it. In reality I have no idea what James's game is, but I'm glad I found him out before I got too involved.

On the Rob front, I don't know what to think. I definitely think he's a pathetic bastard with less emotional integrity than a cream cheese sandwich. (Where did that come from? I guess it's because I'm so hungry and I know I'm not going to get any food until I get on the plane. I've checked the kitchen already and there wasn't a single edible crumb.) But I guess this is the kind of thing that can happen if you get yourself stuck in a relationship you're not really sure about. You waste loads of energy trying to do the right thing and make it work out and then you find out that the other person couldn't give a fuck about you either. He was a wet fart anyhow. I was only ever kidding myself that I liked him. Maybe in a month or two I'll cry about it for thirty seconds or something. But I doubt it. I would have left him sooner or later anyhow. At least this way I don't have to feel bad about it. Sofia's just about tedious enough for him with her crappy Gappy outfits and uptight little family. I hope her brother manages to get away from them all. He should just leave and get on with doing what he wants. I wonder whether he reads English. I have their address. I could start encouraging him with a few anonymous letters. I don't think I'll be too bothered about him by the time I arrive at Stanstead Airport though. Even now I'm beginning to see the whole past few months as a memory rather than something that's still going on.

I'm completely ready to go except for one naggy detail. The print-outs I made on Friday are still down the back of Sofia's bedside table and there's actually a padlock on her door now. It's really badly fitted – I bet Rob did it before they left at the weekend. The lock annoys me so much I feel like busting the door down just to let them know I don't care what they think of me. But I obviously do care because I can hardly stand to consider the fact that they might find the copies when they pack up. If I break the door it'll just look like a mindless bit of violence – especially if I don't touch anything in the room. I can handle them thinking I'm just brutal. What I don't like is the idea of them remembering me as creepy and fucked up.

I wonder whether I could get the door down. Maybe with an axe, but I don't think there is one. I could try it with a breadknife or one of those saddo iron candlesticks Sofia put in the living room the other day (for her candlelit soirées with Rob, presumably). But I can't really see the point. If they find it they find it and if they don't they don't. It's not as if I'd want to keep the copies anyway. I'd much rather forget the whole story.

★

[Ed: This, really, was the most wonderful part of my entire editorial job. The copies weren't in the box and I feared the worst. But, as I said at the beginning, the house had been left in an awful mess and it was clear that the exodus hadn't been too carefully planned. I knew, of course, exactly which cabinet to look behind and rushed straight up to see whether or not the missing pieces were still there. I think the truth is that I didn't expect them to be. I didn't particularly imagine that any of the others had come across them either. It was more a case of not believing entirely in the reality of what I'd been reading. Although I occasionally empathised with Daisy and her difficult situation (or, more frequently, inwardly castigated her for her foolish and misguided notions) I couldn't quite register the fact that it had all happened so recently – so corporeally – under this very roof. Theoretically, I understood, but in practice I found it quite fantastic. The emotional shock of discovering the pages wasn't unlike the tremor one feels on seeing the brushstrokes of a really marvellous painting, or on encountering the coat or pen that once belonged to one's hero. It was surprisingly moving to uncover this relic of Daisy's being, under the very guidance of her journal.

The texts themselves are another matter. There is nothing particularly *moving or revelatory about either – although the second at least functions as a curiosity in relation to Daisy's understanding of events.*

Please accept my apologies for failing to deliver the diary in its original Technicolor glory but I'm sure you'll get the general idea. I've also edited it down to the bare minimum as the repetitiveness of Jo's text could hardly be justified in a book that attempts to pass itself off as entertainment. It will begin on the day of Daisy and Rob's arrival – the previous dates seemed somewhat superfluous – and will only include entries that consist of actual sentences or where the lettering reproduces well in black and white.

In another of my bouts of editorial bossiness, I strongly suggest that you skim briskly through this section rather than allow it to break the rhythm of Daisy's closing thoughts.

19th Sept.
Two new people moved in today. From Las Vegas!!!

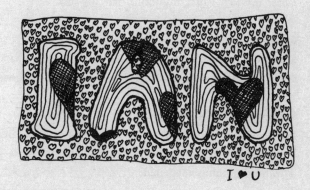

I ♥ U

22nd Sept.
New girl is quite nice.

28th Sept.
Bad day at work. Sarah made me miss my hair appointment. I hate Tony.

263

2nd Oct.

Went to pub with flatmates. Daisy, the new one, fainted. Don't like Leni. Said I wanted to marry Ian. I do.

11th Oct.

This weekend I really knew how much I love Ian.

31st Oct.

Halloween today! Whoooohhoooohoohhh!!!!!! (That was meant to be a ghost!)

1st Nov.

Pinch and a punch. Stayed in bed at Ian's until 9.00 in the EVENING! NICE DAY!!

5th Nov.

I hate my job. I hate my job. I hate my job.

6th Nov.

I hate it more than I even did yesterday. Tony asked Sarah if she could work this weekend. What's he like? I think she fancies him.

Friday 13th of Nov! &%!!!!!!!!!

I'm not superstitious but last time I lost my credit cards and a bus splashed my new suede shoes driving through a puddle. This time nothing happened.

17th Nov.

Had a dinner party. Sarah seriously fancies Tony. Don't think he likes her.

21st Nov.

Nothing much to say.

27th Nov.
Ian.

1st Dec.
Christmas again. I like Sophia the best in the house. The others are alright too except Leni. She's a right fucking stuck-up bitch.

8th Dec.
Might not want to work in TV anyway. Could be full of Lenis.

17th Dec.
Stayed in with others and made dinner. Daisy talks like that Lloyd Grossman. Rob must be really clever to do what he does. Daisies a good cook.

22nd Dec.
Dinner at home with just Sophia and Rob. Sophia puts garlic in everything. I felt more relaxed with just those two. I like Daisy, but she's nervous – or "nervous" like Sophia puts it.

25th Dec.

Got everything I wanted – a phonecall from Ian. He gave me a bear, *again*! He's so soft!

28th Dec.

Dad said Ian was a good lad. I think Mum likes him too.

3rd Jan.

4th Jan.

Back to work already. Tony and Sarah got engaged. She only told me and told me not to tell anyone until she gets another job. I hope she doesn't get one before me.

8th Jan.

Don't like 1999 much so far. Glad it's the weekend again.

22nd Jan.

I, me, Jo, am going to be an ASSISTANT FASHION BUYER!!!!!!!! My feet haven't touched the floor all day. Paris, Milan, New York HERE I COME!!!!!!!!!

Ian Northwick, I wanna marry
you!!!

25th Jan.
Ian is sex on legs. Shall I wait for him to propose or do it
myself? Why hasn't he done it yet?

28th Jan.
Dear Diary,
   Yours sincerely,
   Mrs. Jo Northwick!!!!!!

Ed: And so passed an eventful four months in Jo's life .
   *I'll begin Leni's script exactly where it left off as I'm sure you'll
have no trouble remembering both the story and the characters.*

Act 2, Scene 1:
It's morning in the house. **Joy** is in the
bathroom brushing her teeth. Cut to the
corridor outside where **Rosa** and **Bob** are
waiting. They are looking at each other
and smiling awkwardly. **Alina** is running
in and out of her room, shouting at **Joy** to
hurry up.

Alina: Joy, sweetheart, what you don't
seem to understand is that the rest of us
also need to have freshly scented armpits
and minty breath if we are going to make

anything of our lives. And this situation must be brought about within the next ten minutes as punctuality is also highly valued in this cut-throat modern world of ours.

Joy: Leenz, it's eight thirty in the morning. Can we not make up some kind of rule about not using big words at home until after ten o'clock at the earliest?

Joy vacates the bathroom. **Bob** gestures to **Rosa** to go ahead.

Rosa: We share thees home. We share thees bathroom. We weell brush ze teeth together, no?

Bob smiles and goes into the bathroom with **Rosa**, and they brush their teeth together, giggling. **Alina** hears them from outside the door and turns to raise her eyebrows at the camera.

Alina: Hmm. I think I smell a plot.

Cut to **Daisy**, still in bed. She is lying perfectly still staring at the ceiling. You might almost think she was dead, until she blinks. **Bob** bursts in and kisses her briskly on the cheek.

Bob: Cheerio, Daze. Whaddyou think you'll get up to today?
Daisy: Don't know.
Bob: Well, whatever it is, you look after

yourself and I'll see ya back here around
seven.

Daisy: I'll miss you.

Bob: I'll miss you too, Daze. Ciao.

Bob blows **Daisy** another kiss and races out
the bedroom door. On the main doorstep he
bumps into **Rosa** and they walk off down the
road together. **Daisy** has hauled herself
out of bed and watches them from the
window as they disappear down the street.
A tear wells up in her eye and she climbs
back into bed.

Scene 2: {Music? *Garbage – Stupid Girl*?
Kraftwerk? Check.} We run through the
events of each character's day. We see **Bob**
in a laboratory with a load of other
engineers, watching an experiment. **Rosa**
sits at a desk in an office, audio-typing
with a dreamy, faraway expression. **Joy** is
gossiping and laughing with the person in
the telephone booth next to hers at work.
Alina is having coffee with a group of
interestingly dressed people. And **Daisy**
is in bed, staring at a small patch on the
ceiling. Now we see **Bob** having lunch in a
canteen, deep in discussion with a group
of fellow students. **Rosa** is walking
around a bookshop. **Joy** eats in an Italian
restaurant with her colleagues. **Alina**
stuffs a chocolate bar into her mouth as
she rushes into a large, modern gallery.
And **Daisy** is still in bed. Finally we see

Bob walking down the University steps and waving to his friends before heading back to the tube. **Rosa** picks up her handbag, puts on a coat made from soft, grey wool and walks through the office. All the men turn their heads as she goes by. **Joy** walks down the road with two other friends, looking in the shop windows and laughing at the mannequins' poses. **Alina** kisses a couple of people goodbye outside a bar and races off into the traffic on her bicycle. **Daisy** finally manages to move. She looks at the bedside clock. It's six thirty. She drags herself slowly out of bed, picks a limp, black t-shirt dress off the floor and pulls it on over her nightie.

Scene 3: Later that night. Everyone, except **Daisy**, is in the living room with the TV on quietly in the background.

Joy: Howcome it's only Tuesday then, eh?
Alina: Because it was Monday yesterday, hun.
Rosa: Pero eez Weddensday oy!
Bob: You're wishing your life away, Rose.

As **Bob** is finishing his sentence, **Daisy** enters the room. Her nightie is hanging out from under her dress.

Rosa: Uh?
Daisy: That's what you say to *me*. Do you say it to all the girls?
Bob: Daze! I thought you were out.

Daisy: Well, I'm back. I've brought some pizza, but it's only enough for two.
Bob: Er . . . great. Thanks . . . er . . .
Daisy: It's in the room if you want some.

Daisy storms out and the rest all look at each other, surprised.

Scene 4: Daisy and **Bob** are eating their pizza on their bedroom floor. There is a long silence before either of them speaks.

Daisy: How were lectures?
Bob: Great! Oh man, I love spaceships. It's like, I'm exactly where I wanna be. It's the coolest thing.
Daisy: Oh . . . great.
Bob: How about you? How'd it go today?
Daisy: Cool . . . well . . . maybe not so cool. I dunno.
Bob: But you were so desperate to come to London with me. What's wrong?
Daisy: I dunno. Now I'm here I feel kind of funny. I feel like whatever it was that I thought was wrong with America might actually be wrong with me. I dunno what I'm doing, or where I'm going and it scares me.
Bob: But it's up to you to find out, Daze. What do you want? You must have some kind of idea.
Daisy (starting to cry): You don't understand! Nobody understands! Even I

271

don't understand! Why can't I just want the things that other people want? Why is it so impossible for me to live like a normal person, Bob? I wish I could move to another planet where you didn't have to do the dumb things that you have to do around here.

Daisy starts to cry hysterically and **Bob** puts his arms around her to try to calm her down. He looks stiff and uncomfortable.

Bob: Shhh, Daze. There, there. It'll be OK. It'll work out, you'll see.

Bob is looking unconvinced and **Daisy** is crying louder and louder.

Bob: C'm on, Daze. I'll tell you what. I'll build you a spaceship to take you wherever you want to go. We'll make the fuel tanks so big she'll fly anywhere in the universe. You can check out all the best planets and take your pick. We'll find a cool one with lots of wild fruit and the most sophisticated kitchens. There, there, baby. It's gonna be okay.

Daisy is starting to relax. She lies back on the pillow and closes her eyes. **Bob** strokes her hair and looks up at the ceiling, focussing on the same small patch **Daisy** has been staring at all day.

Daisy (very quietly): But will you come with me?

Bob pretends not to hear. He waits a few seconds before tiptoeing over to the desk in the corner to study.

Three months later. {*Sign? Titles?*}

Act 3, Scene 1: Alina is on her own in the kitchen making toast. Her hair is slightly longer

Alina (to camera): Just to keep you up to date; things have been carrying on pretty much in the way they began. Bob studies, Rosa types, Rosa and Bob flirt, Joy goes to work and looks forward to the weekend, I enjoy life as I labour away at my great novel (winks at camera) and Daisy sleeps, cries, eats, worries and sleeps again. I don't know how she keeps it up.

Joy (bursting through the door): Bollocks! I thought if I did it quick enough I'd catch you talking to yourself.

In walks **Bob**.

Bob: Hi girls. Howzit hangin'?
Joy: Howzwhat?
Alina: It's fine. You?
Bob: Cool.
Joy: Daze?
Bob: Er . . . cool . . . cool. She's . . . er . . . great.

Enter **Rosa**.

Bob: Hey! You ready?

Rosa: Jes!

Bob: Let's go then!

Joy: Where are you off to?

Bob: Daze isn't feeling too good today, so I thought I'd let Rosa show me around. I've been so busy with the space sheep I haven't seen much of London.

Alina: Great idea! But just remember, don't try to talk to the men in tall furry hats and if you need to know the time ask a policeman.

Joy: Have a nice day!

Bob and **Rosa** leave together and **Joy** and **Alina** look at each other knowingly. Meanwhile **Daisy** is watching out of the window again as **Bob** and **Rosa** disappear down the road. When they are barely visible in the distance they link hands. **Daisy** passes out.

Scene 2: Daisy wakes up and finds herself staring at the dot on the ceiling. The longer she stares at it, the darker it gets. It forms a perfect circle. The circle starts expanding, taking over the whole room. **Daisy** floats upwards and out through the circle into a huge night sky. She moves higher and higher and the wind blows her hair. She smiles.

Her body begins to rotate and she sees planet earth receding further and further into the distance.

Meanwhile back on earth we follow the characters through their day. **Bob** and **Rosa** go to the park. They kiss meaningfully by a huge pond with ducks. **Joy** is buying a short dress with pink sequins on it, posing in front of the shop mirror like one of the mannequins she laughed at earlier. **Alina** sits at her computer typing furiously, ignoring the incessant ringing of a telephone. **Daisy** floats further and further into outer space. She is laughing, smiling and looking genuinely happy.

Act 4, Scene 1: Rob, Rosa, Joy and **Alina** are in the living room at home.

Bob: You were here all day. Didn't you notice anything?

Alina: No, not a peep.

Joy: You didn't hear her leave the house?

Alina: No! I told you. She didn't make a single sound all day. I always notice the front door shutting because it's right under my desk and I tell you I didn't hear a thing.

Rosa: But eez eempossible she deesappear so altogezer wizout leaving. We look everywhere and she not here. Sometheeng feeshy, no?

Bob: Well it for sure ain't an everyday occurrence that Daze leaves the house. I think you're right, Rose. Something's funny.

Joy: I think we should have one last check and then we should call the police. I can't believe this is happening.

They all head off to **Daisy** and **Bob's** bedroom. They look behind the curtains, under the bed and inside the wardrobe. **Joy** picks up a corner of the duvet and a little piece of paper flutters to the floor.

Joy: Hey look!
Everyone: What does it say?
Joy: It says, 'Dear Bob, Got tired of waiting for your spaceship to come, so I decided to make my own way. I hope you can be happy and that Rosa will look after you. (Don't think I don't know.) Cheers, Daisy (*not* Daze).'
Bob: No way!
Rosa: (Crosses herself.)
Alina: Bloody hell! (To camera) A clear case of fiction being stranger than truth.

Act 5, Scene 1: We see glimpses of the characters five years on. **Rosa** is sitting in a big bed, playing with her one-year-old daughter. **Bob** enters in a smart suit and kisses her goodbye. They both look very happy. He has grown a beard. **Joy** is on the telephone in her own private office. Her hair is well cared for, her clothes obviously expensive. She has a gorgeous male secretary. **Alina** is signing books in the middle of a heaving crowd of fans. Her clothes are strange and futuristic but she looks mature and serious in her new spectacles. We see the title of the book – *Darling Daisy*.

Titles roll.

Final scene: Daisy is sitting on a fabulous beach surrounded by exotic fruits. The beach is dotted with shiny, designer ovens. All around her are strange, but obviously peaceful, creatures. **Daisy** is smiling.

The saturated sunlight begins to drain from the picture. The sand turns into a hard, shiny floor. The fruits become wooden toys, the ovens turn to cupboards and the creatures transform into nurses and patients. **Daisy's** expression remains unchanged.

End]

★

I'm not even sure what I'll do with my own notebooks. I can't bear just to drop them in the trash, but I don't think they show a side of myself that I really want to stay in touch with. Maybe I could put them in a safe at the Bank of England, to be opened forty years after my death. But who'd open it? One of my kids? – if I have any. They'd be in their nineties or something. I don't really like the idea of it. Perhaps I could make it two hundred years. Or maybe I could put them on a shelf in the

British Library for someone to stumble across by chance one day. What would they think? How should I know? They could be anyone, and I don't have the time anyhow. I could always leave them in a pub or café to make sure someone got hold of them straight away. But why? Or I could give them to Souazik if she promised not to look. Perhaps I could leave them on the bed for Rob so he knows what I think of him. The idea makes me pretty nervous, but there's something about it I find kind of exciting. The off-putting part is the fact that I actually wrote so many nice things about him. I think I'd still rather deal with him in a note. In the end I don't suppose it really matters what I do with my journals. One thing's for sure, I won't be showing them to Mom and Dad. I guess it's time I stopped writing. I've got a plane to catch – although if I leave now I'll be about three hours early. It's OK at the airport though. Lots of people to watch and you know that none of them will be Rob, James, Sofia, Leni or Jo. I feel like I've left already, so I might as well make my body (and my suitcases) catch up.

So what shall I do with this? I could toss a coin. But then I'd rather decide for myself. I'm very confused and excited and I want to get going. I feel like I've stopped writing already too.

That's it then. No more words, it's time for action.

[Ed: And this must have been the absolute low-point of my editorial mission. I didn't know for a fact that Daisy had written a farewell note to Rob, but somehow felt quite sure she must have. It just didn't seem possible that she could allow herself to leave without retaliation. I don't know Daisy – I have no real idea what she looks like, what she sounds like, how she behaves, or whether or not I would like her if I met her — but I refused to believe she would go without claiming the last word.

I decided that, if she had written the letter at all, it might still be amongst the rubbish left behind by the others. Naturally, one of my first actions on arrival had been to heave all the refuse sacks out into the large, black dustbins Lewisham Council kindly supply to the lucky residents of this illustrious neighbourhood. (The box of books only managed to escape this first bout of home improvements thanks to a folded newspaper sitting on the top with a curious picture of a woman with a cabbage for a head. I'd picked up the paper to read the caption, thus uncovering the infinitely more intriguing 3D flower notebook underneath.)

It wasn't until two days later, after I'd read the whole lot, uncovered the missing print-outs and sat down alone with a bottle of wine to mull over such important topics as where to place the sofa and which room I ought to use as my office, that I suddenly found myself overcome with a mania for finding the letter. I imagined it might tell me something I wasn't getting from the journals — something somehow closer to life. In a rather Daisy-like manner, I wanted to see another part of the person whose writing I'd been reading, something presently hidden from view. I also wanted to know what she'd said to Rob. I like to believe it sprang from my professional need for a satisfactory conclusion — it irritated me to allow for the notion that Daisy might simply have slipped off without a definitive parting gesture — although it may have had far more to do with my being an objectionably nosy old blighter.

The rubbish is collected on Thursdays and hadn't yet been touched. Hoping the neighbours wouldn't see, I slipped out the front door and stealthily reclaimed the black sacks from the forecourt. As Daisy has informed you, the bathroom was the only uncarpeted space in the house. (Of course this is no longer the case — I, at least, have had the good sense to rip up the carpets and to sand and varnish the floorboards.) I *piled the bags up beside the bath, ready to face the worst. Wearing rubber gloves and a jumper tied around my head to protect my nose and mouth from the smell, I began unloading the bags, one at a time, into the tub. I don't particularly want to discuss the specifics of what I saw, but suffice to say that a houseful of young people is liable to produce a large amount of the type of rubbish you'd rather not know existed – especially the girls. With my stomach churning and a constant gagging in my throat, I sorted through every available shred of paper. There were about nine bags in total and, by the eighth, I'd all but lost hope. Whereas, at the beginning, I'd searched with an avidity fed by the belief that one of the countless scraps would surely be the item I was hoping for, by the eighth bag I could no longer see any point in the disgusting task I had set myself. I'd just about come to the conclusion that to continue would be foolish (a decision heavily influenced by the fact that the ninth and final bag was heavier than the rest and clearly filled with waste from the kitchen)when I unfolded a ball of lined A4 paper covered in Daisy's writing.*

So here it is. Perhaps you'll enjoy it more knowing the pains I endured in order to procure it for you:

3rd Feb. 1999

Dear Blob,

I was going to leave without telling you what I thought of you, but then I didn't see why you should get off so easy. You are the biggest scumsucking cowardly piece of shit. And if you stop reading this you'll only prove my point.

It wasn't only you who had doubts about the relationship. If you want to know, I've been pretty bored and have only ever enjoyed having sex with you about two times. I always hoped things would get better – I kept on kidding myself that there was more to you than that lamo streak of piss that passes for your character. Now I see I was wrong. When I was under the bed listening to you slopping around with that dumb yoyo – you know, the one you'd only just told me you weren't attracted to – one of the first things that went though my head was that the two of you were probably quite well-suited. Both of you are about as interesting as the contents of a vacuum cleaner and have the dress sense of a pair of toilet seats. I can see already that you'll bore each other shitless before the end of next week, but that's your problem. I'm just glad I got away before I actually started to believe in my own fantasy that you were a worthwhile person.

Why didn't you let me leave you when I wanted to? What was that whole stupid crying joke about? (And, by the way, the sound you made was completely fucking ridiculous. I only fell for it because I was generous enough to turn my repulsion into pity.) I gave you a second chance just so you could go stick your dick in that pile of sick (pardon my poetry). Are you really so vain that you had to organize everything to look like *you* were the one who'd had enough of *me*? Grow up shithead. You're the one who's going to have a crap life if you don't start noticing that you're not the most important person in the universe. And another thing. You weren't the only one who was being unfaithful, but at least I did it with more dignity. I'm not telling you who it was, but don't imagine that he wasn't a million times more interesting than you, in bed *and* out. (And if you think I'm only pretending to make you feel bad, then where do you think I'd been those times I came home late?)

I hope for your sake some terrible things happen to you. It's probably the only way you'll ever stop acting like such a small-minded piss-cutter.

All the worst (I mean that nicely),

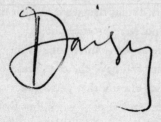

For Daisy <u>only</u>

**I'm being serious.
GO AWAY.**

First of all, please accept my sincerest apologies for making public your confidential musings. But if this note (with its accompanying book) should ever come to your attention – and I'd be lying if I claimed I hoped it would – believe me when I tell you my greatest wish is that you might eventually come to feel glad, proud even, to see your words in print. You really did give enough hints that this was what you wanted – although I understand that a longer gap might have been desirable. I also beg forgiveness for the editorial liberties I have taken. I hope my 'embellishments' on the James Wissen affair weren't too grating – you really ought to allow yourself more freedom when discussing subjects of a romantic nature. Although I must concede your 'bubble of immaterial bliss' had a certain mawkish charm. As for the letter to Rob, my editor made me do it. I hope I didn't overestimate your wrath – it *was* perhaps a dash crueller than he deserved.

I also apologise for being so dismissive of your poetry. It just isn't the sort of writing I personally enjoy. Even so I tried to track down 'Souazik's' (*you* know who I mean – I can't trust *everyone* not to read this) journal, but couldn't find hide nor hair of it. No one in either the British Library, the Poetry Library, Senate House or even Brompton Rd Library had a clue what I was on about. I thought I might be able to contact you through 'S' about the potential publication of your *real* writings. I imagined I might act as your agent and do the whole thing with your consent. But it wasn't to be. At least the widespread unavailability of *'Persimmon UK'* means your surname can remain a secret.

The main point I wanted to make here concerns your career. It may well turn out to be true that you'll make a perfectly good psychotherapist (or art therapist or hypnotherapist or whatever branch of the profession you choose). But it seems to me you'd be better off getting on the couch yourself and devoting more time to improving your writing. I think a few years of therapy would not only help with your interpersonal difficulties, but may also make you a kinder, more thoughtful littérateur. Within a few years I feel sure it would start to pay off. There are countless magazines and newspapers queuing up to pay for the naïve cogitations of young things like you. 'Woke up this morning *in New Cross* . . .' What could be more *de rigeur*? – if only I liked to write as much as you do I'd probably still be living in Bayswater. I know that doing anything as a job – even wine tasting! – can remove some of the pleasure. But writing really isn't a bad profession compared with most of the others. It's true that a few too many years of hackwork can begin to feel somewhat demoralizing, but you can wake up whenever you like (if the guilt doesn't niggle at you) and get tax relief on your cinema tickets. All I'm trying to say is that, if the studies prove disappointing, there might be other options worth trying before you let yourself get into another impossible situation. So you see, I really do have your best interests at heart.

Also, about the fox. I didn't mention this in the public part of your book as I was reluctant to butt in and ruin the description of one of your happier moments, but she and I rather came to blows.

After reading your journal, I dutifully popped off to the corner shop for a few tins of doggy chunks. That evening I put out bowls of food and water and crept inside to watch from the back window. I must have waited ten minutes before impatience took over, but by next morning the food had gone.

The following night I couldn't resist the temptation of a little fox-spotting. That vile blanket was still here (it's since been incinerated) so I wrapped myself up, dished out the dogfood and lay down in the nearby grass. Just as you described, the fox appeared. She eyed me warily before limping over towards her dinner. After wolfing it down she fixed me in the eye and started creeping towards me, her nostrils 'going crazy' in precisely the manner you'd recounted. The little terror must have been within a foot of my face when she realised things weren't quite the same as they used to be. She froze for a second before contorting her mouth into the most horrific snarl. I quickly wrenched the blanket up over my face. The sudden movement must have given her a shock and she sprang forward with the crazed air of a cripple flinging away her sticks in an ecstatic, instantaneous recovery. The little darling clamped herself to my covered head, kicking, gnawing and grappling, as I struggled to get myself upright. At an opportune moment I allowed the whole mangled bundle of mad fox and manky wool to slip to the floor before beating a hasty retreat to the back door. Once inside, I looked back to see the adorable little creature disentangle herself and slip away into the night.

Out of some misguided largesse I continued to feed the ungrateful devil until one day, about a fortnight ago, she pulled up all my bulbs. Right now we are on a trial period – if she lays off my plants she can stay, if not it's the dreaded diesel rag. Still, I assure you that the hobble has entirely disappeared and I am sure she would re-house in no time.

One final suggestion for your writing – why not experiment with making a few things up? The way you're going at the moment you'd probably either end up a columnist, or slopping around your own self-cannibalising stew-pot (or both). Fiction is a wonderful thing and well worth having a crack at. I may even be able to organise a few useful literary contacts – just say the word.

Then again, perhaps you'd rather just use the royalties from this book to pay your way through University (although I fear I may be being rather optimistic about sales).

Either way, the very best of luck.
Yours,
H.P.

Suzannah Dunn

Venus Flaring

'Suzannah Dunn is a gifted writer'   *The Times*

Ornella and Veronica are the very best of friends, inseparable throughout the trials and minute details of their lives, sharing everything, hiding nothing. They grow up and find their way into the world together – Ornella, flamboyant and domineering, becomes a doctor, Veronica, observant and self-possessed, a journalist. But then something goes horribly wrong between them, and what was once the truest of friendships disintegrates into an obsessive nightmare of smouldering resentment that can barely be controlled. As Ornella's loyalty fades, Veronica's desperate need for reconciliation becomes a matter of life and death – and if you can't trust your best friend with your life, then who can you trust?

In prose that soars and fizzes with startling truths, Suzannah Dunn has created a deliciously disturbing and stylishly compelling tale of loyalty, love, memory, obsession and ultimate betrayal.

'Dunn writes with a warm attentive style which makes her characters compellingly real.'   *Time Out*

'Suzannah Dunn writes in loaded and knowing prose, like a hip Edna O'Brien or Muriel Spark in a gymslip.'
                                        Glasgow Herald

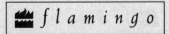 *flamingo*

Barbara Gowdy

Mister Sandman

'Highly acclaimed Canadian novelist Gowdy masterfully notches up her third novel . . . Her prose is a dream which will keep you up all night.' PAULINE KENNEDY, *Time Out*

'This book begins with the birth of its central figure, a tiny, white-haired, angelically beautiful child, who is thought to have cried, "Oh no, not again!" at her first sight of the world, and is thereafter mute. She takes up residence in a closet, and becomes the repository of all her family's secrets; and very odd secrets they are. Then she refashions them into her own explosive work of art. Barbara Gowdy surprises and delights; she also – which is rarer – gives us moments which are at the same time preposterous and strangely moving.'

MARGARET ATWOOD

'Barbara Gowdy has a sharp, surreal edge and a beguiling sense of humour; her prose comes from a darker place whose other residents include Lorrie Moore and Alice Munro. *Mister Sandman* is funny and moving at the same time – strange rather than wacky; touching rather than sentimental. Gowdy invites the reader's complicity, and makes us fall in love with her characters . . . a subtle and original talent.'

JESSAMY CALKIN, *Observer*

'One of the most extraordinary books I have ever read. Gowdy takes the ordinary and turns it inside out.'

ALICE THOMPSON, *Scotsman*

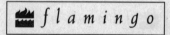

Douglas Coupland

Girlfriend in a Coma

'I was amazed by it. The dialogue is some of the most brilliant I've ever read in a novel. It's a great wake-up call to young Americans everywhere.'   MARK LAWSON

'At the start of Douglas Coupland's new novel, 17-year-old Karen loses her virginity to boyfriend Richard on a ski slope in Vancouver. An hour later she collapses at a party and falls into a vegetative coma . . . Fortunately, Coupland's concern isn't a teen-sex-is-death homily, but the need to live life to the full. *Girlfriend* is a richly associative novel, ranging from the dysfunctional teendom of *Twin Peaks* to the chilly metaphysics of *The Sweet Hereafter*, *en route* to winding up as a post-apocalyptic version of *It's a Wonderful Life*. This media literacy is one of the conspicuous pleasures of Coupland's fiction . . . Coupland's "end of the world" is a brilliantly constructed setpiece, and very scary: you'd have to be cold as ice not be truly engaged and stirred.'   *Independent*

'A millennial novel of a very subtle and interesting kind . . . it's visually brilliant, full of extraordinary imagery, fresh like new paint. I was absolutely knocked over by it.'
TOM PAULIN, *Late Review*

🏭 *f l a m i n g o*